who needs magic?

Also by Kathy McCullough

don't expect magic

who needs magic?

KATHY McCULLOUGH

delacorte press

randomhouse.com/teens

Educators and librarians, for a variety of teaching tools, visit us at
RHTeachersLibrarians.com

Library of Congress Cataloging-in-Publication Data
McCullough, Kathy.
Who needs magic? / Kathy McCullough. — 1st ed.
p. cm.
Sequel to: Don't expect magic.
Summary: Working at a vintage clothing store during the summer, teenaged fairy godmother Delaney Collins struggles to find her next client who needs a life-changing, happily-ever-after wish, while her romance with boyfriend Flynn sputters.
ISBN 978-0-385-74014-2 (hc) — ISBN 978-0-385-90825-2 (glb) —
ISBN 978-0-375-89892-1 (ebook)
[1. Fairy godmothers—Fiction. 2. Wishes—Fiction. 3. Magic—Fiction. 4. Dating (Social customs)—Fiction. 5. Summer employment—Fiction. 6. Vintage clothing—Fiction.] I. Title.
PZ7.M478414957Wh 2013
[Fic]—dc23
2012019177

The text of this book is set in 12-point Apollo MT.

Printed in the United States of America

10 9 8 7 6 5 4 3 2 1

First Edition

★

for my friends

ACKNOWLEDGMENTS

First of all, thanks to my editor, Wendy Loggia, for her guidance, encouragement and wisdom, and to all the people at Delacorte Press. Thanks as always to my agent, Alyssa Reuben, and my manager, Dana Jackson, for their loyalty and support. I'm also grateful to the book blogging community, notably Shanyn Day, Senator Sipes, Alethea Allaray, Alyson Beecher and Lissy Goode.

I dedicated this book to my friends not only as a clever way of covering all bases, but also because I've been so awed by their support. Special mention to my top "sales team": Polly, Bud and Anne (Northeast region); Paula (Southwest); Lee & Paul (West Coast); and Rose (Great Britain). To chauffeurs and hosts Kevin & Jo, Missy & Sarah, Paula & Stan, Paul & Bronia and Bud & Polly. To cheerleaders Jen & Beth, Steven & Michael, Judy & Dave, Nancy, Janet, Lindsay and Marty. The Above and Beyond Awards go to Justin, Connie, Lupe and especially Cappi (aka Rebecca).

Essential feedback on early drafts of *Who Needs Magic?* was provided by my writing group (Mindy, Kate and Ellen) and by Eliza, Paula and the amazing Justin. Thanks to Max for all manner of brilliance, to Judy Y for allowing one of her Floor Model photos to make a cameo appearance, and to my author friends who are both confidants and mentors: Randy Russell, Catherine Gilbert Murdock, Carrie Harris, the LAYAS, the Elevensies and my fellow SCBWIers.

chapter one

It's taking all my willpower not to point my Popsicle stick Theo's way and recharge his phone battery so he can keep playing his war-on-the-high-seas game. But I'm forbidden from using magic in front of Theo. Dad and Gina don't want to tell him about the whole f.g. thing until the time is right.

Like there's ever going to be a right time for Dad to tell his girlfriend's ten-year-old son, "Hey, I'm a fairy godmother." I really think they should let me tell Theo that *I'm* a fairy godmother first, because at least I'm female.

I did manage to grant one wish for Theo without using magic. I insisted that Dad and Gina let us have Popsicles to tide us over until Dad finishes scraping off the layers of burnt hamburger, hot dog, ribs, steak and whatever other mystery meats have built up on the park grill from holiday barbecues gone by. Not that I got a "Thanks, Delaney" or anything. Theo went right back to waging his electronic naval war with one hand while devouring the Popsicle he clutched in the other.

Now the Popsicle's gone, the phone battery is dead and any second the whining will—

"I'm *bored*."

Ah, there it is.

"Why don't you and Delaney play tag?" Dad proposes. Theo and I, who have nothing in common, since I'm five years older and a girl, experience a moment of complete synchronicity as we both stare at Dad in disbelief.

"They're a little old for tag, Hank." Gina shoos another fly away from the side dishes she's set out on the corners of the picnic table to hold the tablecloth down.

"Not to mention, I'm wearing a skirt," I point out. "And boots."

"It was just a suggestion."

What's next? Patty-cake? "I'm taking a walk," I say.

"We're eating soon, honey," Dad warns.

"I'll be back in time," I promise. As long as I make it back this century, I'll still have returned before he's gotten the first hamburger on the grill.

I cross the grass to one of the intersecting walkways that loop through and around the park, linking the soccer field, the baseball diamond and the playground. In between are tiny tree-shaded pastures and lots and lots of picnic tables and grills, all of which are filled with families and packs of friends celebrating the Fourth of July.

Now that I'm free to use my magic, I subtly aim my Popsicle stick to stop paper napkins from blowing away, repair leaky balloons and send Frisbees back on their intended paths. I usually carry a chopstick with me, but a Popsicle stick makes an equally effective wand.

I'm ready to move beyond these little point-and-shoot wishes, though—the bit of Object Transference here, the dash of Atom Manipulation there. I want to experience the big f.g. magic—the powers I earned by granting my first big wish. But I can't access those powers until I find my next client.

It's been three months, which seems a pathetically long time. Not that I have a lot of fairy godmothers to compare myself to. The only other one I know of is Dad, and he got his second client in like two weeks back when he started out. Whenever I ask him why it's taking me so long, he gives me a lecture about "Trusting the Process" or "Cultivating Forbearance" or some other chapter title from the latest "Dr. Hank's Self-Help for the Hopeless" book he's writing (so that non-clients can also benefit from his wisdom). To prevent myself from choking him to death, thereby eliminating the one parent I have left, I've "cultivated" the "process" of not bringing it up anymore.

I can't believe I'm supposed to just sit around and

wait, though. That means big wishes are going ungranted and my full powers are going untested. It's not like I can randomly pick somebody. The small wishes I can do for anybody. They're just guesses. But the big wish is a meant-to-be thing. In the sense that I'm meant to be that person's f.g. and meant to grant their major, love-finding, life-changing, happily-ever-after wish. It's an emotional connection that only happens with one person at a time, and it's why you feel their wish as strongly as they do.

I know from watching Dad that it takes more than wielding a wand to make a client's big wish come true, and that magic, even if it is major pumpkin-into-coach, rags-into-ball-gown magic, is only a tool. The powers go beyond that, but if I don't get more practice at it, I'm never going to know just how far beyond they go.

Shrieks of laughter and calls to dinner and shouts of "Heads up!" as softballs fly by rise and fall as I wind around the park. I pause in my small-wish granting to concentrate. Today might be the day. Could my next client be one of the kids in that family over there with all the pizza boxes? Or one of the two boys playing Frisbee? How about that couple making out on the beach blanket? Hmm, probably not any of them.

A cool breeze blows past. Back in New Jersey, July was hot and humid, but as Dad likes to remind me, here in the golden part of the Golden State, where everything is perpetually pretty and perfect, summers are all sunny seventies and dry desert nights. Maybe the wish I'm meant to grant is being carried off on that same breeze, over my head, out of reach.

I make my way down to the playground. There's a swing free, so I take a seat and kick my legs out. If I can get high enough, maybe I can catch the wish as it floats by. I'm not sure wishes work this way, but it's worth a try.

"Be careful, Ms. Collins. Swing too high and you may fly off." I glance down and see Flynn leaning against one of the swing-set poles, grinning his goofy adorable Flynn grin. I hadn't expected to see him today, but here he is: *my* big wish, my first client *and* my boyfriend, all wrapped up in one oversized-army-jacketed, photography-obsessed, yearbook-editing prince. He lifts up a digital camera to take my picture. "Unless flying is another one of your powers."

I leap off the swing and my boots crunch down into the sand. "Not so loud, Mr. Becker."

Flynn wraps his arms around my waist and smiles. "Haven't you heard? Paranormal is the new black. You should know that. You're the fashion designer."

"Shut up," I say. "I mean it."

"Make me shut up," he says. And so I do.

You know how people say "there were fireworks" when they kissed? I always pictured that as fireworks going off overhead, in the sky, above and around you. But it's not like that. The fireworks are inside; little explosions of energy and heat in every limb, every cell. Tiny sparklers igniting behind your eyes, in your ears. My whole body flushes hot while my skin prickles from the cool air, and it almost seems like maybe *I'll* explode. "Happy Independence Day," Flynn says when we pull apart.

"Go red, white and blue, or whatever."

Flynn grins and takes my hand, and we start up the path away from the playground. It's ironic that this Independence Day has come at a time when I suddenly have all these connections. Back in New Jersey, Mom and I would spend the Fourth of July inside, in the air-conditioning. Sometimes Posh, my best but also my only friend, would join us and we would watch marathons of old black-and-white TV shows, happy to be away from the heat and the crowds—independent.

Now I have a boyfriend, and Dad and Gina and Theo, and the yearbook people, and Cadie and the other kids at Allegro High I've only started to get to know. Plus, here I am today, in a crowded park, willingly, actively seeking yet *another* person to add to my life. It's all pretty strange to me.

"A dime for your thoughts, Ms. Collins."

"Happy Interdependence Day," I say. "I'm glad you could come."

He smiles. "We drove home early because—guess what?—I got the job I applied for at the paper. And Skids got one too. We start tomorrow."

"I didn't know writing Facebook status updates for Brendan's skateboarding fan page qualified Skids to be hired as a journalist."

"It's an internship, it's how you learn. We can't all be paid professionals like you, Ms. Collins." We circle around the soccer field, where a couple of dads are teaching drills to a confused gaggle of toddlers. I wave my Popsicle stick to stop the soccer ball from rolling into the trees. "Skids'll be writing copy," Flynn says, "and I'll be taking photos. Even without a paycheck, it'll be like I'm a full-time photo-journalist for the whole summer."

"Full-time? But I thought it was called the *Sea Foam Weekly*." My heel catches on the edge of the concrete and I lose my balance for a second, but Flynn pulls me upright.

"*Sea*side *Weekly*. And just because they don't publish every day doesn't mean they don't work every day. News doesn't only happen once a week."

"I know, but . . ."

Flynn laughs. "Were you expecting me to hang around outside your store every day and wait for you to get off work?"

"No." I didn't expect him to hang out doing *nothing*. He could pop in now and then to keep me company. He could even leave for a while, take a few pictures around the mall and come back. As long as he didn't go too far.

"Anyway, aren't you going to be busy, making boots and granting wishes?"

"I guess." I haven't gotten started on either yet, but I don't tell him this.

I'm feeling on shaky ground again, even though my boots are now solidly on the path. Flynn and I have been going out for three months, but it seems like we've barely started. First there was finishing the yearbook, and then finals, and then as soon as school ended, Flynn went off on some camping trip with his family for two weeks. If you subtract the group outings with Brendan and Skids and the yearbook staffettes, our time together has been microscopic. This is another area where I need practice, but until now I hadn't been worried about it, because I'd expected we'd have the whole summer together. Just like I'd expected to have another client long before now, but here we are, back at our picnic table, where Dad is still scraping, Gina is still shooing and Theo is now sinking ships on Gina's phone. And I am still client-free.

"This is a stupid Fourth of July," Theo says after Flynn wishes him a happy Independence Day. "We don't even get to have any fireworks."

I squeeze Flynn's hand and think, *Some of us do.* Flynn smiles, which means maybe he's thinking the same thing. This is one of the things I would have been surer about after we spent some serious quality and quantity time together this summer, which now won't be happening.

"I was saving these for later." Dad takes a break from his scraping to retrieve a bag from under the table. "But you can each do one now." He lifts out a box of sparklers and hands it to Gina.

"That's a great idea!" she says, opening the box. "Our own individual fireworks! Right, Theo?" Theo grunts, noncommittal, but he puts down the phone.

Soon we're each holding a lit silver stick, fiery sparks snapping off the end. Theo waves his in a big circle, the most energetic I've seen him all day. Flynn makes figure eights in the air.

It occurs to me that a sparkler should make an excellent wand. Maybe it's attracting client energy right now. I swing my arm up high over my head, but a second later I hear a sizzle and look up. The sparkler's gone out. I hear Theo moan as his fizzles too.

Flynn's is still burning. "Make a wish, Delaney," he says.

I close my eyes. What should I wish for? That I find a client? That my full powers work once I do? That Flynn's job won't get in the way of our relationship? And what about my boot-making business?

"Hurry!"

"Okay, okay! I wish for all of my wishes to come true." I open my eyes and blow as Flynn's sparkler sparks its last spark.

"Leave it to Delaney Collins to find a way to get everything she wants." Flynn smiles at me and I smile back.

It's not until he's tossing the burnt-out sparklers in the trash that I realize I forgot something. I forgot to say *when* I wanted the wish to happen.

chapter two

Ugh. I hold the boot up, examining it. This is beyond frustrating. I'm at Treasures, and luckily for me—and not so luckily for Nancy, the owner—there aren't any customers. So I can do what I like. Except I'm not liking what I've done so far today. I have this fantastic summer job at Treasures, a secondhand store/antiques shop. (It's fantastic partly because it means I'm not working for Dad. He'd offered to pay me to be his "office assistant," helping him with filing, typing, proofreading and stuff like that. But that was pretty much a job *I'd* pay *not* to do.)

It was Cadie who told me about Treasures. She said that

Nancy occasionally got boxes of clothing and accessories mixed in with the lots she buys at estate sales to stock the store. Nancy never unpacked any of the clothing boxes, though. Instead, she put them in a smaller room connected to the main room, and vintage shoppers would come in and sort through the boxes, hoping they'd find something they liked. Because this is the land of sunshine and sandals, secondhand boots aren't big sellers, which means there were a lot of them. But I know how to redesign them to make them new, and saleable, so I persuaded Nancy to hire me for the summer to overhaul the vintage clothing room in return for minimum wage, an employee discount and permission to work on my redesigns when business is slow.

My plan is to get started on a boot business. Why wait until I've gone to college? Especially when Cadie and her cheerleader friends, plus a bunch of other kids at Allegro, have told me they'd buy them. My goal is to have at least twenty pairs finished by the time school starts in the fall.

But I'm already behind schedule, because it took me three weeks to unpack all the boxes and sort and organize and stack and hang everything. Today, finally, I was able to try out my first design. And it's a flop.

Literally.

It looked so great in the sketch: the calf of the boot sliced into strips, and the strips braided and clipped at the top. But the one boot I've finished looks like it's been mauled by some mad scientist trying to build Frankenboot. The clipped strips keep collapsing, so I stitched a band beneath the clips to hold the strips up. But now I realize there's no way anybody could ever get the boot on—unless their leg was the width of a pencil. As I pull out the stitching, a customer about my age flits past my view, darting in and out from behind tilting bookshelves and dusty lamps in the main room of the store. She's wearing a pink ruffled skirt, a sparkly silver headband in her wavy blond hair and a kaleidoscope of pastel-tinted jelly bracelets on one arm. She reminds me of Tinker Bell. She flutters past a couple more times and then I guess she leaves, which is no surprise. This doesn't seem like her kind of store.

I return my gaze to the Frankenboot. I stare down at it, trying to will myself back in time, before I sliced it to bits, and then back before that, when I was sketching it and should've known that the design wouldn't work. Unfortunately, f.g. powers don't include time travel. And you can't use magic to grant your own wishes anyway. Making boots is supposed to be the thing I'm *already* good at. But I can't concentrate properly when I'm worrying all the time about when I'm going to get my next client. And I can't stop thinking about Flynn. I haven't seen him since he started working at the paper. It's only been a week and we have a date tonight, but *still*. I miss that goofy Flynn grin.

I toss the boot in the corner. Maybe I'll reorganize the accessories again to take my mind off it all. I'll put the hats on the shoe rack, the belts on the hat rack and the shoes on the shelves. It's the "meditation of doing," as Ms. Byrd, the yoga teacher at Allegro, says. I know I'll feel a hundred percent better when I'm done.

By the time I get to the belts, I'm feeling about half a percent better. At this rate, if I keep redecorating and reorganizing for another hundred years, I may succeed in advancing from feeling severely depressed to merely seriously bummed.

Hmm. Maybe having a screaming fit and ransacking the room is a better idea. The "meditation of flipping out."

"Do you have anything with wings?" I glance up to see Tinker Bell, a lemon candy stick clenched in one hand, glitter-covered sandals on her feet, perched on the threshold into the room like she's about to take flight.

"Wings? Like . . ." I flap my hands, imitating a bird. She nods. Is she putting me on? "Sorry. Only regular clothes in here. You might want to try a costume shop."

"No, no, not real wings. Things with wings. I collect them."

"There's a denim jacket over there with a butterfly embroidered on it." I indicate a folding screen, where I've hung some of the nicer shirts and jackets.

"Ech, not insects." She shudders. This is not a reaction I've ever seen to butterflies. "*Magical* things with wings," she clarifies. "Like angels. And fairies."

"No, sorry."

"Are you sure?" She glances around suspiciously, as if I've secretly stashed a family of fairy dolls somewhere in the room.

"You're welcome to look around."

Tinker Bell steps into the room and then stops, her blue-eyed gaze locked onto the hat rack, where I've just hung a trio of blue belts over one of the hooks.

"That's a hat rack," Tink informs me as I drape a white canvas belt over another hook.

"Yes, it is," I confirm.

"But those are belts." She directs her lemon stick to the remaining belts in my hand, to make sure I understand.

I lift up the belts and study them closely. "They are indeed," I say, and then resume hanging them.

Tink folds one arm across her stomach, rests the elbow of the other on her wrist, and bites off the end of her candy stick with a frown. "The hats are on a shoe rack," she says between chews.

She may not like insects, but she's starting to remind me of one. The pesky, buzzing kind.

"In case you were curious, there *is* a belt rack." I tilt my head toward it. "That's where the scarves are." I make a sad face. "No angel scarves, though."

"But it's wrong." Tinker Bell waves her half-eaten candy stick around the room, like she can make it all go away.

"It's *cre-a-tive,*" I explain, sounding it out slowly in case she's never heard the word before.

"Hmm." She taps the candy stick against her teeth, as

if she's considering whether or not discipline is in order. Unfortunately, I don't have a human-sized flyswatter, so I'll have to come up with another way to get rid of her.

"Thanks for coming in!" I say brightly. "Hope to see you again soon!" Not.

She doesn't leave. I notice she's studying my mangled boot, lying on its side like a soldier fatally wounded in battle. I truly won't be able to endure any snide comments about *that,* so before she provokes me into swatting her for real, I say, "I may have seen an angel pillow in the other room."

Tink cheers up, forgetting all about the abomination of my decorating choices. "Can you show me?"

That backfired. I sigh, drop the belts and stride into the main room of the store, Tink on my heels—heels with which I'd like to crunch her pink-frost-painted toes. But that would be bad customer service.

Behind the counter, Nancy, swaddled in the eight million scarves she's wrapped around her shoulders, reading glasses slipping down her nose, is hunched over one of the ratty paperbacks she's taken from the selection that fill the store's bookshelves. "Hey, Nancy. Do we have any angel stuff?"

Nancy is too deep inside her cocoon of 1980s-trashy-novel bliss for the question to penetrate. "Mmm" is all I get. I shrug apologetically to Tinker Bell and lead her around a three-legged coffee table that's been propped up with old board games, past a pair of scuffed easy chairs, to a sagging couch. Sifting through the pillows that've been piled onto the couch, I find the perfect one and pull it out.

"Oops, sorry," I say oh-so-sincerely. "It's a duck, not an angel." I show her the pillow: a faded needlepoint mallard on a threadbare pond. "It has wings, though." Tink doesn't seem amused by my joke.

"This room is very unorganized," she says.

I happen to agree with Tinker Bell on this, but there's no way I'm going to admit it. "Not my department."

Tink picks up a Porky Pig saltshaker and lets out a disapproving huff. "You should have some new stuff in here. To mix in with the old."

"It's an *antiques* store."

"So? Lots of the regular stores have retro stuff too now. It's the same thing, right? Just in reverse. I think you'd get more customers."

I don't bother to tell her that we don't *need* more customers, because every other week some interior designer comes in and pays Nancy a few thousand dollars for some old piano or a clock that's apparently the last one left in the world. "I need to get back to the area that *is* my department," I tell Tink. "You can keep looking if you want, see if any *antique* mythical creatures with wings are lurking about."

"What about chopsticks?" I freeze for a second when she asks this. "You know," she continues, "the fancy shellacked kind, with the Chinese letters painted on them."

Why would she want chopsticks? They don't have

wings. I worry she's toying with me and I glance down at my boots. It's my "Fires of Hell" pair, with orange flames shooting up the sides, and I've sewn a pocket inside one of the skinnier flames. But it's zipped up now, my chopstick out of sight.

Tinker Bell is staring at me, waiting for an answer, and I realize I've overreacted. Her family probably just orders takeout a lot.

"No, no chopsticks. We had some, but we sold them all." To *me*.

"Oh, okay." She surveys the room one more time with a mix of frustration and disappointment. I can tell she's used to getting her way. "Well, I have to go now. Sorry." As if I'll be crushed she's leaving. "I might be at the mall a lot in the next couple of weeks, though, so I can check back. If you find any angels, will you save them for me?"

"Of course. I'll make it my sole purpose in life."

Tink cocks her head. I think my sarcasm has finally penetrated her very dense filter. She bites off another piece of the lemon stick and casts a final disapproving look around at the all-old-stuff-all-the-time clutter and then flits out.

"A little less of that, Delaney," Nancy says without looking up from her book.

"Less of what?"

"You know."

"Sorry. I'll be nicer the next time she comes in." Which I pray never happens. Nancy turns another page in her book without saying anything, so I guess I'm forgiven. I return to the vintage clothing room and head to the corner to retrieve my mangled boot so I can toss it in the trash, but I find the unmarred one instead. I must've tossed the wrong boot.

I carry it to the worktable, but the boot on the table is unsliced too. I lift up the boot in my hand and study it from all sides. It's the left boot, the one I *definitely* hacked up and ruined. Except it's not ruined anymore. It's back to where it was before I cut the first strip—back in time, like I wished. . . .

It can't be. It *can't*. Just because she sparkles and dresses in pink and collects chopsticks?

And *fairies* . . .

I drop the boot like it's on fire and race out to the counter. "I have to take a break," I tell Nancy. "It's an emergency."

"Honey, I told you, you can use the bathroom in the office anytime."

"No, it's not that, it's . . . I have to . . ." *Think, think.* "I'm really hungry."

"Good idea. Let me give you some money." Nancy puts down her book and opens the cash register.

"No, that's okay."

"I want you to get me a Nutri-Fizzy. Something different. Hmm . . . pomegranate and walnut, maybe."

I snatch the twenty out of her hand without even

bothering to make a retching noise at her flavor request. "Got it."

"If they don't have pomegranate, acai is fine—and buy whatever you want for yourself. My treat!"

I wave the money and yell "Thanks" as I dash out the door.

chapter three

It's always a shock when I leave the Annex, the old part of the mall where Treasures is located, and enter the huge, new, glossy Wonderland section. The new mall's real name is the Alcove, which suggests it's some small, quaint, set-off area, but it's actually this sprawling outdoor pseudo-paradise three times the size of the Annex. There's a curving path that winds through the Alcove, past all the gigantic storefronts, and although the path is made of cobblestones, it might as well be a Yellow Brick Road, because when you enter the Alcove, it's like that scene in *The Wizard of Oz,* when the black-and-white shifts to color, and everything is shiny and rainbow bright. It even smells different here, like a mix of sunshine and citrus and some faint flowery scent that they probably pump into the air from little misters hidden in the artificial ivy draping the pretend balconies on the top floors of the stores. As I dash around modern-day Munchkins and their mothers, I scan the crowd for a sign of Tinker Bell. She couldn't have gotten far. I hope.

I text Posh, but there's no response. This is no surprise. I've barely heard from her since she and her new boyfriend, Christopher, went off to NASA summer camp. She's my sole link to my life back in New Jersey, and the one person aside from Flynn, Dad and Gina who knows I'm an f.g., but our worlds barely intersect anymore. She'll email me back eventually, but it'll only be to tell me about some Mars moon that's gone out of orbit or a new ring discovered around Jupiter. The email will include three million "links to more information," approximately zero of which I'll click on and exactly zero of which will relate at all to what is going on with *me*.

I could call Dad, but he gets pissed if I interrupt his "writing time," even though, from what I can tell, his writing time involves a lot more Internet searching, snack making and desk reorganizing than writing. But whatever. The one person I'd really like to tell is Mom, but I can't. I could "imagine" talking to her, or talk to her "in heaven" like people do sometimes—but it's not talking to her that I miss, it's her talking back, and that won't be happening.

I wade my way through bickering families and

awestruck out-of-towners and clusters of BFFs (male and female) that always seem to be around on the weekends. The beach is twenty-five minutes away, but instead of surfing or sailing, they're all *here,* strolling happily along the curvy mall avenue, wandering in and out of the high-end chain stores with their enormous window displays of expensive furniture and clothes and vases and jewelry, all of which will be on the sale rack tomorrow (and in Treasures fifty years from now). It may be outdoors, but whenever I'm over here, I feel like I'm suffocating from all the plastic newness.

In the middle of the mall, across from the movie theaters, is the fountain. It's currently playing some song that isn't exactly "Over the Rainbow," but it's close. The water sways along with the music, and toddlers lean over the side, reaching their hands toward the dancing droplets. Parents clutch their kids' belt loops to keep the urchins from face-planting into the penny-filled pool.

This is pointless. Tinker Bell's not going to stand out here where *everything* is sparkly and candy-colored. And now, because I promised Nancy, I have to join the five-mile-long Nutri-Fizzy Bar line, which winds past the surf shop, the organic chocolate boutique, Brennan's bookstore *and* the custom-designed kids' furniture emporium. I should've brought a book. I could run inside Brennan's and get one. I think Gina's working today, so I could use her manager's discount. But then I'd end up even farther back in the Nutri-Fizzy line.

"Nutso-Fizzy" is more like it. I don't get what the thrilling appeal is of combining carbonated water with disgusting flavored powder mixes. But I've stopped being surprised by the weird behavior of the bleached-brained locals in this part of the country. I only hope I don't suffer the same mental sun damage. I should've brought a book and a *hat*.

A few days go by as I inch forward in line. Why did I even come out here in the first place? I already know what Tinker Bell is—a bossy, irritating, angel-collecting brat— and *nothing else*. I was looking at the wrong boot back at the store, that's all. There was another pair, unsliced, and I got the two pairs mixed up. This is obviously the ex- planation, because it's too much of a coincidence for my suspicions to be right. And whoever heard of an f.g. who actually looks the part? Look at me. Look at *Dad*. Maybe I can tell Nancy that they ran out of the fizzy part of the Fizzy. I'll wait until the current fountain song (something about seagulls and star beams) is over, and if I'm not any closer, I'll leave. Through the spouts of waltzing water, I can see a group of kids dancing on the mini-lawn on the other side of the fountain. A little girl trips on the sash from her dress, which has come untied, and it rips off. She grabs the sash off the ground and presses it onto the dress, as if it might repair itself. Her eyes go wide in pre- tantrum warm-up as she presses harder and harder with- out success.

I reach down toward my boot to unzip the chopstick

sleeve—just as the little girl's eyes go even wider with delight when the sash *does* repair itself. The girl smiles, pleased, not at all surprised by this tiny miracle, and she goes back to dancing. None of her friends are fazed either, but then, magic is nothing special if you're young enough to still believe it's a part of daily life. I, however, feel my breath catch, and then I glimpse a slash of a pink skirt disappear behind a vendor cart selling Crocs accessories. I dart out of the Fizzy Bar line, making the thousands behind me thrilled to move up a micro-inch, and race after her. Now that I've seen her, I'm able to keep her in my sight, despite the gaggles of camera-snapping tourist couples, app-playing boys and stroller-pushing nannies that get in my way. Tinker Bell holds a green candy stick now, and she points it this way and that as she strides along. Around her, falling sunglasses make slow-motion soft landings, pacifiers are restored—clean—to babies' mouths before their mommies see, and melting ice cream cones re-freeze mid-drip. Small wishes granted all around, and they happen so fast, I've only just spotted the last before she does the next. There's no effort either. No sense that she's concentrating, willing her energy through the candy stick. To anyone passing by, it looks like she's licking the candy and then pausing briefly and then licking again. No one would ever suspect her.

Except another f.g.

Tink interrupts her wish-granting marathon to check the time on the big clock that hangs over Taylor & Taylor's

24

for Men. She holds the lime stick in her mouth, pressed against the inside of her cheek like a lollipop, and reaches into her pink vinyl purse to lift out her phone (pink, of course). She glances at the cell's screen and then takes a seat on an empty bench nearby. Behind her, a spray-tanned male model seems to stare down from an ad for sunglasses that's posted on one of the stand-alone pillars that line the mall's weaving walkway. Sunglasses Man and I watch as Tink reads a text and then types a reply. She taps her foot as she types, her frosty toenail polish firing off little flecks of reflected sunlight. The sun glints off her headband. This girl really is too sparkly—I expect Sunglasses Man to come alive and push those designer shades all the way up to block the rays. Tink puts the phone away, takes the lime stick out of her mouth and taps it against her teeth, deep in sparkly thought.

I should go up to her. Now is my chance. But what do I say? It's not like "how to greet a fellow f.g." is in the rule book anywhere. Partly because there *is* no rule book and partly because Dad told me there *aren't* any f.g.s except him and me. Of course, he initially thought I wasn't one either, and he was wrong about that too.

Suddenly I feel nervous, but why? What am I afraid of? *Tinker Bell?* I force myself to walk up to her. She raises her head and shields her eyes with her hand as I approach. "Oh, hey," she says. Her tone is one-quarter surprised, one-quarter curious and one-half wary. "Did you find an angel?"

"No. Something else."

"Really?" She sits up straight, eyes wide, *all* curious now. I lower the zipper at the top of my boot and pull out the chopstick. "Why are you hiding it in there?" She lowers her voice. "Did you steal it? You didn't have to do that. I can pay for it."

"It's mine. This is where I carry it. I'm one too."

"One what?"

"You know." I wave the chopstick in the air and then point it at her. "You fixed my boot."

"I don't know what you're talking about." Her voice has now gone as frosty as her nail polish.

Striding up behind Tinker Bell, a woman with moussed hair and lots of chunky gold jewelry bats at a crease of dirt that zigzags above the knee of her bright white slacks. "Watch," I tell Tink. The woman has stopped to retrieve a bleach pen from her power purse. While she's involved in screwing off the top of the pen, I clamp down on the chopstick and focus—because unlike Tinker Bell, über-f.g., *I* still have to concentrate. Now that she's got the cap off, the lady leans down to attack the stain, pen poised—and frowns. The stain is gone. She glances at the other leg, as if the dirt might have migrated, but that leg is as blindingly bright as the first. The woman shrugs, laughs to herself, returns the pen to her bag and saunters off, problem solved.

Or rather, wish granted. I blow on the end of the chopstick like I'm a sheriff in an old western movie and return the chopstick to its boot pocket. As I straighten up, I'm thrown off-balance by two arms grabbing me, squeezing me in a ribs-crunching bear hug. "Oh my God, oh my God, oh my God. I can't believe it! It's true, isn't it? It is! Oh my God!" I flex my arms and she finally lets go. "You have to tell me everything! Are you in disguise? I've never heard of a"—she lowers her voice to a whisper—"you know"—then back to regular volume—"who dressed like you." She whirls the lime stick in a big oval loop to take in my black boots, black tights, black minidress and black neckband, stopping before she gets to my long black hair. "But then, the only other ones I know about are my mom and my grandma." She claps her hands together and her eyes gleam. "I can't wait to tell my mom I've met another one, and my age too! She'll flip out."

"So will my dad."

"Your dad?"

"It's a long story. . . ."

A little while later, Ariella Patterson, f.g., and I are sitting cross-legged on the grass at the far edge of the mini-lawn, away from the stage and the tiny toddling dancers, eating ice cream and talking about magic wands and fairy godmothers like we're kindergartners during story time. But what we're talking about isn't made up. It's real. And we're living it. Ariella is the perfect name for her. Very Tinker Bell–like. Even sitting, she flutters constantly, waving her hands as she chatters on in enthusiastic bursts, as if this is the most exciting conversation she's ever had in her life. It's not really a conversation, though, so much as Ariella talking and me listening. Despite about five more pleas to "tell me everything," Ariella Patterson is the one doing most of the telling.

She moved here from Phoenix two years ago and lives in a house near the beach with her mother and grandmother (both of whom are f.g.s) and her dad, her little sister, Justine, and her dog, Razzle (who aren't). In addition to collecting "things with wings" and chopsticks, she's also got two bookshelves that are crammed with (1) fairy tales from around the world, (2) all of her picture books from when she was little, and (3) scrapbooks she's made of every vacation she and her family have ever been on. She loves big, warm slippers and musicals, and her favorite book of all time is *The Secret Garden*. She thinks jigsaw puzzles keep the f.g. mind sharp, that having a dog helps with empathy, and that making up cookie recipes is good for practicing improvisation, which an f.g. often needs on the job. It's like she's been bottling up all this information for years, waiting for somebody to tell it to. I can relate to that, but it feels more like she's been practicing for a cover story in *People* than confiding in a fellow f.g. Meanwhile, I haven't had a chance to ask her the questions I *really* want answers to.

"It's so amazing that we found each other. How did

you guess? Oh, right—the boot! I didn't know we could do small wishes for each other, did you? But why not, really?" Her spoon makes a little loop on the way to her mouth, and I know somewhere behind me an iPod battery has been recharged or a ripped shopping bag mended. "My grandma met a couple of us when she was younger and lived in France. We thought maybe they were all European. It makes sense, right? The Grimm brothers were from Germany and Hans Christian Andersen was Danish. Is your mom European? Although, according to my fairy-tale books, there are fairy godmothers all over, they're just called different things. It would be so cool to meet one in South America or Africa, don't you think? There must be lots more of us we don't know about. I looked online once, but I didn't find anything." She stops suddenly and stares at me. "What's wrong? You haven't said anything. You're not in shock, are you?" She snaps her fingers in front of my face.

I grab her snapping hand and push it down and away. "I'm waiting for a pause so I can 'tell you *everything.*'" I'm sorry the second I say it, because I no longer want to smoke her with one of my signature clouds of sarcasm, even if she was asking for it. Plus, I started it—I followed *her,* after all.

She doesn't seem offended, though. She smiles and scoops up the last bite of her melted strawberry-vanilla swirl. "Hey, I'm excited, right? Aren't you? I *do* want to hear everything." She sets down the empty bowl and opens her handbag. "Candy stick? I have lots." She tilts the purse toward me, displaying a dazzling bouquet of sugary sticks in every color.

"So I see." I grab a red-and-white peppermint one, to go with my mint chocolate chip ice cream.

"Who was your first?" Ariella asks, immediately shifting back up to verbal warp speed. "Mine was my cousin Lucy. She had this puppy she loved. He was so cute, some kind of doodle. You know—one of those mixes, like jacka-doodle or maybe yorkadoodle. But he was a rescue and was scared of her. My powers were super-limited then, so all I could do was make Lucy smell like a steak bone. It worked, though! After that it was easy. How many have you done? I'm aiming for a hundred big wishes granted by the time I turn fifteen. February seventh. Oh!" She slaps her hand over her mouth for a second. "I'm doing it again! You go."

"A *hundred*? How many have you done so far?"

"Eighty-two."

I accidentally bite off a huge piece of peppermint stick and cough wildly when it goes down the wrong way.

"Don't feel bad," Ariella says. "It's exceptionally high. My grandma says so. It's partly because I started so early. I was nine when I granted Lucy's wish."

"Nine?"

"I know! Right? I used to keep track of small wishes too, but I stopped counting after five thousand. My mom's totally jealous, even though she won't admit it. We're kind

30

of competitive. How old were *you* when you started?" She presses her lips together, like she's determined to let me get more than ten words in finally. My luck, it's the one question I don't want to answer.

"Older."

"That's okay! That's normal. It's better to be normal. Less pressure. I don't know why I feel this need to hit a hundred, but I do. I'm obsessed." She chirps on, explaining how she once granted two big wishes in the same week. She's so energetic and wound up, it's tiring me out just listening to her. I thought I'd feel more of a connection to her: finally, somebody who gets it, who shares the secret, who knows the frustrations. But she's never felt frustrated at all. She's an f.g. Einstein. Instead of feeling like I'm not alone, I feel even more alone.

"It's so . . . *fulfilling* when you grant one, don't you think? It's such a gift we have. We're like that guy I learned about in school who planted all those trees— Johnny Appleseed. Doing good, spreading good. So how many have *you* done?"

I take it back: *this* is the question I don't want to answer. "Not that many."

"Come on, you can tell me. Are you working on one now?"

"No, I'm sort of between jobs. I wanted to ask if you had any advice—"

There's a tinkling sound like wind chimes and Ariella lifts up a finger: "Hold on." She pulls her phone out of her purse and turns off the alarm. "Shoot. I have to go. Fawn's on break now. She works at the Elegant Imprint—the card store? Fawn LaSalle. Do you know her? I met her at a concert at Otter Beach Pier last weekend. There was this huge crowd, and she was like halfway across the boardwalk, but that didn't matter because—*ping!*—I felt her wish. Has that ever happened to you? Fawn and I are meeting now so we can check out the 'target.' I like to do a cruise-by and assess the difficulty level, and then I can work out a strategy. How do you work it with your beneficiary?"

"That's what you call them? Isn't a beneficiary someone who inherits money when somebody else dies?"

Ariella stands and straightens her skirt. "A beneficiary is someone who benefits. And our beneficiaries benefit from our magic. Why, what do you call them?" Before I can answer, her phone chimes again. "Sorry, Delaney! Gotta go. But I promise I'll stop by your store the next time I'm here." Ariella drops her cell back into her purse and adjusts her headband. Behind her, the swaying fountain seems to frame her in a halo of glittering watery light. "Feel free to call me anytime, day or night. There's so much more we have to talk about!" She sprints off, unwrapping a new candy stick—orange—as she goes. She must be a sugar addict. With all her sweetness and sparkle, I wouldn't be surprised if she was *made* of sugar.

My whole body relaxes now that she's gone. Without her voice chirping away, the sounds of the laughing kids

32

and chatting lunch-breakers and jazzy fountain music flood into the vacuum and blend together in a soothing audio haze. The calm is accompanied by the realization that Ariella Patterson and I could never be friends. I don't care if she's the only other f.g. I'll ever meet. The one thing I wanted to ask her—how do you find your next client?—she wouldn't be able to answer anyway. She doesn't *have* to find them. Their wishes storm through crowds to find her. *Ping!* I won't be calling her. I'll delete the number she programmed into my phone when we were in line at the Ice Cream Cottage. If she comes into Treasures, I'll just be "busy." She'll get the message, eventually. And if she doesn't, she'll have probably granted her "beneficiary's" wish by the end of the week anyway, so she'll be out of my life.

When I walk into Treasures, Nancy looks expectantly up from her book, and I realize that I forgot all about the Nutri-Fizzy.

"Sorry," I say. "The line was endless, and then right before I was going to order, the carbonation machine broke or something." I hand Nancy back her money and avoid her eyes, though I can feel the skepticism wafting off her.

"That's all right, honey. I'll live. You will too."

Whatever *that* means. Do I look like I'm dying? I trudge back to the vintage clothing room but pause at the doorway. Across from me stand the boots. I'd almost forgotten. I walk over and pick up the repaired one and run a hand down its smooth, unmarred surface. It's definitely as good as new. Well, good as *used,* but better than it was.

It wasn't all a waste meeting Ariella. I still don't have a client. I still don't know how to get one, and the extent of my full powers remains a mystery. But at least one thing that had gone wrong today went right.

chapter four

"Dad! I have to talk to you!" I slam the door behind me and dash through the dining room to the kitchen. After tossing my backpack on the counter, I open the pantry, looking for the Pop-Tarts I slipped into the shopping cart the last time we were at the grocery store. The surreal experience of meeting another f.g. has made me crave something warm and toasty and junky. Not a lot of that in Dr. Hank's House of Health, but I've been staking my claim, slowly. I have nothing against vegetables, but Dad goes overboard. For instance, the leafy greens taking up the bottom shelf of the fridge look like they've been dredged up from a swamp or harvested from somebody's front-yard ground cover.

I find the Pop-Tarts behind a box of ten-grain crackers. Soon one is heating up in the toaster and giving off that nice burnt-jam smell.

"Dad!"

His car's here, so I know he's home. I yell again and finally I hear his footsteps approaching from the hall, but it's his cologne that enters the room first. It's so intense and eye-watering, it's like a special-effects monster. A fog of cinnamon and musk come to terrifying life. It's completely crushed my little Pop-Tart's nice grapey aroma.

"What did I tell you about the screaming, Delaney?" Dad says when he catches up to his cologne.

"I wasn't screaming. I was calling. I have to tell you something earth-shattering."

"Then you could have come down the hall and told me. In a civilized voice."

"You said never to disturb you when you're in your office." I pop my tart onto a plate and lean close to inhale. Nope. The cologne has won.

"Yelling at the top of your lungs *is* disturbing."

"You weren't in your office anyway. You were in the beauty parlor." I take a bite of the Pop-Tart and wave the rest at his slicked-back hair. "Why did you do that to your hair?" I say between chews. "It makes your receding hairline look even more receding."

Dad pats his forehead worriedly. "No, it doesn't." He peers at his reflection in the door of the microwave.

"Like a wave pulling away from the shore. Farther and farther. Out to sea."

Dad frowns. "I don't need the metaphor, thank you. Is that your dinner?"

"I'm going out with Flynn, remember?"

"Be sure you're home by eleven. I'm having dinner with Gina, but I'll be home before that. Now, what did you want to tell me?" Dad waits, listening intently, a Dr. Hank–type "I'm standing by to help you solve all your problems" expression on his face.

I swallow my last bite of Pop-Tart and feel a flutter of worry. He's the one person who would truly understand the significance of what happened today, but whatever I say needs to come out just right so that I'm not subjected to a life-coach session on how "this experience is an important part of your individual learning path," in which I'm then ordered to create a ten-step plan on how I can use the experience to "empower my choices for action" or "choose my actions for empowerment" or whatever.

Talking to Dad is the opposite of how it was to talk to Mom. She would say things like "Wow" and "It's okay, that's how I'd feel too." When I talked to her, I could get to the end of things, but with Dad it's like you're just starting. I don't want an action plan, because part of it would be seeing Ariella again, which I will *not* be doing.

"Delaney? Did you want to tell me or not? I'm already late." Dad pulls on the jacket he's carried in with him.

"Gina's taking Theo to his father's and then I'm meeting her at the restaurant, so I have to get going."

"Will you promise not to give me any advice?"

Dad pauses in his jacket-buttoning and gives me a look. "The reason I give you advice, honey, is because I'm trying to help—"

"Never mind."

"Delaney—"

"No, go on. It's okay. It was nothing big. I had a problem with a boot design, that's all."

"Are you *sure* that's all? You said it was earth-shattering."

I pluck his car keys off the key ring on the wall next to the door and hand them to him. "I was exaggerating. Like I've done a million times before."

Dad smiles and takes the keys. He leans over and kisses my cheek, his cologne cloud enveloping me. "Okay, we'll talk later. And don't forget. Eleven o'clock." Then he's gone, out the door, his monster cologne fog dragging behind him, leaving just a dying vapor.

My cell buzzes. Posh must be calling me back. Thank God. Finally, I can tell *somebody*. On the cell's screen, a starburst flares and the name "Ariella P" glows underneath. I hit Ignore and dial Posh.

"Delaney!" Posh squeals, but before I can say anything, she launches into a giggling fit and there's a *thunk*, like she's dropped the phone, and then more giggles, and a guy's voice saying something I can't understand, and Posh saying, "No more tickling! I'll get hiccups."

Ugh. I end the call. You'd think I'd get more respect when it was me who made all these happily-ever-afters happen. Dad never would've gone out with Gina if I hadn't tricked him into it, and if I hadn't moved away and left Posh with no one to dominate her time, she never would've ended up in her backyard one night with Christopher, watching shooting stars and embarking on geek romance.

Not that it matters. Who cares about any of them? Flynn's coming in half an hour and I haven't changed yet.

Finding the perfect outfit for tonight. *That's* what matters.

★ ★ ★

Ten minutes left until he gets here and I still can't decide.

When I texted Flynn to ask what I should wear, he texted back that whatever I chose would be perfect because everybody will probably be dressed in black. I'm not exactly thrilled at the idea of being like "everybody," even everybody at an art gallery, but it does make getting ready a little easier. I've narrowed it down to the black dress with the lacy trim, the long black beaded tunic, and the black velvet skirt with the black satin tee. I circle my bed, where I've laid them out, with different black boots propped up on the floor below each outfit: the dragon boots, the snake boots and the "Attitude #3" boots with the crisscrossed slashes.

This is another one of those times when I really wish Mom were here. She could help me decide.

Not that I ever went out on a date back in New Jersey. It wasn't something we even talked about. She never gave me any tips about dating, and I never asked. It'd been just the two of us for so long, I guess I thought it would be that way forever—although I never really thought ahead very far. It was enough that it was the two of us in the present. Until it wasn't.

But now I wish *Mom* had thought ahead, a little, to the possibility that I might actually one day have a boyfriend and need to know something about how it's all supposed to work.

The Tinker Bell night-light winks up at me from beside the bed. I bet Ariella would love to give me advice. She's just the type. She'd have me outfitted in bubble-gum-colored boots and a matching pleated dress, with a big bow in my hair.

Why am I thinking about *her*? Possibly because I still haven't purged the bedroom of the kiddie décor Dad dressed it up in before I came. I should at least pack up all the stupid dolls, and the frog prince alarm clock, and the Snow White lamp. But the first thing to go is that night-light—

Stop. I don't have time to obsess over this now. The clock is ticking and I'm starting to feel nervous, like this is a first date or something. It's because this will be the first time we've been alone together, without friends or family around, in over a month. Which is like forever.

Yet, weirdly, our first night together feels like it happened only a week ago. Not even a week. The memory of it has crystallized in my mind so sharply that the time-travel restriction doesn't apply to it. I can go back and relive it, and every detail is vivid, like I'm watching it happen now. I like to rewind a little first, to the night before, when we went to the carnival together, when I thought Flynn still liked Cadie. It feels as if my heart is being squeezed when I think about it. It's like when you're watching a movie, and you know the boy and girl belong together but some tragic misunderstanding has caused them to misinterpret each other's actions. It's a weird sort of psychological torture, but it makes it even better when I skip ahead in the movie to the happy ending:

It starts with me standing barefoot on the sand, my boots in one hand, my other hand grasped in Flynn's. Seagulls and waves and the laughter of the body-surfing beach-partyers are the background music for the scene— for the moment our story had been building to.

The beach sound track fades as we walk along the sand to the wooden steps that lead up to the pier, and a new tune kicks in, a mix of children's voices and merry-go-round music and snippets of conversations that sprinkle over us as we move through the crowd.

This is the part of the memory where it becomes more than a movie. It's as if I've been transported there. All five senses come alive. I feel the rough, sandy surface of the boardwalk press into the soles of my bare feet as we walk. There's the smell and taste of the damp salty air, and the cool bloom of the lavender sky as the sun finally sinks into the sea. Through it all, there's the warmth of Flynn's hand in mine.

That warmth stays there, all the way to the Ferris wheel, a miniature version of the one from the carnival, but this one has music, and tiny green and purple lights that blink and beam along the perimeter. As we rise, the tinny music from the Ferris wheel speakers becomes our new background theme. The wheel pauses when we get to the top, and Flynn looks over at me, and even though the sun has set and his eyes are shadowed, I can tell he's gazing at me in a way that signals an impending kiss. But I have to tell him everything first. About him and Cadie, about Dad, about small wishes and big magic—but he only lets me get halfway through the story before he stops listening.

And then it happens.

We're kissing. My first real, official teenage kiss. It's a kiss that starts off soft and hesitant. It breaks, just for a second, and then I lean in or Flynn does or we both do, I'm not sure—it's the one detail I don't have nailed down. It changes every time I remember it, but it doesn't matter, all of the versions are so . . . spectacular. It's the only word that fits.

It was the most corny, clichéd, wonderful happily-ever-after ending you could ever want, and sometimes I rewind and replay just that one little loop over and over again. We kiss, we kiss, we kiss, and every time it's for the first time.

It wasn't really the happy *ending,* though. It was the happy beginning, since it's where we started, not finished. And tonight, we can finally get the story going again.

Oh my God, he'll be here in five minutes! This is the problem with memory-driven time travel. You don't return to the same second you left. I grab a random pair of boots. Flynn will like whatever I wear; I don't need to stress about it. I don't need advice. I just need to redo my mascara and put on lip gloss.

My cell rings. He's here. "I'm almost ready," I say into the phone. "Do you want to wait in the car or come in?" Maybe that purple gloss that's so dark it's almost black. Hmm. I rifle through my makeup drawer, but I don't see it.

"That's why I'm calling."

"Okay. Come to the door. I'll let you in." I pull out the drawer and dump everything onto the bed.

"Uh. No, I mean—I'm really sorry this is so last-minute, Delaney, but they found the top of this lighthouse washed up on Aurora Beach. They have no idea where it came from."

"You want to go to the beach instead of the gallery? I'm not dressed for that. I'll need another ten minutes."

"We'll go another time, Delaney. I promise. I have to run. Skids is picking me up."

"Wait, wait, wait. You're not coming here at all?" I watch myself in the mirror as I fling my arm out in frustration.

"You're blowing me off? For a waterlogged lighthouse?" I look so good in this outfit. Even pissed off. And it's completely wasted.

"It's breaking news, Delaney."

"If you want something broken, I'll be glad to take care of that for you."

Flynn laughs as if I'd made a joke. "I knew you'd take it well. You're the best."

"I'm not the best." I put my hand on my hip—an even better look. "The only superlative that applies to me is 'most enraged.'"

"I *am* sorry, Delaney. I'll call you tonight when I get home. Okay?"

Is it okay? If I say yes, am I being supportive or wimpy? If I say no, will he laugh it off or cancel his plans?

"We'll go out this weekend. Whenever you want. Wherever you want. We'll declare it Delaney Collins's day."

"I'm not sure there's a greeting card line for that."

"Then we'll design it together."

Together. The magic word. "Okay." And for a second, it is.

But after I hang up, the emptiness of the evening ahead rolls in, and doubt comes with it. The rules of romance are as confusing to me as the rules of fairy godmothering, and it makes me wonder if being an f.g. and being a g.f. are somehow linked. I'm supposed to be helping people land their true loves, but how can I do that when I have hardly any experience in the subject? And maybe if I'd granted more wishes by now, I'd know exactly what to say, do and feel when I'm talking to, with or thinking about Flynn. I'd know when I should worry about us, and whether I should worry a lot or just a little.

I flop back on the bed, tempted to transport myself back again to the Night of the First Kiss, to fill the time and blot out the angst—but I can't just dwell in fantasy.

What I'd like is for the conversation with Flynn to have been the fantasy. One of those dark ones that come sometimes at the end of a long worrying jag, before I drag myself back to the present and realize I imagined it all and everything is fine.

But no, it happened, because there's Flynn's name, right at the top of "recent calls." Right above Ariella's . . .

How can I even be tempted? Didn't I decide I was done with her? Do I want to make myself feel worse? No. I do not. Absolutely not.

I am *not* calling her.

chapter five

"The crimson halter dress with the black sling-backs." Ariella's mom, who's just as blond and high energy as Ariella but less sparkly and more serious, gives clipped orders into her Bluetooth as she drives. "No. The ones with the open toe."

"She's on with her beneficiary," Ariella explains. "She likes them to pre-dress to her specifications before the transformation. It's not a technique that I embrace, personally. But every fairy godmother has their own style, my grandma says."

I'm not really sure how it happened. It was like some horrible self-destructive impulse caused by Flynn abandoning me to photograph debris, and before I knew it, I had dived off the bridge—or rather, tapped Ariella's number. The phone dialed and Ariella answered and then I was calling Dad to tell him and then it seemed like only a second later Ariella and her mom were pulling up outside my house in this long pale green car that had to be from like fifty years ago but looked brand-new.

It's one of those cars with the fins like you see in old movies. Each corner of the car's body, where the headlights and taillights are, juts out, as if the metal had been pulled away and pinched to a point. It had never really occurred to me that there might be an f.g.-mobile, like a Batmobile. Dad's boring blue Honda definitely doesn't qualify. But *this*. This is a car for magical women bearing wands.

We're on our way to yet another mall. This one is in the same area of town where Ariella's mother's client lives. "She drops me off and I walk around and do small wishes until she picks me up." Ariella told me this over the phone, and I could picture her eyes gleaming in manic f.g. glee as she said it. It's like she's a wish-granting junkie. Either that or all of the sugar she consumes makes it impossible for her to turn off or even power down.

She hasn't stopped talking since I got in the car. ". . . and then there was this boy at the beach who'd broken up with his girlfriend and wanted her back, and she was there that day with her sister. That one went so fast, I never actually even *met* him! At the end of June, just before Fawn, was Hannah, who lives two blocks over from us. She was in love with this piano. Isn't that funny? To be in love with a piano? But she was. So I got her a job at the piano store, where she can play it all the time. Tell me about some of yours."

I give her a second, in case this is just her usual brief pause before another ten-minute verbal assault, but she continues staring at me in eager anticipation. "I don't really keep a list," I say. This should get her started again on the pros and cons of lists, or list organizational strategies, or examples of lists she keeps of things besides clients: candy stick flavors, headband colors, types of wands, things with wings.

But no, instead, I get another question. "Tell me about the last one. When did you grant it?"

I could change the subject, ask her another question. But if the reason I'm here is to learn how to improve my f.g. skills, which will help me gain confidence in the g.f. area too, then I need to tell her the truth.

"April."

"But that was like three months ago," Ariella says in a hushed voice. She leans back and regards me with barely veiled horror. Her mom, too, pauses to glance at me in the rearview mirror, lips pressed together, either disapprovingly or disbelievingly, I can't tell—and the little "mm" she lets out doesn't clarify it at all.

Ariella's mom returns to her client conference a second later, but Ariella remains quiet, possibly in shock, which

48

confirms everything I've suspected: it's taken me a grotesquely long time to get another client.

Ariella continues to stare and her silent, stunned gaze is infinitely more annoying than her nonstop chatter. "I wouldn't have called you if I wasn't desperate," I finally say, but she takes it as a compliment and squeezes my arm, her horror softening into sympathy.

"Don't feel bad, Delaney. I told you it was fate that we met. And it was fate that you called me! And that mom had to go out tonight to meet her beneficiary! Who happens to live near the Castle Gates Mall! And . . . what do you think it was that your house is on the way?"

"Fate."

"Right!" It wasn't exactly multiple choice. "Our destinies have collided, Delaney, because I'm destined to help you get your next beneficiary. I already granted a small wish for you—why not a big one?"

"So *my* big wish is to grant somebody else's big wish?"

"You should be proud. It's the most admirable wish there is. Totally selfless."

"I'd rather find a way to hang on to my 'self' *and* get a client."

Ariella lets go of my arm. "You call them 'clients'? That's so . . . clinical."

"It's because my dad—"

"Mom! You're going to miss it!" Ariella flings herself between the front seats and stretches one arm toward the windshield, straining against her seat belt, as she indicates a curved indentation along the sidewalk where a couple of other cars have pulled in to drop off or pick up passengers. The mall version of the elementary school car circle.

We get out of the car, to the left of an escalator that leads up to the mall. All that's visible from down here is scattered pinpricks of light poking through the hedges. There's also a low hum, the sound of many voices too far away to distinguish but close enough to recognize what the sound is.

Ariella rises on the escalator a few steps above me. "What you need to do first is get your motor up to speed." She tosses this advice to me over her shoulder. When we move up through the shadows of the lower-level pedestrian drop-off and into the golden glow of the mall's lights, the sequined angel embroidered on the back of Ariella's pink denim jacket gives off more and more flecks and flicks of sparkle, making it look like the wings are fluttering and propelling Ariella forward. "I aim for fifty small wishes a day."

"Fifty!"

"At least."

Ariella's silver headband, her twinkling triple-star drop earrings and her angel jacket are brought to full shimmering brightness as she steps off the escalator, onto the shiny-stoned path that opens before us. Meanwhile, my outfit, "perfect" for an art gallery, is completely wrong here, where it's all about reflecting and glowing. I'm like one of those cutout silhouettes—a shadow, an absence of color and light.

"And you need to do them as fast as possible. Once you've done like ten, pause for a second. Wait and see if anything hits you. Mom says granting a lot of wishes at once shakes up the molecules in the atmosphere and deep-seated wishes rise to the surface."

The glow and glare of the store window displays add to the luminescence from the giant globe streetlamps that seem to march down the middle of the walkway, set off in pairs that each bracket an S-shaped slate-gray metal bench. "We'll start in Fermier's. It's up here a little ways." I follow Ariella past several clothing stores and a travel shop. We turn a corner and pass another row of similar stores, at the end of which there's yet another corner that leads to more of the same. It's a dizzying maze, and it makes it impossible to tell how big the mall is, but it feels like it might go on forever, one corridor angling into another, on and on and on to infinity.

After another turn, there's finally something different: a department store that spans one whole side of the passageway. Ariella leads me to the revolving door and we push through. As big as it looked from the outside, it's even bigger inside, the ceiling angling up like the interior of a cathedral. The air is cold and clean, as if it's being pumped in directly from heaven. Everything about it is artificial, disconnected from reality. After spending all day in a mall, I'm feeling seriously stifled, but I remind myself why I'm here and that the suffering will be worth it.

Unfortunately, this hope is soon dashed on the linoleum that crisscrosses the store. First, Ariella expects me to see through the walls of the dressing rooms in order to tailor tacky dresses and boxy jackets for the women trying them on.

"I'm not Superwoman. I don't have X-ray vision."

"Study what they take in. Like that short, skinny lady over there. The hems on those skirts are all going to be way too long, and that shirt is way too wide in the shoulders. Right? So now you just time it so that you fix them *as* she's putting them on."

"How would I know when to do that?"

Ariella stares at me, mystified by the question. "Instinct."

I have no response to this. She gave me a lime stick after we entered the store, but I don't think it's granted me the superpowers it's apparently given her.

Ariella cocks her head to the left and studies me as if I've only now begun to come into focus.

"You're further behind than I thought. . . . That's okay, though. We'll go back to elementary wish granting."

Great. Doing small wishes was the one thing I thought I had down. Now I find out I'm still in the slow learners' class.

We crouch behind a circular rack of 30-percent-off

blouses and spy on a woman trying on a crimson velveteen jacket over her shirt. The woman's not old, exactly, but she's definitely not young. Her brown hair is gray where the roots are showing, and there are tiny lines fanning out from the corners of her eyes. She frowns at her reflection in the pillared mirror, the permanent furrows between her eyes deepening.

"Go ahead," Ariella whispers. "It needs to be let out in the back—see? Try making it a little longer too, but be subtle."

I study the woman for a second. I don't think it's the jacket she's frowning at.

Ariella pokes me. *"Delaney,"* she hisses. "Come *on.*"

I aim the candy stick over the top of the rack. The woman blinks, and then her expression softens. She leans back, considering herself. She smiles, takes off the jacket, hangs it back up and walks away.

Ariella steps out from behind the rack. "Why didn't you do what I said?"

"I fixed her roots instead. Now she can skip the salon this month."

"She didn't buy the jacket."

"That wasn't her wish."

"Yes, it was. Or she wouldn't have tried it on."

"Didn't you see her? She smiled."

Ariella's attention is caught by a revolving jewelry display on a nearby counter. "Most people have multiple wishes, Delaney." Ariella removes a thread-thin silver necklace from a hook. A tiny angel charm dangles from it. "But you have to pick one. Fast. The jacket would've worked too. Or you could've done both together. But you can't waste time *thinking* about it. You'll never get to fifty if you're too busy analyzing everybody's secondary wants. Save that for your beneficiary."

"Client."

Ariella rolls her eyes and carries the necklace to a nearby cashier. I wait for her to tell me I'm hopeless. That I'm a stubborn, impossible student and she's through with the lesson. But when she turns away from the cashier, itty-bitty shopping bag in hand, the stern look is gone. Instead, she's beaming, bright with a new idea.

"I know exactly where we should go next. It's like a shooting gallery of small wishes. You'll definitely score there."

★ ★ ★

"This is such a great place for granting small wishes," Ariella says as we step off the escalator that leads to an upper level of the mall. "Once you figure out what movie they want, you make it happen. I once did four at the same time!"

She guides me through the tangled web of moviegoers gathered outside the mall's multiplex. Some are messily bunched up in front of the box office, where giant flat screens play scenes from the movies, above digital schedules in blinking red. The rest of the would-be ticket buyers serpentine off from computer kiosks. We "excuse me" our way closer, until we're near enough to see the grumpy men and swearing women repeatedly pressing the Back button on the kiosks or inserting their credit cards for the twelfth time.

I raise my lime stick and peer over the shoulder of a woman who's squinting at the monitor through her reading glasses. She taps *Luckless in L.A.* but gets trapped in the backup loop when she keeps pressing the wrong time. I check the box-office display for the next show, but it's playing on three screens.

"Delaney." Ariella waves her grape stick and the ticket spits out for the woman.

"I was about to do it," I complain as an older couple, grandparent age, step up next. The man pouts at the screen while the woman tells him what to press, but they end up stuck anyway. I get them their tickets, but it takes a beat. Or two. I don't know what the matter is. It usually doesn't take me this long, although having Ariella watching over my shoulder doesn't help. I try to ignore her, but my next wish feels just as slow. I shake the candy stick like a thermometer.

"That's not the way it works, Delaney. You can't shake the energy down to one end."

"I know that." Although it's what I was trying to do. "I need to use my own wand." I hand her the candy stick and retrieve my chopstick from its holster in my boot. I head down to the other end of the kiosk row, getting Ariella out of my sight line. She seems to understand and hangs back, giving me some space.

I try to concentrate, but I'm finding it hard to care whether these people see the generic action movie or the generic slasher film. Doing a zillion wishes every thirty seconds may shake up the molecules or whatever, but it feels pointless—and I'm not saying that just because my magic seems slow-motion compared to that of Ariella P., super f.g.

Ariella catches up with me. "Hmm." She taps her grape stick against her teeth. "Let's get something to eat," she says finally. "Maybe your blood sugar is low."

★ ★ ★

"You missed another one." Ariella waves her grape stick toward the front of the line, granting a wish I didn't catch because the second we entered the food court, starvation kicked in from all the hunger-inducing smells—curried rice and spicy pizza sauce and sizzling stir-fries—reminding me that I hadn't eaten anything since the Pop-Tart. My blood sugar probably *was* low. I couldn't even decide what I wanted to eat, so I let Ariella lead me to some Japanese noodle place. *"Delaney."* Ariella elbows me and points her chin toward two women exiting the line with their trays. Before I can even try to figure out which one has the wish and what it is, Ariella waves her candy stick over my head.

"But that *is* brown rice," one of the women says.

"Oh, you're right. I guess I didn't forget to ask for it."

Ariella snaps off a piece of the grape stick with her teeth and regards me with concern. "Did you have any problems with your last big wish?" There's a careful, suspicious tone in her voice, like she already knows the answer.

"Sort of."

"What about before that?"

I keep my eyes on the people in line. "I can't focus if you're going to distract me with questions."

"You need to be able to grant small wishes no matter what's going on, without even thinking about it. I just did three more while I was talking to you."

"You wish."

Ariella folds her arms, miffed. "You wanted my help, Delaney."

I did, but her nonstop condescension is seriously bugging me. I look around, determined to grant at least one wish before we order, to get Ariella off my case.

At the pickup area, a customer lifts his tray, causing his miso soup to spill. I point my chopstick and really concentrate and the spill vanishes. Thank God.

But, unfortunately, Ariella remains on the case.

"You didn't answer me. Did you ever have any, you know, *glitches* before the last wish you granted?"

"No."

We reach the counter. Photos of the entrées are projected on a monitor and they dissolve from one to the next, like the movie previews at the multiplex. I study the sequence of the noodles and the toppings as they flash by on the screen. The captions are in Japanese, which makes it challenging to choose. I could ask for a translation, but I'm too hungry to listen, so I narrow it down by color scheme to the noodles with the flecks of purple and green, and the noodles with the strips of orange and red. "The last time was the first time you had a problem? Everything was fine before that, right?"

"Not exactly. There weren't any glitches before, because there wasn't a before."

"What do you mean there wasn't a before?"

I ignore her and step up to the counter to give my order. "I'll have that," I say, pointing to the orange-red dish on the monitor. The counter guy raises his eyebrows a little in . . . surprise? Amusement? Wariness? It must be some kind of spicy peppers. Luckily, I like spicy. "And a root beer," I add. This gets me a frown. I'm guessing root beer is not an authentic Japanese beverage. Either that or it goes better with the purple and green flecks.

Ariella orders, using the Japanese names for both her meal and her drink. She receives a smile for each, and the guy hands her a bottle of bright orange soda from some secret stash under the counter.

We pay and move off to the pickup counter. "You need to be honest with me, Delaney, if we're going to get to the root of your problem. If it's been hard for you from the beginning, just say so. For instance, how long did it take you to grant your first wish?"

"I already told you. My first was my last. My last *was* my first."

"The one you did three months ago? That was your first? How could it have taken you that long? Didn't your mother give you any coaching at all? Wasn't she worried?" Ariella holds her Japanese soda bottle at shoulder height and is tilting it in a way that makes it obvious (to me anyway) that she's using it to do small wishes. *A soda bottle.* I'm not impressed anymore. I'm annoyed.

"I've tried to tell you, but you don't listen." I grab the top of her bottle, preventing any more wish-granting, forcing Ariella to look at me and pay attention. "I inherited the f.g. thing from my dad, not my mom. She didn't know. Neither did I until I moved here."

Ariella pulls the bottle out of my grasp. "That's not how it works. It goes from mother to daughter."

"It's how it works in my family."

"I think you're confused. Maybe your mom sensed that your powers were sort of . . . remedial, and so she didn't tell you until later, but you misunderstood what she said. You need to talk to her—"

"I can't talk to her. She's—"

"You have to. This confusion is probably half of your problem. Just ask her—"

"She's not here—"

"She didn't move with you? Are your parents divorced? You can call her, can't you?"

"No, because—"

"Why not? I don't understand. Where is she?"

"She's *dead*!"

All the blood drains from Ariella's face, while the opposite happens to me. My whole face is on fire and I haven't even had a bite of the mystery pepper noodle dish yet—which is being held out to me by a different counter guy, one who's wearing the same awkward expression as everybody else around us in the pickup area. I'm surrounded by the jittery energy of twenty pairs of eyes trying not to look at me.

"Thank you," I say, and carry my tray through the silent crowd. I wade out into the sea of tables, but I have no idea where to go. I even forget for a second where I am, because I've been snapped back into that nauseating clutch of grief that hits me sometimes, like a punch in the stomach from out of nowhere.

"I found a seat." Ariella's voice is soft and calm in my ear. She takes the tray out of my hands and I follow her like a robot to the narrow table where she's already set her tray. She places mine opposite hers, and I sit down. The chair is hard and cold, but the noodles are spicy and hot, and the mix of tastes is so intense that I'm able to experience it without thinking at all.

The conversations of the zillion other diners spin a giant cocoon around us. Ariella leans forward, head bent over her food, eyes only on her plate. I know she thinks

I'm mad at her, but I'm not. It's not her fault. If I had kept quiet for a few seconds, let her figure it out without me having to scream it, I wouldn't have had to suffer the gut punch that always comes when the memory hits me this hard, leaving me emotionally deflated afterward.

The food is helping, though. "The noodles are good," I say.

My comment completely inflates Ariella, whose head snaps back, body straightening, perkiness revived.

"I know! It's my favorite place. Although Taco Wrap is great too. And Pasta Plus. I really like their veggie bolognese, but I try not to do mushrooms too much. It's fungus, you know. It interferes with the energy flow." She spins her soy-stained bamboo chopsticks in the air.

"Huh. That's interesting."

Ariella's cheeks flush pink, a companion shade to her purse. "I'm sorry. I . . . I'm sorry."

"It's okay."

"It's amazing you've been able to do any magic at all. If anything happened to my mom, I'd definitely be . . . I don't want to think about it."

"Neither do I. But I do."

There's another moment of quiet between us, but Ariella stays alert, gaze focused on me. She's trying to show me that she's *listening*. But I don't want that anymore. I'd rather hear her talk.

"What's it feel like?" I ask her.

"What?"

"The wand. When you do the big magic. Is it like electroshock?"

Ariella thinks a moment. "It doesn't really feel like anything. Not in your hand. It's more like you get really awake, as if you've just eaten a big cupcake with lots of frosting and drunk three Cokes."

I dig around in my noodles for the biggest pepper I can find. If I can't have the sugar rush, I can at least perk myself up with some spicy warmth.

"Maybe it's happened already," Ariella suggests. "Maybe you've passed right by your next beneficiary, but it's so new to you, you didn't pick up on it."

Not what I need to hear. I chomp down on the pepper— and my tongue is instantly on fire. I snatch up my root beer and guzzle it down.

"Want to try some of mine? It's not spicy." Ariella pushes her bowl my way. I twirl a few of the noodles onto my fork and stuff them in my mouth to put out the fire. She's right. The noodles are tangy and herbal, soothing. "Lime zest and lemongrass!" She smiles, takes a sip of her mystery soda and gazes around at the other tables. "It's nice to have somebody to come here with for once."

"Don't you come with your friends?" I say when I get my voice back.

"Oh, you know. You have to keep your distance when you've got a big secret like this. I mean, what're you going to talk about? 'What'd you do this weekend, Ariella?' 'Oh, nothing.' I can't exactly say I went around waving a magic wand and granting wishes, right?" She stabs her chopsticks back into the bowl and twirls. "I can't even talk to my family. Mom's always busy with her latest beneficiary, and my sister's a brat and jealous, and Dad doesn't get it. Grandma's the only one who listens, but it's not like having somebody your own age to talk to." She smiles, but it's a little off and I can see it now—the crack in her outward confidence that's probably always been there but I was too dazzled by her rapid-fire f.g. sorcery to notice. It's nice to know she's not totally invincible.

The weird thing is, hearing this is like hearing my own thoughts. Without the sister, and with Dad in place of her mom, and no grandmother. The "no one really understands" part—that's the part that matches.

"I wouldn't even be able to tell my boyfriend, if I had one. Because what if we broke up? I'd have to be sure he's the One—but you need a fairy godmother for that." She smiles again, and there's that same sad light in her eyes. "I'm not allowed to go out with boys until I'm sixteen anyway, so I don't have to worry about it now. That's all right with me. It would distract me from my work." She scoops up more noodles.

"My boyfriend knows I'm an f.g."

Ariella's chopsticks freeze in midair, noodles dangling. "You *told* him?"

"He was my client."

Ariella drops the noodles in the bowl and leans back,

incensed on my behalf. "Your boyfriend was in love with somebody else?"

"He wasn't my boyfriend at the beginning. And I thought he was in love with this cheerleader, Cadie Perez. But it turned out she was in love with somebody else. A girl, Emma, who loved her back."

"Wow."

"Yeah. Flynn's wish was actually me all along." I feel a flush of pleasure when I say this. The thought of it transports me to the Ferris wheel again and also makes me believe, right now, that everything really is and always will be okay with us. I *was* his wish, after all.

"Isn't that weird, though, now that you're going out, knowing what he's wishing for all the time? There's no mystery."

"That was then. I don't know what he's feeling anymore. It's *all* a mystery now, believe me."

I take a sip of my root beer. My tongue hasn't completely recovered from the pepper attack, and the bubbles sting. Next time, I'm ordering milk.

Ariella scoops up the last few noodles in her bowl. "So the beneficiary's wish was for the fairy godmother." She chews thoughtfully. "I've never heard of that."

"You've never seen an f.g. who looks like me either, right? That's what you said."

"That's true." Ariella pulls a fistful of candy sticks from her purse and fans them out like cards for me to choose. I pick another green one. I expect it to be lime again, but it's not. It's something else, something un-tangy, almost milky. Is this even a fruit?

Ariella unwraps a pink stick and holds it between her index and middle fingers like a cigarette, one arm folded across her stomach, contemplating. "I wonder . . ."

"Wonder what?" Melon. That's what flavor it is. Honeydew. Blech. At least it's not kiwi. That would be even worse. Ariella takes a lick of her grapefruit stick or pomegranate or whatever and her eyes light up, as if an internal switch has been turned on. She definitely runs on sugar. "I've got another idea . . ."

"Don't you *love* it?" If Ariella had a visible aura, it would be bursting with dancing exclamation points. Pink ones. Pink and purple and honeydew melon green, the colors of pretty much everything in this store.

I am in hell. Hell has a name. It's called the Princess Shop.

"Are you kidding?" I ask. "Look at me. Do I look like somebody who would *love* this store?"

There are pink dresses. Pink shoes. Necklaces with pink lockets, and bracelets with purple charms. Matching green and pink notebooks and notepads, pink pencil sets and pink and green pens. Pink purses and backpacks, and laptop cases with big purple daisies on them. Desk lamps shaped like ball gowns and clocks with glittering fairy-tale castles etched on their faces. Sparkly hats, sparkly barrettes, sparkly headbands and sparkly tiaras. *Tiaras.*

It's such a gruesome visual assault, I'm scared I might go blind. Actually, I'm not scared. I *hope* I go blind. Or at least black out. Anything to end the horror.

"That's why I brought you here! You need to look the part to be the part." Ariella holds up a pair of twinkly beaded earrings to her ears and studies her reflection in a narrow mirror that runs along the side of the twirling countertop display.

"Um . . . no way."

You'd think the customer base would be primarily the preschool/kindergarten set, and there *are* plenty of little girls running around, squealing in delight. But there are a terrifying number of older girls too. Some even older than me.

Ariella returns the earrings and tries on a thick wooden bracelet painted green with white polka dots. "I know green's not your normal princess color. It used to be a preppy store a long time ago, but it evolved." She holds out her arm to admire the bracelet. "Green's nice to have as an accent, though. They could use a little baby blue too, if you ask me."

A mix of floral and fruity scents, gardenia and pink grapefruit, swirls in the air, and a pop ballad plays oh-so-faintly from hidden speakers, low enough so you can't hear the lyrics and be distracted, but loud enough to pulse an electro-funk feel-good "buy buy buy" vibe throughout the store, which seems to be working on Ariella.

"Ariella! Don't you look adorable! Let me see that jacket." Ariella does a half spin for a pink-frocked employee whose name tag identifies her as Sapphire and who applied a little too much lilac-frost eye shadow this morning. "I was just saying to Helen, 'We haven't seen Ariella P. in a while.' Wasn't I?" Sapphire calls the question over to a weary-looking older employee who's rehanging an armload of mini-sweaters in the toddler section.

"Oh, yes. Hi, Ariella!" Helen waves to Ariella, her weariness lifting for a moment into the same genuinely happy smile Sapphire wears. They actually know Ariella's name. She must drop a lot of doubloons in here, or whatever the official princess currency is.

"Are you finding everything all right?" Sapphire asks, casting a dubious look my way, having finally noticed me.

"Yes, thanks," Ariella says. "This is my friend Delaney." Sapphire gives me a veiled once-over, clearly put off by my completely pastel-free, princess-free look. "We're just looking around."

"Okay, let me know if you need any help."

"Thanks!" Ariella leans over toward me as soon as Sapphire moves away, and whispers conspiratorially, "I have a member's card." Of course she does. "I get a ten percent discount on everything. So pick out whatever you want and I'll buy it and you can pay me back."

"I'll say it again, since you're obviously lost in a pink haze: 'Um. No way.'"

"Come on, Delaney. There are boots!"

"Yeah, I saw them." One pair. Pink plastic rain boots with yellow daisies on them. "I'm not three years old."

"Those would be too big for a three-year-old," Ariella replies, completely missing the point. The air in here is definitely numbing her brain cells.

She leads me over to a wall where the "New Summer Fashions!" clothes are displayed.

"Just try a couple of things on. See if they make you feel any different." Ariella grabs a pine-green sweater off a hanger and holds it out to me with a green-and-pink-striped headband.

I fold my arms, tight. "Do you mean different as in 'my blood cells are already messed up from being caught in this princess vortex, but if I let any of this stuff touch my body, I'll turn totally toxic'? That kind of different?"

"That"—Ariella swings the sweater at me in an effort to wave off my negativity—"is exactly what I'm talking about."

I could argue more, but it feels like a show-don't-tell moment is called for, so I grab the sweater and tug it on over my shirt. I snatch the headband and shove it onto my head. I was joking, but they actually do feel radioactive. I catch a glimpse of myself in one of the floor-length mirrors that bracket the clothing racks. I'm surprised the glass doesn't shatter in protest at the unnatural image it's been forced to reflect.

Ariella takes a couple of steps back and studies me.

"No. It's not working." Big surprise. I keep the sarcasm to myself, as hard as this is to do. Ariella circles me, to get all angles. "You're right. It's really not you."

"Thank you." I can*not* get the sweater and headband off fast enough. I hold them both out to Ariella, clutching them between two fingers like a dirty diaper. Ariella takes them but doesn't return them to where she got them, because she's still looking at me like I'm some complex math equation that she's *this close* to solving.

"I wasn't sure, but now I am: You're not one."

"One what?"

Ariella waits for a pair of pink-and-green-clad tweens to pass by. *"You know."* She twirls a wandlike finger in the air.

"I am so."

Ariella hangs up the sweater and slides the headband over her hair. Naturally, it looks perfect on her.

"Think about it, Delaney. You're fifteen and you've never done any real magic. You haven't granted one big wish."

"Flynn got his wish."

"See, that doesn't make any sense. You can't be emotionally involved with your beneficiary. And then there's the way you look." Ariella glances into the shatterproof mirror and adjusts the headband.

I step between Ariella and her reflected self. "I have the wand. I've felt the wish. I can do the magic. You've seen me."

69

"You felt *one* wish, and you got it wrong. It doesn't count."

"My dad *told* me I was one."

Ariella takes off the headband and waves it at me. "There you go. More proof. A fairy god*father*? There's no such thing. When Justine was little, she called herself my fairy godsister, but her powers were all pretend."

"My dad's not a pretend anything. He's granted like a million wishes." I follow Ariella to the cashier line. "I have the phone number of one of his clients, because we're going to her *wedding*. You want me to call her?"

Ariella lowers her voice when we get in line. "Okay, maybe you're some sort of distantly related magical entity."

"Like because my Dad's half-Irish, maybe we're leprechauns?"

"Sure! That's possible."

"Then I would *want* to wear green." I say this *loud* and get a barrage of quick glares from the princesses in line behind us.

Back outside the store, Ariella swings her shopping bags in one hand and gestures with her other. "Don't you see, Delaney? It explains everything. Your people, whatever they are, start later in life. They don't have as much magic, and they look like . . . you." As she waves and swings, the big bold mall lights bounce twinkling beams off her headband and off her embroidered jacket and even off her hair. I'll admit this difference between us: she reflects light; I absorb it. "So that means there's nothing

70

wrong with you at all! You're probably only *meant* to do small wishes."

"But my dad——"

"You said he's some kind of therapist guy, right?" I'd told her about him on the way to the Princess Shop. She'd never heard of "Dr. Hank." ("Oh, I don't have time for TV or any of that sort of stuff, and I get all my books from the library.") "That means he's good at figuring out what people's wishes are. And then he uses his minor magic to help them come true."

"He turned a rusted heap of metal into a red convertible. That's not minor magic."

"But he's been doing magic for a long time, right? So he's gotten better at it. Twenty years or so from now, you'll be a tiny bit better too."

"You are so completely——"

Ariella's cell tinkles its wind-chimes tune. "Hold on." She checks the text. "Mom's here."

On the way to the car, Ariella continues her pep talk, offering to take me "small-wish hunting" anytime, because I should definitely keep trying to improve my skills even if they're limited by my inferior birth. She babbles on as if nothing's wrong, saying we should come to the mall again soon, because she didn't get to show me the Accessories Plus store or the Starlight Organic Makeup Bar, and wouldn't it be cool if I slept over one night?

I say nothing, because what more is there to say? She's wrong, that's all. I know what I felt with Flynn and it *was* a wish. Even though I got the wish wrong, it was still a wish. And Dad's magic is *big*. Plus, he wouldn't say he was an f.g. if he wasn't, because he *hates* being one. If I told Ariella any of this, though, she'd just argue it away like everything else, and I'd be even more frustrated and pissed off than I already am. So I vow to stay silent until I get home.

"I got this really cute angel necklace, Mom," Ariella says once we're back in the car. "And some earrings. I'll show you." Ariella leans forward, brandishing her tiny shopping bag.

"Later, honey," her mom says, waving her away and resuming her Bluetooth conversation with Ariella's dad. "Can you take Justine to camp tomorrow? I'm meeting with Beth in the morning for a debriefing."

Ariella plops back down onto the seat, hurt by the dismissal, having forgotten me. But the memory lapse is temporary.

"I hope you're not sad, Delaney. I was trying to make you feel better. You can't be happy unless you accept who you are."

How ironic that I said almost the same exact thing to Andrea, Dad's client, owner of the magic-made red convertible, a few months ago. But I was talking about accepting who you really are. Not accepting who some sugar-crazed clueless winged-thing collector *thinks* you are.

"I *have* accepted who I am. An f.g." Now I've broken my promise to myself to never speak to her again.

"Once you have time to think it over, you'll realize I'm right."

I break another promise, to avoid eye contact, and I twist in my seat to face her, the pressure of the seat belt preventing me from sticking my face right into hers. I hope it's not too dark in here for her to see the sparks of anger flashing from my eyes.

She either can't see it, or she's doing an excellent job of pretending not to, because instead of shriveling under my gaze, she smiles a sympathetic smile that's illuminated by the headlights of the car behind us, and she pats my hand. "I don't look down on you, Delaney. I'm not that kind of person. Different doesn't mean less. We can still be friends."

I yank my hand free and press my body into the corner between the seat and the door. The headlights have gotten closer and Ariella's face glows ghostly gray, like she's some f.g. ghoul come to torment me—which she is, even without the ghastly glow. I'm tempted to scream "Let me out of here!" at horror-movie-shriek-level pitch, when I notice that Ariella's mom has pulled up in front of my house, and the lights behind us sweep past as the driver veers around.

I unsnap my seat belt, open the door and practically fly out, relieved to be in the cool air of night, free. Dad's car is in the driveway and the living room light is on. Another thing to deal with. I have to go in, though, or Ariella's mom will never leave.

After I unlock the door, I wave the all-clear signal,

ignoring Dad's "Delaney? Is that you?" Who else would it be? Ariella's mom returns the wave, still on the phone, and shifts the car into drive. I purposely keep my gaze from the backseat, but the car advances before I can turn away and I spot Ariella. Thankfully, she's in the shadows. But then a streetlamp casts a brief spotlight on her face. She's still smiling at me sadly. Not a sad-for-her smile, because she's sorry about her idiotic accusations regarding my supernatural DNA, but a sad-for-me smile. A pity smile.

By the time I think of the perfect comeback, the car's already at the end of the block, its red taillights blinking into darkness as the car turns the corner.

I run down to the end of the front walk and shout it into the air, on the chance it might be carried on the night breeze to Ariella's ears.

"We can't still be friends—because we never were!"

chapter six

Dad's in the living room, sitting in the easy chair, squinting through his glasses at a tiny folded-out piece of paper. "What are you reading?" I ask.

I don't feel like talking, but mindless conversation should, by definition, clear my mind, which has already started replaying my conversation with Ariella. Once again I try to mentally fix the past, coming up with great arguments—which she immediately shoots down.

Even in my imagination, I lose.

"It's the instructions to the lights we bought for out back. I thought I'd put the lights up tonight, since I was home early."

"What instructions? Don't you just plug them in?"

Dad drops the paper on an end table and stands. "Since you're the expert here, why don't you help me put them up?"

"It's dark out, in case you haven't noticed."

"Isn't that the best time to hang them? So we can see what they look like up? We're not going to have them on during the day."

It's a good point. And Ariella's going to keep creeping into my brain if I try to read or watch TV, so although it seems insane, the only way to *maintain* my sanity is to agree.

"Don't forget to bring the instructions for walking down the hall," I say. "And the ones for opening the door. And the ones for—"

Dad takes my arm and guides me out of the room. "You're not always as hilarious as you think you are, Delaney."

But obviously I am, because he's smiling when he says it.

★ ★ ★

Dad carries the stepladder out from the shed as I lift the rest of the lights out of their boxes and set them down on the new patio table. The yard is eighty times better than when I arrived, when it was nothing but weeds and dust. There's lavender along the brick wall that separates our yard from the one next door, and red bougainvillea spidering up the side of the garage. It still needs work, but the lights, which were my idea like everything else that's been added, will help a lot.

"We should start behind the gardenia bush and then string them along the top of the back—"

"Um, excuse me," I say. "Which one of us is the one with taste?"

Dad sets the ladder down on the grass. "I don't think this requires a fancy design, Delaney. You're the one who commented that you only need to plug them in."

"Do you want it to look pretty or boring? I'll let you decide."

Dad sighs and gestures at me to take over, which I do, directing him to drape the strings in a series of spirals and waves around the trees and along the walls. This was a good idea. The air is floral and sharp and full of mind-cleansing, confidence-juicing oxygen.

"So did you have fun with your friend, Delaney?"

"She's *not* my friend."

"You said you knew her from the mall."

"I said I *met* her at the mall. And I should've followed my instincts and never talked to her again. Then I wouldn't have had to spend all night having her tell me *I'm* the freak."

Dad repositions the stepladder along the wall. "She told you you're a freak? Why?"

I hand him another string of lights. "Because I've only had one client, my magic is lame and I don't sparkle."

Dad stops halfway up the ladder and turns to me. "You told her you're a fairy godmother?"

"She's one too. The supercharged version. Eighty-two wishes granted and she's not even fifteen yet. She got her first client when she was *nine*!"

Dad steps down to the grass. "That's not possible, Delaney."

I grab the lights from Dad and climb up the ladder. "That's what I thought. Until today." It was a *horrible* idea to come out here. My brain was almost Ariella-free and now she's stomped her way right back in. I concentrate on stringing the lights, but my mental picture of Ariella won't go away. "You should see her. She fits the part perfectly, with all her glitter and blondness. She's practically sprouting wings."

"Maybe she came from a costume party."

"I didn't say she actually *had* wings." I pause mid-string and think about this for a second. "At least not that I saw, but who knows?"

"I'm sure you misunderstood, honey."

"You're as bad as she is! Everybody's calling me a liar."

"I'm not saying that, Delaney, but it seems strange that in my whole life, I've never met another one, and my mother never met another, and as far as I know, my grandmother never did either."

"As far as you know? That's not very far. You never have an answer when I ask you things like why can't we do wishes for ourselves or why we only have one client at a time."

"That's just the way it is." Dad reaches up to help me, but I yank the lights out of his reach.

"That's not a real answer. And it makes it difficult to argue back when somebody like Ariella says you're not a real f.g." I climb off the ladder.

"That's ridiculous."

I march past him and pick up the last string of lights. "What's ridiculous is a fairy god*father*. And an f.g. who hates pink and hates people."

"You don't hate people."

"I may not hate all of the people all of the time, but I hate all of them some of the time, and I hate some of them all of the time." I plug the new string into the last one and then zigzag the lights down along the little looping wire fence bordering the lavender.

"That's definitely a new spin on the quote. But no matter what this Ariella says, the fact is, you *are* a fairy godmother."

"A fact is provable, and you can't prove it. In *fact*, it would be easier to prove it wasn't true. I need an extension cord."

Dad disappears into the shed and emerges with a nest of tangled green cable. But instead of handing it to me, he holds on to it, as if he's absorbing some silent message it's giving him. Finally he's come up with something supportive to say that will crash a hole through Ariella's logic and crush my doubts. "Maybe she's right."

"*What?*"

Dad carries the cord over to me. "We already know the genetic makeup in our family has mutated over time. The ability isn't supposed to pass from a mother to a son, or from a father to a daughter. So maybe it's morphed into something else. A lesser version."

I grab the cord out of his hand and yank the tangles apart. "I am not a mutant *or* a morph. And I am *not* 'lesser.'"

"That was the wrong word. I don't mean lesser in the sense of inferior."

"Really? Because if I looked 'lesser' up in the dictionary, I'm pretty sure that would be the definition." The cord practically unwinds by itself, like it's afraid of me, which it should be, because I am *pissed*.

"Your powers may not be as strong in some areas, but you'll make up for it in other ways."

"What ways?" I slam the plug end of the light at the socket end of the extension cord, but it won't go in. When Dad tries to take it out of my hands, I spin away from him.

"Well . . . we'll have to see."

I give up on the stupid lights and throw both cords onto the grass. "I've already had my identity messed with enough in one year. I really don't need this existential torture." I put my hands on my hips and face Dad. "I *am* an f.g." I'm vaguely aware that I've assumed a superhero pose. I can see why they stand this way. It gives you confidence.

Dad picks up the cords and attaches them. "What we should do is get together as a group."

"Why? So you can gang up on me?"

"No. Because you're right when you say I don't have all the answers. I was so resentful of inheriting the ability myself, I barely asked my mom anything. By the time I was curious, it was too late." He carries the plug end of the extension cord over to the outdoor outlet. "Wouldn't it be great to meet and trade information?"

I picture sitting across from Ariella and her mother and her grandmother at a big conference table, like in the movies when lawyers meet. The three supreme f.g.s smile their snide superior smiles at me while Dad types away on his laptop, taking down their testimony—which details the many reasons why he and I are an inferior breed.

No, thank you.

"Oh, yeah. Great. But, um, unfortunately, they're going away for the summer," I lie. "Starting tomorrow. One of those RV 'let's visit every state park in the Pacific Southwest' trips. Maybe when they come back, though." If Dad asks again in the fall, I'll say Ariella's father was transferred somewhere far away, like Budapest, and then I'll be safe until Dad gets an international book tour that includes Eastern Europe, which will hopefully be never.

Dad pauses before he plugs in the cord and glances over at me. I can tell from his expression that he thinks there's something I'm not telling him, when the truth is I've told him too much. I should've kept this all to myself.

That's been my mistake—asking for advice, begging for reassurance. All that does is let people see your doubts. It allows them to think you're weak.

I don't need any help. Help gets in the way. I'm on my own here. Like always.

The lights blink to life, shining together for a moment, illuminating my perfect design of spirals and loops and waves. Then they begin to twinkle, like little Tinker Bells, mocking me. I don't care what Ariella thinks, or Dad. I *will* find a client. I *will* grant the big wish. I'm so sure of it, it's like it's already happened.

I'm going to show them all.

Later that night, Flynn calls, like he said he would, and tells me all about the lighthouse and the disgusting dead marine life inside it. I lean back on my bed and listen, relieved not to be discussing me and my inadequacies after a whole evening of it.

But then Flynn runs out of things to say about barnacles and algae and rusted treasure, and he asks me what I did while he was out snapping photos of architectural debris.

And there it is, the opening I need to tell it all to someone who is on my side. But I can't start with Ariella's claim that I'm a non-f.g. I'd have to go back further, to before meeting Ariella even. I'd have to tell Flynn that I haven't had a client since I granted his wish.

On the Night of the First Kiss, after I told Flynn that I

was an f.g. and showed him some small wishes, he was so amazed. I explained that we only get one client at a time, and when he kept asking if I had a new one yet, I finally said I couldn't talk about the big wishes because it was against the rules, that there's an f.g.-client confidentiality that I can't betray.

I planned to tell him everything once I'd granted a big wish or two and got my magic up to speed, because then my flawed abilities would be in the past. In the present, I'd be the amazing supernatural creature Flynn believes me to be. But my next client is still stuck in the future. It doesn't matter that Flynn liked me before he knew I was an f.g. He knows now. Without my powers, I'm no longer amazing. I'm ordinary.

So when Flynn asks what I did tonight, I tell him, "Not much. I helped Dad put up some lights in the backyard." I can't see Flynn, but I can sense from his silence that he, like Dad, suspects there's something I'm not telling him. Luckily, I know better now. I'm keeping my flaws to myself until they're fixed.

chapter seven

Okay, I'm open. I'm focused. I'm ready.

So where is the client?

I've searched and sensed and listened for the *ping*. I've even ramped up the small-wish granting—which is a lot easier to do without Ariella watching and judging—but I don't feel any closer.

I really thought it would happen, that my inner declaration of impending triumph would be the trigger, but it's been two days and I'm still waiting.

Waiting in a general sense and, at the moment, in a specific sense. Specifically: waiting in the Nutri-Fizzy line.

As much as I don't like venturing into Wonderland, this part of the mall does offer a constant crush of humanity. And among those hundreds of humans, I have to believe there's *one* in major need of an f.g. So I've spent every break over here, mainly in the snack-food lines, where humanity is particularly crushed. There are lots of opportunities to magically refill napkin dispensers, aid snackers in coming up with correct change, and avert spills—while also trying to tune my f.g. vibe into the big-wish frequency. During my last break, I hit the Ice Cream Cottage, the Pretzel Palace and the Cinnamon Bun Barn. Most of the time I don't buy anything, but today, out of desperation, I ordered and devoured a double caramel sundae, a chocolate-covered pretzel and an extra-large pecan roll. I wanted to see if a literal sugar rush would jump-start my client-perception powers, but it's not working, and the need to find the big wish is inching beyond urgent now, edging toward panic. I know that sounds extreme when it's only been two additional days after three whole months of nothing, but the nothing has built to a critical mass, thanks to Ariella. Meanwhile, the snacks have all sunk to the bottom of my stomach in a big, fatty, sugary lump.

So here I am at the Nutri-Fizzy Bar in the hopes that something carbonated will dissolve that lump. I've spent half of this break in line, but at least I'm inside the store now, and there's actually a fizziness to the air in here, which perks me up a little. I step onto the mosaic that covers most of the floor: blue and white glass tiles illustrating a giant tumbler, asterisks of popping bubbles exploding all around it.

I scope out the Fizzy fans eagerly awaiting their Fizzy fix. Ahead of me are three women in classy waiter wear— skinny black pants, white shirts, skinny black ties, hair back in ponytails—and a heavy man with a shaved head in hospital greens talking on his phone. Behind me is a tall guy around my age, shifting his shoulders to whatever's playing on his iPod and rocking back on the heels of his brand-new unlaced high-tops, and two women in business suits talking office gossip. Farther back, just outside the entrance, there's somebody texting, somebody reading a magazine, somebody counting their change. Nobody sending any big wishes my way.

I'm starting to suspect there's something more to it than numbers, that there's some element I'm missing. But for now, speed-granting is the only strategy I have.

What if it's not that I need to do more small wishes, though? What if it's that I'll never be able to do enough? I'm scared that my client, the one I'm supposed to help next, is actually in Minnesota. Or India. Dad says there are big wishes everywhere and we just have to pick up on them, but what if the frequency I can read is only in a few people in the world? As I move up in line, the conversations of the other customers blend with the Nutri-Fizzy orders, which are like a rhythmic backbeat: "I'll have a large star fruit with lime and mint, extra fizzy." "Small triple berry with agave and vitamin D boost." "The antioxidant special, hold the banana."

I wish I could order up a client like that: One extra-large wish, please. Light on the resistance. With a double magic boost. Too bad that's not on the menu.

My phone goes off inside my purse. Not the "you've got a text" chime, but the full-blown crashing-cymbals ring tone. The doctor/nurse/orderly/radiology technician/ whatever guy in front of me glares over his shoulder, like he has any right to be annoyed when he's been on his phone the whole time he's been in line. His might be a medical-related life-or-death call, but then why is he wasting three hours waiting in line to order carbonated water when he could just stick a dollar in the hospital vending machine?

I check the phone. Ariella. Again. I punch the Ignore button, cutting off the animated fireworks mid-spark.

She's texted me about eight hundred times and left about twenty voice mails. I've stopped reading or listening to any of them after the first message, which was mostly suggestions of dietary changes that might improve my small-wish-granting skills: "You're probably low on iron, Delaney, so I'd recommend more leafy greens. And you should cut back on caffeine." No apology. No "I was being a jerk—of course you're a real f.g." In fact, she made a point to emphasize *small* in "small-wish-granting." Her tone was totally friendly, but I know she only wants to be friends so she can feel superior. Dream on, Peppermint Stick Girl. It's not happening.

I've made it to the popping bubbles at the top of the mosaic, and the spicy citrus scents of the drinks grow sharper. I get an extra-strong whiff of something that smells like a cross between pineapple and damp soil, and my stomach clenches and then flops. Just as I was feeling better. I wonder if the pecan roll gave me food poisoning. I hope I can make it to the counter without passing out, because I'm feeling light-headed too. Suddenly an intense, pained yearning joins the woozy seasickness. It's not a yearning for the watermelon parsley special with the zinc infusion, though. . . .

Oh my God. This isn't food poisoning. Wow. I forgot how physically unpleasant it is. But who cares? It's happened! *Finally*.

I peer around again at the customers in line. No one looks lovestruck or lovelorn. Please don't tell me that after all this searching and waiting, my next client has already gotten his or her Fizzy potion and left.

Wait. I still feel it. It's coming from in front of me. The last two of the three waitresses are giving their orders now, but I don't think it's either of them, and I hope it's not Hospital Greens Guy. It's not. He's too close to me. The vibe is coming from slightly farther away, which means it's got to be one of the "Fizz Masters." There are two girls taking orders and a guy filling them. The guy could be in love with one of the girls, or one of the girls could be in love with him. I remember Cadie and realize that one of the girls might be in love with the other. After handing an order to a customer, the guy says something to the girl on his left, a pixie-faced redhead with glassy gold nail extensions. Pixie laughs, but it's too light and easy.

There's a sadness in the wish I'm feeling. Hopelessness. The girl on the right, closer to me, whose name tag reads "Jeni," isn't looking longingly at anybody, but that's because she barely lifts her eyes from the ground, even when she's talking to a customer. Her voice is so soft I can barely hear it, and I'm only two customers back. She's short, a little heavy. Her skin is the color of a fading tan. Her hair is a dull brown, pulled back in a plain ponytail. "Plain" is the word for her all around. No makeup, no color, no style.

Cinderella before the ball. It has to be her. It's beyond perfect. She *needs* a fairy godmother. This is going to be a snap.

The guy in the hospital greens steps up to Jeni to order. "Medium pecan nectarine with a ginseng shot."

The waitresses have stepped aside to wait for their drinks, and Pixie calls, "Next!"

I need to make sure I get Jeni and not the other girl. "Go ahead," I tell the bopping high-tops guy behind me. "I haven't decided yet."

He thanks me and smiles like I've made his week and I wonder if that counts as a small wish. It should. As he slips around me, over to Pixie, I feel another tidal wave of f.g. longing roll over me, coming straight from Cinder-Jeni.

Now I *know* it's her. One of the businesswomen behind me taps my shoulder. Hospital Greens Guy has paid and moved off. I'm up. Here goes.

When I step up to the counter, I realize I have no idea what to tell her, though. Do I just introduce myself? "Hi, I'm Delaney Collins, and I'll be your f.g. for this wish. Whatever it is."

Damn. *This* is what I should've asked Ariella's advice about. Why didn't Dad ever talk about this? "How to Greet Your Client" should be Fairy Godmothering 101.

Jeni glances up at me, almost making eye contact. "Are you ready to order?" she asks, her voice tentative, as if she's worried I might be offended by the question.

"One large pomegranate with walnut." This is for Nancy, since she never got the one she asked me for the other day. "And, hmm . . . what do you recommend?" I expect the question to break the ice, but Jeni's eyes go wide in utter panic at the request. "That's okay," I say quickly. I decide to keep it simple. "A small plain lemon." As she rings up the order, I get out my money and try to come up with a way to make at least a small connection now so I'll have an excuse to talk to her later. I notice she's wearing tiny amethyst earrings. Little teardrops. She's not entirely plain after all.

"I like your earrings," I tell her.

"Oh!" She touches her ear with her free hand. "Thank you." Her cheeks flush and her gaze drops. Maybe I can get her to come by Treasures to look at the jewelry. I hold out a ten, and when she takes it, I feel a shock, a little one, like static electricity. Jeni must feel it too, because her eyes fly up to mine and lock for a second. She yanks her arm back in alarm.

I remember Dad saying something about there being a connection, an electrical current that passes between you, but it didn't work like that with Flynn. I hadn't granted a wish yet, though, so I was still operating with only minor magic. But now I'm fully charged.

"What was *that*?" Jeni whispers.

I lean in toward her. "How open-minded are you about the existence of the supernatural?"

Jeni's eyes widen. "Are you a ghost?" There's a touch of fascination in her voice, under the fear.

"No. And I'm not a leprechaun either." I lean closer and lower my voice. "I'm your fairy godmother."

You'd have thought I told her I was a zombie come to chomp her face off the way she goes stiff with fright, from her dull brown hair to her ugly brown shoes. Really? The idea of a ghost triggers curiosity mixed with mild caution, but "fairy godmother" freaks her out?

"We have to talk," I tell her. "When's your break?"

Jeni shakes her head. "Next!" she calls out in a squeaky voice.

"Hold on," I tell the woman behind me. "I need another minute." I return to Jeni, craning myself over the counter, prompting her to back up until she hits the carbonation machine behind her. "I'm here to help you, Jeni."

The remaining blood in her face drains completely out. I'm worried she's going to faint. "How did you know my name?"

I tap my chest and Jeni glances down at her own, seeing her name tag. She relaxes. A little.

Now that I have the big magic, I hope I can control it, since this will be the first time I've used it with a client. I need to do *something* to make Jeni believe me, but it'll have to be subtle, so it won't be noticeable to anybody but her.

I grab a straw from the container on the counter and hold it directly in front of me, blocking the view of the people behind me. I aim the straw at Jeni's shoes. *Please work, please work, please work.* The straw takes on a greenish, ghostly glow, and then there's a flash of light, exactly like the first time I saw Dad use his big magic with a client. The light bounces off the carbonation machine, illuminating the whole area behind the counter, as if somebody snapped a photo with a giant camera. I feel it—the boost Ariella had described to me. It's the sugar rush I'd tried to get with the sundae and the pretzel and the pecan roll. "What was that?" the guy worker asks. "The machine better not have shorted out again." Jeni steps to the side to let the guy inspect the machine. Her eyes lower as she moves, and I know it's because she's avoiding looking at me and hopes I'll just go away already. But that's okay, since it also means she's looking *down*. To her shoes. Which are no longer the dull Nutri-Fizzy standard-issue dung-brown orthopedic horrors and are now a pair of pretty robin's-egg-blue flats.

"Ah . . ." I barely hear her. It's like she's trying to scream, but fear has sucked all the oxygen from her lungs. I wait for her to raise her gaze to me—in amazement, in gratitude, in Cinderella-in-her-glass-slippers delight.

Instead, she whirls around and vanishes into the back of the store, leaving me alone with a line of perplexed Nutri-Fizzy addicts behind me. I don't get it. How could she not like those shoes? They were adorable.

chapter eight

Shockingly (not), nowhere in my searching have I found any version of a fairy godmother who uses a chopstick for a wand and ends up with the prince. Although I guess, technically, Flynn wasn't the prince, he was the boy Cinderella. And anyway, I'm not supposed to be researching *my* story. I'm amassing information to help advance Jeni's story beyond "Once upon a time, there was a shy Nutri-Fizzy clerk with f.g. phobia."

I spent the rest of yesterday at Treasures, separating all the jackets into denim, corduroy, tweed, leather and "other," and then subcategorizing by color, sleeve length, width of collar and type of closure (buttons, zipper, snaps, clasps), while also mentally sifting through the possible reasons for Jeni's freak-out. I finally concluded that Jeni either has me confused with some mythic creature who means her harm, or she's suffered through a bad romance—or two—and doesn't realize that she's guaranteed to have a happily-ever-after ending this time.

Therefore, I need to present her with the facts. (Although the facts are technically fiction. But they're only *called* fiction by people who don't know the facts.) I hear the *click click click* of a camera shutter echoing around the library reading room, and I glance up. Flynn moves along the railing of the upper level, snapping photos of the scenes from famous books—*Charlotte's Web, Oliver Twist,* something with an old guy fishing in a boat—that are painted around the edges of the ceiling.

Flynn was surprised when I suggested visiting the main branch of the county library for the start of our "Delaney Collins's Day" date. "But the weather's supposed to be super-amazing," he said. "We should do something outside."

"The weather's always super-amazing," I pointed out. What I didn't say was that running around Wonderland for the past several days has made me need a break from sunshine. An afternoon inside a dark, grand, book-lined room is the perfect antidote for the sunniness, shallowness and cultural bankruptcy of the mall. Because I couldn't tell

Flynn the true reason I wanted to go to the library, I pretended that I needed to do research for my boot business. "I'm out of fresh ideas. Maybe if I check out some examples of boot design through the ages, it will replenish the well or restock the fish pond or whatever."

Flynn completely fell for it and even spent the fifteen-minute car ride here explaining how he looks through photography books all the time for inspiration. "Different angles, processes, subject matter, color. I've gotten a million ideas that way." The downside to Flynn's enthusiasm is that he offered to sit with me and go through photography books while I looked through books on boots. Luckily, I persuaded him to take photos of the building instead, which has lots of the weird architectural details that Flynn likes. "Great idea! I could do a photo spread for the paper!" It really is cute how excited he gets about everything, even things I trick him into doing. We arranged to meet in the library's coffee shop at noon. Although I hoped Flynn would keep busy filling up film rolls, I still lugged an armload of ten-pound illustrated design books to my table, in case he came by before I finished my real work. It's a good thing, because by the time Flynn spots me from above and waves, I've already flipped open *The Complete History of Footwear, from Ancient Greece to the Present,* and the book is so big, it covers all four of the fairy-tale books. Flynn may be too far away to see what I'm doing, but it's better to be safe.

While I wait for Flynn to move on, I go over my notes. Last night I did as much research as I could on the Internet. I found a lot of clips from the million or so movies and plays and TV episodes based on "Cinderella," and way too many boring doctoral dissertations on the Political Implications of a Jungian Interpretation of Medieval Fairy Lore, or whatever.

What I wanted was stories of other fairy godmothers, not just the Cinderella one. I need more evidence, to prove to Jeni that her happily-ever-after is really just one f.g. away. I haven't found any fairy godmothers, though, just helpful witches and magical fish, along with talking capes and birds and mystical voices without bodies, all of whom do the same thing an f.g. does: help the hero or heroine get his or her wish.

I've also found examples of heroes and heroines who resist the help, who don't trust the magical fish or talking cape. These stories usually end with the hero or heroine dying a gruesome death or being trapped in some agonizing situation—blind and enslaved, forced to clean out some king's pigsty forever after. I might be able to use these as a warning to Jeni to let me help her or else, but the punishments are harsh even by my standards, and I'm pretty sure that if she's not completely terrified of me now, *this* would make it complete.

"Hey, how's it going?"

I'm so startled when I hear Flynn's voice that I

accidentally slam *The Complete History of Footwear* shut—and then quickly open it again when I realize what I've done. "You scared me."

"Boo," he whispers into my ear. He smiles and glances down at the open book. "Those aren't boots."

I notice that I've opened the book to a two-page spread filled with drawings of sandals. "I have to be aware of the competition," I explain. "And I think it was Flynn Becker who once said that inspiration can come from anywhere."

"He must be very wise, this guy."

"He has his moments."

"How about heading to the coffee shop and I'll share some more Becker wisdom with you?"

"Um, yeah, okay. I'll meet you there in five minutes. I just have to put the books away."

"I'll help you." Flynn reaches for one of the books, but I flop my arms across it.

"Great!" I say, too loudly, causing the other studiers in the reading room to glare my way. "Can you ask at the information desk if they have any magazines that focus solely on boots or shoes? I don't need to check them out now. Just get their names. While you're doing that, I'll finish up this section I was reading and then we'll put the books away. Together."

The second Flynn is out of sight, I gather up all of the books and run them over to a "For Reshelving" cart, straining my arm muscles. Research, note-taking *and* phys ed. It's like being in school. If life were fair, there'd be a way for me to get extra credit for all of this.

★ ★ ★

Because the weather is still super-amazing (of course), I let Flynn talk me into going outside with our drinks and walking through the maze that winds around the gardens behind the library. At least the bushes provide some shade, so it's not too oppressively sunny. Strolling through the maze—chai latte in one hand, Flynn's hand in the other— should be relaxing and romantic, and it would be if my mind wasn't already filtering through all the information I've gathered.

"Did you get any ideas?" Flynn asks.

"Oh, sure."

"So?"

I try to come up with something boot-related to say, but my mind's too focused on quasi–fairy godmothers. "I can't talk about it right now. I need to let the ideas . . . flow. You know, subconsciously."

"I get it."

We don't say anything for a few minutes. There's a buzz of tension between us. I can feel it in Flynn's grip on my hand. This is the first time we've been together, in person, since I met Ariella. And since then, so much more has happened. The things I can't tell Flynn about are multiplying exponentially, and I feel the secrecy building like a force.

Flynn's phone beeps. While he reads his text, I drop his hand and walk ahead, exiting the maze and entering a grassy clearing with a green-tiled pool in the center. A boy and his father steer a mechanical boat across the water, and two older women inspect a patch of lilies planted around the perimeter. I'm jealous they're all so "in the moment," but I remind myself that it's because living under cloudless skies has fooled them into forgetting to be cautious.

Even if there were a forest nearby where I could lie down for a second and just *be,* the calm wouldn't last. Growing up in New Jersey taught me that you always have to be on guard, because the bad weather is always there, hovering, waiting to rain down on you and wash away any memory of the sun.

Flynn catches up to me. "Brendan has a skateboard competition at three in Hannah Park. You want to go?"

It's always entertaining to watch Flynn's friend Brendan perform senseless aerial flips off a concrete ramp and nearly break multiple limbs when his feet fail to reconnect with his skateboard, but this will mean sitting next to Flynn, and more hand-holding and gaze-sharing. There was a time—the Night of the First Kiss to be specific—when these were things I'd hoped to be doing with Flynn all summer, repeatedly. But that was so long ago, back before I could even imagine the complications coming my way.

I may know about the hidden storm clouds, but another couple of hours out in the happy sunshine, with our knees and hands touching, and my willpower will collapse. It'll all come out. The pressure will be gone, but I can just picture Flynn looking at me like Ariella did: pitying, doubtful of my abilities. It's too risky. I just have to hold off a couple more days.

"Actually, I think I'm going to go home and sketch out some of these ideas while I'm energized." I back away, toward the maze.

"You're leaving now?"

"I have my roller boots on, so it won't take long."

"That's not what I meant."

I wave as I slip behind the bushes. "I'll call you later." I know this is the right thing to do. Soon, I'll have Jeni on board, and I'll grant her wish, and I'll be able to tell Flynn everything.

As I hurry through the maze, I wait for relief to come, but instead, I feel worse. That's because doing the right thing is like medicine. It may taste awful, but you know it's good for you and that in the end you'll be better off.

There she goes. Again. Dashing off to the back room to hide from me.

I've gone through two entire Frequent Fizzy cards and drunk an ocean's worth of Beta-carotene Berry Blasts, and every time I get to the front of the line, Jeni vanishes the second she spots me. Ducking behind the Nutri-Fizzy machine, crouching under the counter, running off to the restroom and locking herself in. I've left her multiple copies of the fairy-tale research I've done. She has to have at least looked at it. I've dropped off gifts—boxes of organic chocolate truffles, jars of scented baby powder—like I'm some heartsick suitor from a fairy tale, when that's not my part in the story! I'm not the one who's supposed to be begging. I'm the one who's supposed to be *begged*.

I've even tried stalking her outside the shop before it opens, and at the end of the day, but I always miss her. I'm beginning to wonder if she has a superpower of her own: the ability to become invisible whenever I get within three feet of her.

This should not be the hard part. Magic hasn't even come into the equation yet. For things to even out, granting Jeni's wish will have to take less than a millisecond—and the odds of that are not good.

It's ironic that my breaks have become more work than work. Although work has been more work too. Since I reorganized and redecorated the vintage room, there have been a lot more customers. When I first started, there were one or two a day. Now the only time the shop is empty is first thing in the morning and at the end of the day near closing—and even then, not always.

I deserve a raise, since this is all due to me, but instead, I asked Nancy for more breaks. "The effort that goes into keeping the vintage room at its aesthetic peak is draining me," I explained to her. "I'm not able to sustain this level of creative supremacy without sufficient time to replenish my mental and physical energy levels."

"I can imagine." I detected a hint of sarcasm in Nancy's

voice. "Just coming up with that excuse must've been exhausting." More than a hint.

But I got the extra breaks. I'd rather have the money, but it's a sacrifice I have to make as an f.g. Yet *another* sacrifice. When will they stop?

Even though one more break has come and gone without success, I'm relieved to get back to Treasures. It's late, so business should be slow. I think I'll pull out my worktable and devote the rest of the day to boots. I'll concentrate on just one pair. I don't even have to finish, as long as I start.

I'm semi-cheered-up—until I enter the vintage room and notice that there's a customer. Not only that, but she's totally wrecked my belt display. I rearranged the design yesterday, mixing up the lengths and colors into an impressionistic sculpture of a weeping willow caught in the morning sun.

Now it looks like a dying tree after an ice storm. Actually, it just looks like a hat rack, because all the belts are draped over the girl's arm.

"I had those organized," I say. The girl turns and glares. She's a little older than me and everything about her is hostile. Her eyes have five times more black eyeliner etched around them than I've ever worn, and her sandy blond hair shoots up in angry spikes, like porcupine quills poised to fire. "If somebody wants to buy one, it'd have to come off, right?"

"Yeah."

"Well, I'm buying them."

"*All* of them?"

"If that's okay with you." I notice she's already got about six belts strung around her waist, over her dress, which looks like a burlap sack with holes cut out for the arms. Her tan, chunky-heeled hiking boots match the color of her hair and the dress and the leather cuffs on her wrists, and even her skin. She's like some comic-book girl Robin Hood rendered in sepia tones.

She follows my gaze to the belts she's wearing. "I didn't steal these," she snaps. "They're *mine*." She glares at me. Wow, it's not just her hair that's prickly.

"I know that. I'm aware of my own inventory. I was just thinking that you seem to have enough belts already. And half of those"—I point my Nutri-Fizzy cup at the belts in her hand—"aren't going to fit you."

"They're not for me. I redesign them and then sell them."

"You do?" I can't help the surprise in my voice. Damn, now she's going to think I'm impressed.

"Yeah. I carve images onto them, paint them, add studs, beads, clamps." She steps closer. I expect her to give off a foresty scent or something earthy, but she weirdly smells like roses. "Like those," she says, and punches her belt-holding hand through the air toward my boots. The buckles of the belts whip around like the ends of a medieval torture device.

"I made these," I tell her. They're my "Artist's Palette" pair, with paintbrushes and fountain pens carved next to stamps of inkpots and paint cans.

"I figured. You seem the type."

"What does *that* mean?"

"You think it's an insult?"

"It is the way *you* say it."

She laughs. "That's just the way I talk." I can tell now that she has one of those cute little-girl faces under the harsh makeup, her features round and soft, babyish. I wonder if her attitude is a way to mask it. I don't see her liking being called "cute."

"I saw the table behind the screen with the boots and tools and all. What're you hiding it back there for?"

"I'm not hiding it. It's a separate business. My main job is managing this room."

"You do good work. I love this, by the way." She swings the cat-o'-nine belts out again, the ends fluttering past the hats on the shoe rack, the scarves on belt hooks, the shoes stacked vertically on the shelves, the left of each pair with the toe pointed up, and the right with the toe down. She's incredibly irritating, but she's got taste. And talent too— I'm guessing she carved the spirals on her wrist cuffs in addition to the snakes and skulls and flames on her belts. I take a sip of my drink while I try to figure out if I like her. The nasty fake fruit flavor hits the back of my throat. Ech.

"Nutri-Fizzy, huh?" the girl says. "You like those?"

"It's disgusting."

"Why're you drinking it, then?"

"It's complicated."

She shrugs. "I've never had one. I won't go to places that don't let you bring a reusable cup."

"They have them there."

"Yeah, you have to buy one of *theirs*." She drops the belts on a chair and hunches a shoulder, letting the strap of her leather backpack slide down her arm. For a second I expect her to pull out a bow and arrows. "I have my own." She shows me a felt pocket with a wooden fork, knife and spoon inside. She's also got a tall steel coffee mug and a collapsible metal canister with a lid.

"You could go camping."

"Most places respect it. If they don't, I go somewhere else."

"You're probably vegan too."

It was a joke, but she sneers at me in response. "Yeah, as a matter of fact. If that's all right with you."

"Then how do you explain all the leather?" I wave a hand from her cuffs to her belts to her shoes. Ha! Got her.

She packs up her reusables, unfazed. "I never buy new. No cow has died on my account."

"I don't buy new boots either." Although this is mostly because old ones are cheaper.

"Glad to hear it, Boots."

"Not my name."

"Fits, though." She shifts the backpack onto her shoulder and nods to the belts on the chair. "So, is that it for belts?"

"We might have more in back." Because of all my client-searching breaks, I haven't had time to unpack the boxes Nancy brought in from her last estate-sale spree.

The girl doesn't say anything. No request to see the boxes. Definitely no "Please," although I wasn't holding my breath for *that*. Which is a good thing, because my lungs would've exploded since all I get from her is "Well?" accompanied by an expectant, demanding stare.

"All right, all right." I find a couple of boxes marked "Clothing +" in the storeroom, carry them out and drop them at her feet.

"You take that one," she orders, pointing to the bigger box. "I'll take the other."

Normally I'd snap back that I'm not her servant, but her bossy style is growing on me. At least *she's* not afraid of me. The opposite, actually. And her hostility is on the surface, where you can see it, and not buried under sugary layers of condescension, like Ariella's.

I kneel down next to her but sigh loudly as I do, just so she knows I can match her attitude. She grins at me and holds out her hand. "Lourdes Taranco," she says.

I've never seen anybody my age shake hands. Back in New Jersey, a college admissions guy came to talk to us about doing interviews and made a big deal about how a lot of women do these wimpy handshakes because they seem more feminine, but that it actually makes you seem weak. So when I say "Delaney Collins," I grab her hand tight, determined to show her I'm the polar opposite of weak—but her grip's even stronger than mine.

She gives me an approving nod, like maybe she had the same guy come talk at her school. "Cool name."

"Thanks."

She lets go of my hand and I wiggle my fingers to get the blood back in them.

Lourdes hunches over her box and starts digging through it. "So what's your problem, anyway?" she asks. "Why were you so pissy when you first came in here? And don't tell me it's because I ruined your precious weeping willow display."

Okay, that's incredible. She knew it was a weeping willow. That's just . . . Nobody else would ever get that. Except maybe Flynn. "I've been dealing with a lot of weirdness the last couple of days," I say. "Something that seems really great happens and then it turns out to be, like, anti-great, if you know what I mean."

She laughs. "Oh, man. I have so been there. Feel free to vent."

"Will you be mocking my pain?"

"Probably."

I smile. I'd like to tell her everything, and it *would* be easier to confide in a stranger, somebody I have no emotional connection to. But I'd have to back all the way up to Mom and moving here and Dad and learning I'm an f.g. and my first wish and Ariella and Jeni—and Lourdes probably wouldn't believe half of it. Even if she did, it'd definitely lead to a nickname a lot worse than Boots.

"Is it a guy thing?" she asks. "Because I am *all* over that. My love life is a tragic farce."

This surprises me, because it seems like Lourdes is somebody who can get whatever she wants on her own. I concentrate on her for a second, to see if I can sense any kind of wishing vibe coming off her. How great would it be if *she* were my client? Hmm. Maybe it's possible to switch clients if you haven't found out the wish yet.

"Yo." She dangles a striped leg warmer in front of my face. "Earth to Boots."

"Sorry." I keep trying to tap into some invisible yearning from Lourdes, but she's vibe-free. "It's not that. It's more of a professional problem," I say, hoping this ends it. To change the subject, I hold up a rope belt I've found. "Interested?"

Lourdes takes it and dangles it by one end, as if she's got a snake by the tail. "How much?"

I always tell customers to ask Nancy the price of stuff that's not marked yet, but I've noticed that she seems to make up the price on the spot, to match the customer. She's pretty good at guessing the person's maximum budget. I don't think she'd mind if I gave it a try, especially since Lourdes is buying every other belt in the store.

"A dollar."

Lourdes thinks a second. "Why not?" She tosses it onto the chair with the others. "So?" She spins her hand in the air for me to continue my story. "Spill."

She's not going to give up, so I try to come up with a good metaphor. "I'm supposed to, like . . . tutor this girl in, um, math. And she really needs a tutor. Bad. But she's freaking out about it."

"Because she doesn't want one? Or she doesn't believe she needs one? She thinks it's an insult? What?"

That's the question. Why? Why would somebody *not* want an f.g.? "I don't know."

Lourdes inspects a long blue-and-white vinyl belt. "Yeah, that's an easy out." She drops the belt back in the box. "Put yourself in her place. See the situation from her point of view." She sits down on the floor cross-legged, facing me. "Imagine you're this girl. What've you got against math tutors?"

I lean back on my heels and think. It doesn't make sense. I've given her written proof that her wish will be granted, that I'm the one who can put her together with what she's been wishing, dreaming, yearning, pining for. And still . . . "She's afraid for some reason."

"Afraid of what? Math?"

Oh my God. That's it. It's not *me* she's afraid of, it's getting the wish. "She's scared because she's never done it!"

"Wait, how old is she?"

"I don't know. Sixteen?"

"She can't be sixteen and never—"

I stand up, excited by the realization. "She's *imagined* . . . adding and subtracting, and calculating the area of a trapezoid, but the reality of it . . . of having a, uh, pencil, and a piece of paper, and having to actually divide eleven thousand by forty-three—it freaks her out."

"Like those people who have that test phobia thing?"

"Yeah!" I pace around the room. "What if I back off a beat, give her an opt-out? She might relax enough for me to move in and get her to admit—to herself, and then to me—that this *is* something she wants, and that it's worth the risk to get."

"I think this is moving beyond math." Lourdes gathers up belts. I lean down to help her.

"Exactly. And I would've figured it out thirty Nutri-Fizzies ago if Ariella hadn't gotten me all screwed up."

"Who's Ariella?"

"She's this other, um, math tutor. She's tutored eighty-two people, but she has no idea what she's doing."

"But if she's taught eighty-two—"

"She's all about the end result, not the process."

We carry the belts out to the main room. When we reach the counter, Nancy holds up a finger for us to wait, and turns the page in her book.

"Thank you," I tell Lourdes.

"Hey, I . . . I have no idea what I did."

"You helped me see it."

"If you say so."

Nancy lets out a surprised chuckle at whatever she just

read and sets the book down on the counter. She peers over her glasses at the pile of belts and gives me a "good work" smile. I didn't do much, but I'm not going to tell her that, because this sale should earn me a few more unscheduled breaks, which I am now going to need again. When Nancy gets to the rope belt, I tell her about the dollar deal I made. She gives Lourdes a wry smile. "Why don't we just throw that one in."

Lourdes and I exchange a grin. After Lourdes pays, I walk her to the exit and she hands me her phone. "Put your number in. I'll call you to see how the psycho-tutoring goes. And I mean psycho as in 'psychology,' not crazed serial killer."

"Thanks for clarifying." I type my cell number in and hand the phone back to her.

"We'll bitch about boys next time. Maybe you can give me some random advice that'll make sense to *me*."

"I'll try."

I stay at the door after she leaves, still smiling at our conversation. Maybe I'm fated to always have the challenging clients. An ordinary f.g. wouldn't know how to help them. But I know how to think outside the wand.

chapter nine

I've been sitting here forever, or at least twenty minutes. The wrought-iron bench has definitely engraved a spiral imprint on my butt by now. I stand up and stretch. The mall is starting to come to life. When I first arrived this morning, the sun was already up and bright, as if it had gotten its wake-up call two hours too soon, but the mall was still empty. A couple of gardeners tended to the tiny pink, white and red flowers planted alongside one skinny patch of mini-lawn, but that was it. Now the store employees are ambling down the curved walkways, sipping their iced coffees and inhaling their last breaths of fresh air until their breaks. Vendors raise the grates on their carts and snack sellers unlock the doors to their stand-alone shops. The last few drops of dew on the lawn evaporate into the summer air, one by one.

I don't have to be at Treasures until noon, so I'm determined to wait here until whenever Jeni comes on shift. I do a couple of mini-lunges. All around me, store doors swing open as if they're synchronized, and here come the nannies and mommies, steering their strollers around the edge of the fountain. As if on cue, the fountain jets, which have been bubbling softly, suddenly shoot up into the air, and a full orchestra intro to some show tune blares from the speakers. I've moved on to shoulder stretches when I spot Jeni, already in uniform, walking alone. Her head is down, and she's several feet back from a couple of other Fizz Masters who fizzily chat, oblivious of their shy mouse of a coworker.

I duck behind one of the skinny trees on the lawn side of the fountain. As soon as Jeni goes inside, I dart over to the sidewalk and then creep closer to the entrance, with its giant bubbly tumbler jutting out from above the door.

The pillar with the Sunglasses Man ad is across from the entrance, a little to the left, and it's perfect to hide behind. I only have to lean out about an inch to get a clear view of Jeni, but she can't see me. She'd have to drape herself over the counter and crane her neck to the right. This means she'd have to be looking for me in the first place, which there's no reason for her to do.

At least, not yet.

Despite having come up with a back-off plan, thanks to Lourdes, I still needed to find a way to let Jeni know I was *willing* to back off.

The idea came to me during a trip with Dad to a craft fair. He'd asked me to help him find a birthday present for Gina. I was initially excited at the possibility of seeing a whole park filled with art, but the first few booths were all sequined scarves and hand-painted plastic animals and lots of sunsets: watercolor, oil, collage, felt. I guess a lot of people out here like to have a picture of the sun on their wall, even though they can just look out the window and see it pretty much every day of the year.

"I think they spelled it wrong on the sign," I told Dad. "They spelled it 'C-R-A-F-T' when it's really 'C-R-A-P.'"

"Eye of the beholder, honey."

"Yeah, well, this eye is beholding a lot of junk."

"Stop complaining and help me find something for Gina."

As we continued on, the offerings got better: handbags made out of grain sacks, benches made out of scrap metal, and sheets of silk-screened wrapping paper. We passed a booth of photographs that I knew Flynn would love. They were black-and-white exteriors, but sun-free. Instead, the skies were filled with clouds that seemed to pulse and swirl even though the images were still. I was tempted to text Flynn, but if he was nearby, he might offer to join us. Although walking hand in hand with Flynn through an art show, mocking and admiring, is something I've been wanting to do with him since he canceled on me the night of the lighthouse, I knew I still needed to wait a little longer, until the Jeni situation was situated. Self-discipline is another f.g. skill I've been getting better at with practice. For instance, Dad still thinks I don't have a client yet, and each time he asks about it, it becomes a little easier to shake my head and say nothing.

"Women like fancy soap, right?" Dad stopped at a table covered with waxy bricks in different colors, each bar flecked with seeds and herbs.

"Gina isn't 'women,' Dad. She's Gina. You don't want to get her something generic. You want to give her something that's *her*."

When I heard myself say this, it occurred to me that the presents I'd sent Jeni had been exactly that—generic—random bribes I'd bought arbitrarily. For all I knew, Jeni hated chocolate and was allergic to scented lotion. But there *was* one thing I knew she liked.

"I'm going to check out the jewelry," I told Dad, and zigzagged through the booths until I found an artist who made exactly what I was looking for.

"Earrings!" Dad said when he caught up with me. "Great idea. Women love earrings."

Dad was hopeless, but he wasn't my problem. And after I borrowed the money from Dad and asked for a gift box, *my* problem was one step closer to being solved.

So now all I have to do is get the box, with the note I wrote, from my hand to Jeni. I can't make it suddenly appear in front of her, or there'll be a replay of the usual running-off-in-terror, even without me there. I decide to try for the far end of the counter, to the left of Jeni, behind the straw-and-napkin display. She won't see it until she turns that way, and one of the other Fizz Masters may see it first. But her name is on the note, so they'll tell her and that'll work just as well.

Although I've done a million Object Transferences by now, they've always been pretty simple. It didn't matter if I was off a little. But today my aim has to be perfect. I can't miss the counter, and the note has to lean against the box, so it's visible.

It's such a minor thing I'm doing in a way, but it feels as big as transforming a dress of rags into a satin ball gown. Bigger, even, because that magic doesn't have to be precise. If the gown is more azure than indigo, who cares?

It's all instinct and intention and timing, like changing the size on a skirt after a lady's already gone into the department store dressing room. A few days ago, I couldn't do it, but now I have to, so I will.

I hope.

The envelope lies flat in my hand, the small silver box on top of it, the tip of my chopstick hovering a millimeter above the box. If somebody sees me, they'll probably think I'm practicing a magic trick. Which is sort of true, but I don't care. I can't let anything enter my mind but what's right in front of me. I close my eyes. My breath falls into a rhythm with the fountain's music, a soft piano tune, an interlude between the water-dancing songs. I imagine the exact spot on the counter where I want the box and note to appear. I picture it in such clear detail, it's like I've created the reality in my mind.

I feel a coolness sweep over my palm as the box vanishes. When I open my eyes, I glance down to the ground, to make sure the box and note haven't fallen.

Nope. They're gone.

In the few seconds this took, the usual endless Fizzy Bar line has already formed, its tail curving out from the entrance, and I can't see Jeni anymore.

There's nothing left to do but wait.

And wait.

I return to the bench, but the wrought-iron seat has gotten hot, thanks to the sun, which is nearly directly overhead now. The shade from the tiny tree has shrunk to nothing.

Why did I tell Jeni to meet me here? I could've given her my cell number and gone to Brennan's Books. If Gina's working, she'd have bought me a chai latte. I could be sitting in the cool A/C'd café, curled up in one of the plush armchairs, drinking tea and reading some random "New for Teens!" novel, until Jeni called. If she calls. To create a little breeze, I reach out my hands and do a swan dive. I arc my arms and then touch my boots, exactly like Ms. Byrd taught us in yoga class. The stretch feels good, but the sun is really heating up now, and I don't think I can wait outside any longer. I should buy an iced chai from the coffee cart in front of the movie theater and get to work early, because Jeni's obviously not coming.

"Um. Delaney?"

The voice blends with the *whish* of the fountain and the blare of the music, so that I can't tell where it's coming from. But when I fly up from my forward bend, Jeni is there, right in front of me, jets shooting up behind her like a watery crown. It worked! She's wearing the earrings I magically transferred to her, a pair of delicate silver strands about an inch long, with tiny pearly beads at the ends.

"Those look very pretty on you," I tell her.

"Thank you." She smiles shyly and her gaze drops to the note in her hand. She lifts it out in front of her. "Is this true? I only have to say . . ."

"If that's what you want." She doesn't answer. I'd made the note sound as ripped-from-the-fairy tales as possible:

Our bond cannot be severed until you release me. You must tell me, in person, that you don't want your wish granted, and then we will both be free.

I've put the power in her hands, which, as I hoped, has lessened the fear enough for her to come out and meet me. But there's also a subtle threat in there, if she's smart enough to get it.

"If I tell you I don't, then that means I won't ever . . . ?" She gets it.

"Never," I say. "You'll never get your wish."

119

Jeni doesn't answer. I can see her struggling with her decision. She may be afraid to have her wish come true right now, but that doesn't mean she wants to give it up forever.

"The fact that you have this wish, and that I was sent to help you fulfill it, means that it's your destiny," I tell her. "If you say no, you'll be altering the entire fated course of your life." I keep my voice low, laden with doom. I almost expect the fountains to chime in with some ominous sound track—lots of gongs and the low rumbling of drums. Instead, it segues into an old *Sesame Street* song about a rubber ducky.

Fortunately, Jeni's listening to my words, not the music, because her tense expression grows tenser. "Would it be bad? If it got, you know, altered?"

"The universe has woven a detailed path for your life, and you come along and rip out all the threads and tangle them up in a ball and toss them? What do you think?"

Jeni bites her lip and considers this. While I wait for her answer, I do an overhead stretch and smile to myself, impressed with my metaphor. Arms still up, I twist to the right, where a few feet away a little boy bobbles his sippy cup and it tumbles free. I wave my chopstick and the cup floats back up to his hands. The little boy giggles and slurps a happy sip.

I twist back and notice Jeni staring at me in awe. I'd saved the sippy cup without thinking, but it was obviously a good non-thought, and perfectly timed.

"See how easy that was?" I say, taking advantage of the moment. "That could be you."

"So I just have to let you grant a wish and everything will . . . go the way it's supposed to?"

"And you'll live happily ever after."

"Um. Okay . . ." She combs her fingers through the ends of her ponytail. "I'd like highlights."

"Highlights are a small wish. I can do that for you, but I can do that for anybody." Behind Jeni, a triple stroller with a trio of sleeping toddlers crosses the mini-bridge toward us. Their mother is talking on her phone as she pushes, not noticing that she's about to run Jeni over. I grab Jeni's hand and pull her away in time. "It's dangerous here. Let's walk around."

"I only have a ten-minute break."

"We'll get back in time. Come on."

We cross the trolley tracks, into the shade from the pseudo-balconies that jut out over the storefronts. "It's the big wish that sets your life on the right path," I tell Jeni as we stroll past the furniture store. "That's the one I'm destined to grant for you." I can't believe how slowly she walks. I have to restrain myself from taking hold of her arm and tugging her along. "And the big wishes are always about love."

When I say the word "love," Jeni stops walking— although she was already moving so slowly, it's not much of a difference. "But . . . that's not . . . there isn't anybody . . ." She whispers this last part so softly, I barely hear it.

"There has to be or I wouldn't feel this way."

"*You* feel it?"

A flip-flopping remote-control car, operated by a nearby vendor cart sales guy, zips through our legs. I kick it aside. "That's how we're bonded. And how I know your big wish is huge, and is definitely about love. *And* how I know you don't really want to send me away and have it never come true."

Jeni doesn't answer. I tilt my head, trying to meet her eyes. "Haven't you imagined holding hands? Going on dates? Having a special song? Kissing?" It could be the breeze brushing past us and causing the loose strands of hair around Jeni's face to flutter that makes it look like her head has dipped, just a little, but I take it as a nod. "This will make it *real*."

Suddenly we're propelled forward by a gaggle of women laden with bagged bounty from Vogel's semi-annual half-off clothing sale. They squeeze in and around and by us, and we're finally spit out near one of the curvy shop-lined alleyways. The pulsing beat of hip-hop vibrates the air outside of Jump Kicks, the athletic shoe store. The sound crashes into the jazz orchestra music from the fountain speakers behind us. A shopper exits the shoe store, shopping bag in hand, and a gust of frigid A/C'd air bursts out—at the same moment that a wave of lovelorn yearning surges next to me.

Aha! Jeni doesn't need to tell me her wish, because she's staring right at him through the window, her longing reflection bracketed by a window display of orange and blue trainers stacked on white stepladders. He's pointing out the features of a pair of high-tops to two guys in their twenties, who listen intently, hooked by Prince Charming's enthusiasm. I recognize him. He's the guy I let go in front of me at the Fizzy Bar line yesterday—when I felt the f.g. vibe for the first time.

"Good choice. He's not only cute and nice, but he's good at his job."

Jeni blushes and turns away from the window. "I didn't . . ."

"Too late. I know who it is now. There's no going back." The blush fades as the blood drains from her face and the panicked look returns. I grab her wrist to prevent her from fleeing. "You don't need to be afraid. This is meant to be."

"But he doesn't even know who I am. I'm so . . . and he's so . . ." She sighs wistfully. "It's impossible."

I have to admit it's going to be a challenge. The adoration is obviously one-sided. The prince has glanced this way a couple of times, but his gaze has moved right over us. "It doesn't happen all at once," I explain. "There are steps. And it *is* possible. Didn't you ever see that musical of *Cinderella*? The fairy godmother sang a song about how nothing's impossible as long as you believe."

Jeni thinks this over. "We're meant to be," she says, as

if she's testing it, seeing if the thought will stick. There's a glimmer of a smile on her face, and her expression grows pensive and dreamy. She's hooked.

"Yes. You are." I take her arm. "Let's go in."

Before we reach the door, a girl in a long teal velvet wrap skirt, ruffled olive top and espadrilles sweeps between us. "Excuse me," she says, after she's already shouldered me out of the way. She pushes open the door, but then hovers there for a second. Then, as if shoved by an invisible hand, she stumbles in.

Velvet Girl walks up to Jeni's Prince Charming and stares up at him, squinting slightly. Her braided hair is tied at the end with a glossy emerald ribbon, and her dangling earrings, made of beads in every remaining shade of green in the big crayon box, sparkle in the store's fluorescent lights. A slight shiver goes through me, as if some inner alarm has gone off. Like some extra-f.g. perception, but I'm not sure why. At the same moment, a shoe display falls off the wall and Prince C. grabs Velvet G.'s arm to pull her away from the hailstorm of cross-trainers. They both look down, then up, then at each other. Velvet smiles. Prince smiles. Their gaze lingers.

"Oh, no," Jeni says. "Is that his girlfriend?"

"No," I say firmly. Because it *can't* be. But my next thought is, *Not yet.*

Velvet's cell goes off. She reads the message and glances out the window. I follow her gaze, but I already know what I'll see—or rather *who,* because my brain has caught up to my extra-f.g. perception. There she is, sitting on the stone wall of the fountain. Her back is to me, but I'd know that blond hair and pink sequined jacket anywhere. I can't believe she can work her powers from that far away. And without even facing the right direction.

This needs to be stopped before it goes too far. Before Prince Charming's down on his knees, about to slip a blue canvas running shoe onto Velvet's bare foot, unaware he's got the wrong Cinderella. I turn to Jeni to reassure her, but she's gone. I spot her running across the mini-bridge, back to the Nutri-Fizzy Bar. I'll deal with Jeni later. First I have to get rid of the pink, sparkling obstacle standing in the way of her wish.

I quickly cross the mall and step in front of Ariella, my shadow dimming her sparkle. She glances up from her texting. "Hi, Delaney! I've been calling you! Is your phone broken? I even went by the store this morning, but you weren't there."

"I need to tell you something."

"Maybe we can get an ice cream later. This isn't a good time, unfortunately." She waves her lime stick in the direction of the shoe store and then goes back to typing. "I'm in the middle of something." Behind her, the fountain's water spouts burble quietly, as if they don't dare disturb her concentration. I dare, though.

"I found my next client."

"You did?" she says, but I can tell she's only half listening.

"I granted a bunch of small wishes in a row, like you told me to, and *ping,* I got slammed with the f.g. vibe."

The *ping* gets her attention. She forgets the phone for a second and smiles up at me. "That's great, Delaney! Congratulations!" It's a genuine happy-for-me smile. This is good. She's willing to accept that she can be wrong. "See? I told you it would happen." She pretty much told me the *opposite,* actually, but I let it slide, because if she wants to be f.g. friends again, that's going to make this whole thing easier.

"There's kind of a catch—"

Ariella's cell chimes. "I want you to tell me *everything,* Delaney. But we have to do it later." She frowns down at the message. "I'm having an issue with my beneficiary. She's not being cooperative."

"That's what I want to talk to you about—"

"I can't afford these!" A girl with frizzy hair and a peasant skirt steps in front of me and thrusts a red plastic shoe bag in Ariella's face. It takes me a second to realize it's Velvet Girl, but the velvet is gone. She's completely transformed—or should I say transformed *back*? Her clothes have gone from elegant and chic to dumpy and dull. The teal skirt is a dreary algae color now, the top is a faded sleeveless tee and the shoes are stretched-out beach sandals. It's impossible to tell if the earrings are still there or not, because her hair has sprung loose from whatever magic had kept it bound in the braid and it cascades down around her shoulders like a teased-up lion's mane.

"Hello?" I say to the back of her head. She whips around and squints at me through brown rectangular-framed glasses, which she definitely wasn't wearing in the store. I try to remember her name. Something woodsy, like Moss or Pine. No, it began with an "F." Flora? Fungus? Field Greens?

"Fawn, this is Delaney," Ariella says. Right. *Fawn*. "Delaney, Fawn. Delaney is a colleague. You can speak freely in front of her."

Fawn studies me for another suspicious beat. "You look familiar."

"I was there," I say. "Outside the shoe store. I saw what happened."

Ariella regards me curiously. "*What* happened?"

Fawn turns back to Ariella. "He didn't ask me out, that's what. He didn't even ask my name! And now I'm stuck with these." She lifts the box out of the bag and opens it, waving the blue running shoes from the window display in front of us. "I don't even like sneakers. I only wear sandals. My feet need to *breathe*."

"Don't worry about it. This was just a way to break the ice." Ariella takes the shoes from Fawn's hands and replaces them in the box. "We'll return these later, when Ronald isn't there, and get a refund."

His name is Ronald? That's not what I would've guessed. "Prince Ronald?" Hmm.

Her hands now free of the bag, Fawn arcs them through the air dramatically. "But he didn't notice my dress or *anything*. I was just a *customer* to him."

"Maybe you have the wrong guy," I suggest. Fawn casts a panicked eyeglass-framed look my way.

"Very funny, Delaney." Ariella slips the shoebox back into the bag. "She's only joking," she assures Fawn.

"No, I'm not. I really didn't see any chemistry there."

"Delaney." Ariella gives me a stern schoolteacher scowl, which is a bit of a joke when you look like Tinker Bell.

"It's my professional obligation to inform you that a mistake has been made," I tell Ariella. "You've targeted somebody else's wish."

Ariella studies me for a moment. She hands the shoe-store bag to Fawn. "Go back to work. I'll come by when your shift is over."

Fawn casts a worried look my way. "But is she—?"

"No," Ariella snaps. "This is about something else. Go on." She flaps the back of her hand at Fawn, shooing her away. Fawn shuffles off in her floppy sandals, throwing occasional concerned looks over her shoulder until she disappears into the growing lunch crowd. Ariella folds her arms and faces me. "All right, what's going on with you, Delaney? Is this about what happened at Castle Gates? Is that why you haven't texted me back? Because you were too busy inventing this silly revenge plot?"

The sun's pouring down on my back, which is not a great thing when you're wearing all black. Or boots. "Can we talk somewhere else? I'm baking here."

"Maybe you should dress more appropriately. It *is* summer. No one wears boots in summer."

I fold my arms, mirroring her. The water jets choose that moment to shoot up, in time to the cymbal crash opening to the fountain's next scheduled dance number. Misty droplets rain down on Ariella, who huffs, barks out, "Fine, let's go," and stomps off across the trolley tracks to the store opposite us. Well, sort of stomps, since it doesn't really work in flip-flops. She may mock my footwear, but boots are much better for stomping.

I navigate through a pack of summer preschoolers and follow Ariella into the store. It's refreshingly cool inside, but it's also so dark it's as if we've stepped into a cave. A cave filled with chanty, chimey music and burning sandalwood incense. Oh God, we're in the Tranquility Den. Ms. Byrd loves this place, but I've never been inside. Yoga mats fan out on one area of the floor like a deck of giant cards. Shelves of candles, books and little plug-in, trickly fountains line the walls, and big velvety pillows with tassels are scattered around everywhere. At the back of the store, a girl with multiple piercings and colorful tattoos decorating one entire arm like a sleeve sits behind a counter lined with displays of crystal jewelry. She glances up from her phone, takes out an earbud and waves. "Hey! Welcome! Let me know if you have questions or need help with anything."

"Thanks. We're just looking," Ariella tells her.

The girl offers her a peace sign and goes back to her music, which I can tell from the rhythm of her hip-swaying is slightly more up-tempo than the Franciscan monks crooning with the whales—or whatever it is that's playing over the store's speaker system.

Ariella steps through a gauzy curtain that divides off one corner of the store. She gestures for me to follow. The space is set up like what I'm guessing is the ideal Zen meditation room, with a couple of big pillows on the floor next to a stone Buddha, trays of tiered candles that reek of vanilla even though they're not lit, and end tables stacked with books with titles like *Be Calm* and *Relax*. Good place for a showdown. Ariella starts it:

"Just because you're mad at me for being honest with you the other night, you don't have to take it out on my beneficiary. If you *are* a fairy godmother, that kind of behavior is not going to help you build your powers."

"I wasn't taking anything out on her. I was being honest with *you*."

"What about this 'client' you found? Did you make that up?"

"No. I have a client. Jeni Gold. She works at Nutri-Fizzy."

"Then why aren't you out there helping her?" Ariella studies me with the same condescending big-sister expression she gave me at the Princess Shop. "Did something go wrong already?"

"No." Although technically yes. But it's not *me* who's wrong.

"Then why are you interfering with me and Fawn?"

"Because Jeni's in love with Ronald."

Ariella takes this in. She retrieves a lime stick from her purse and peels down the plastic. "He's a cute guy," she says. "A lot of girls probably have a crush on him."

"This isn't a crush. I *felt* it. This is the real thing."

"You're being oversensitive to a small wish."

"No, I'm not." A high-pitched whine has crept into my voice and I glance down at the end table next to me. *Be calm,* I remind myself. "I know the difference between a small wish and a big one," I say. "Jeni is my client, and Ronald is her wish."

"Delaney . . ." Ariella shakes her head as if I'm some clueless loser she feels compelled to set right. "We've talked about this. You've had one beneficiary. *Ever.* In your whole life. And you got the wish *wrong.*"

"I've done the major f.g. magic with Jeni." I take my chopstick out of my boot and wave it in the air. "That proves she's my client. And it proves her wish is a big one."

Ariella leans her hand on the Buddha's head and takes a bite of her candy stick as she thinks this over. "Maybe you got the stepsister."

"What stepsister?"

"You know. In *Cinderella,* the stepsisters were in love with Prince Charming too."

"Neither of them had an f.g."

"They might have had a lesser version. Somebody with weaker powers . . . like *you.*"

"That's the stupidest thing I've ever heard. If it was true, it would've been in the story. I mean, that's a pretty big plot element to leave out."

"It's a really old fairy tale, Delaney. Practically a myth. Parts of it have been lost along the way." She points the lime stick at me. "There isn't any fairy godmother in the Grimm one at all. It's a bird."

I already know this from my library research, but it doesn't prove anything. "So what? I know what I felt."

"I believe you connected with her wish, Delaney. And I also believe you mean well. But which one of us is more likely to have sensed the *real* wish? The fairy godmother who's been doing the job for only a few months and has never granted a big wish correctly? Or the one who's been doing it for *six* years and has granted *eighty-two*?"

I point my chopstick at her. "Did you ever think maybe you've been rushing it a little? Grabbing the first wish you feel because you're so determined to get to a hundred by your birthday?" I step near her, pointing the chopstick. "All you're focused on is upping your numbers so you can show up your mom." We circle the pillows, wands out in front of us like daggers. Ariella glares at me, but there's a glimmer of doubt in her eyes. "When all you care about is the goal, you're going to make mistakes."

"I'm a *professional*," Ariella snaps. "I don't make mistakes." As she says this, she stumbles on the edge of a pillow and loses her balance, dropping her lime stick and knocking her elbow into a stand of wind chimes. The little metal tubes ram into each other in tinkling protest as Ariella lands, butt-first, on the pillow.

It's really hard not to grin, but I repress it. Not very well, I guess, because Ariella's glare gets sharper and colder. "This is *not* how a fairy godmother behaves," she says. She pushes herself up from the floor.

"Maybe you're right," I tell her. "Maybe I *am* something else. A superior version that's evolved over the years. Look at you, with all your pink and glitter." I circle my wand at her, making a big lasso in the air, with her in the middle. "You're totally old-school."

Ariella fixes her headband. "I'm the real thing," she says. "And you're just a wannabe." She smoothes out her skirt, snatches up her lime stick and brushes past me, batting the gauze curtain aside. I follow Ariella back out to the main room of the store. She stops at the door. "I don't want to fight you, Delaney," she says as she drops her candy stick into a trash can painted with swirling spirals.

"No, you just want me to cave."

Ariella doesn't answer.

"But I'm not going to. I'm getting Jeni her wish."

Ariella shoves open the door, setting off another cascade of chimes.

"*Namaste!*" the girl at the counter calls out to us.

"Same to you!" I say, and then step outside—to find Ariella waiting for me, blocking my way.

"I'm warning you one last time, Delaney. Don't do this."

I feel a flicker of worry, but I quickly tamp it down.

"I'm not afraid of you, or your fruit-flavored pseudo-wands, Tinker Bell."

Ariella's blue eyes narrow and take on an icy gleam. "If you insist on marching your carved-up, out-of-season boots down this dangerous path, you and your 'client' are going to be very sorry."

I hold up my chopstick in a salute. "May the best f.g. win."

chapter ten

"All you have to remember is the code."

"P.W.F.S.L."

"Right. Follow the code and you'll do great, okay?"

Jeni nods one of her barely perceptible mini-nods, which I'm able to detect only because I'm staring at her so intently. She squeezes the iron armrest on the bench and nervously murmurs the letters to herself while I lean back, breathe in the calming, suntan-lotion-scented air wafting out of Fiji Escapes and picture Ariella's horror when I tell her that my Cinderella has beaten hers to the prince.

I also imagine Flynn's awe when he hears about my f.g. triumph. He'd invited me out to a concert last night, but I told him I was doing something with Dad. I have to get this wish done first before I can say yes to any plans. Luckily, now that Jeni knew it was either go after Ronald or risk unraveling her destiny, I was able to reel her back in pretty quickly. I explained that Fawn was the girlfriend of Ronald's best friend. "She was in the store to buy shoes for her boyfriend, for his birthday," I told Jeni. Either it's getting easier to lie, or Truth Altering is yet another advanced f.g. power.

Because Ronald and Jeni don't know each other, I've come up with a plan for their "meet cute," which is what they call it in romantic comedies when the hero and heroine first connect. I read it in a movie review when I was doing my online research, and I thought it was a good technique for an f.g. to use.

The best sort of "meet cute" is one where it later seems like fate was behind it all. And it will be fate, because aren't fate and fairy godmothers the same thing?

After doing a little spying on Ronald, I discovered that every day, on his two breaks, he buys a Nutri-Fizzy (morning break) or a coffee (afternoon break) and hangs out at the fountain to check his text messages.

Then I came up with my plan.

I wanted the meeting to be relaxed. Not something farcical and crazy that could only happen in the movies. All I needed was a trigger to get the conversation started and a couple of prompts for Jeni to use to keep it going, until nature and chemistry kicked in and the romance took off on its own. A torso-less male mannequin in a Hawaiian (or I guess Fijian) shirt and straw sunhat stares coolly down at me from the Fiji Escapes window like he doubts my plan. What does *he* know? He's a brainless piece of plastic who's been sliced off at the chest. He should stick to his own problems and not waste time trying to knock down my high expectations, which can't be done anyway.

"What do the letters stand for?" I might as well quiz Jeni for the tenth time, since we've still got a few minutes.

"Pomegranate walnut Fizzy with selenium and lime."

"Right. That's how to remember it, but what is it really?"

"Um . . . take my *place* . . . the *wallet* . . . um . . . uh . . ."

"The 'F' is the easiest one, Jeni. It's the same."

"Right! Fizzy! 'S' is shoe store, and 'L' is 'What are you listening to?' "

"Yes! Perfect. It's going to go great."

Summer shoppers shuffle past us, their shopping bags hanging from elbows and stroller handles, temporarily blocking our view.

Then the crowd clears, and—

"There he is!" Jeni's eyes brighten. At the fountain, Ronald is taking up his usual space at the stone wall. His back is to the water and the sun hits him like a spotlight as his body bops in time to a beat only he can hear, thumbs tapping and scrolling. "It's like the space is reserved for him," Jeni coos, as I think the same thing. The rest of the rail is packed with shoulder-to-shoulder grade-schoolers and camera-clicking tourists, but somehow Ronald's butt has managed to slip right in—to the exact place I'd seen him before, like there's some magnet in his pants that repels the crowd and draws him to the spot.

"In a second, you'll be right next to him." I take Jeni's hand and pull her to her feet. "Repeat it again."

"P.W.F.S.L."

"Good."

"But aren't you supposed to . . . you know."

"What?"

Jeni waves a hand up and down in front of her.

"The whole servant-girl-to-beauty-queen magic makeover? That would be superficial, and wrong. Magic is a tool. I'll use it to help you but not to change you. You need to be *you*, because that's who Ronald's meant to be with, not some fake fairy-tale princess. The whole ball-gown thing's for people with no confidence."

"*I* have no confidence."

"I mean f.g.s with no confidence. You don't need confidence. I mean, you do, but that's easy because all you have to do is be yourself, which you already are. Okay?"

"Well . . ."

"We're wasting time." I spin her around by the shoulders. "You're meant to be. Just keep telling yourself that."

"*We're meant to be. We're meant to be.*"

"Right. Don't forget the code, though."

"P.W.F.S.L., P.W.F.S.L."

I guide Jeni forward a few steps and then let go. Miraculously, she keeps walking. I see her fingers curl one by one and then straighten again as she repeats her mantra.

I sprint over to observe from behind a vendor cart selling sun hats. When Jeni gets close enough, I pull out my chopstick. It's another one of those mysterious f.g. rules that allows me to use my wand to perform magic that no one is actually wishing for, as long as it helps with the client's big wish. I narrow in on a girl eating a salad from a plastic container. I hate to litter, so I won't send it flying into the pond. Too bad there's no recycling nearby, but if Lourdes were here, she'd say that nobody should be ordering meals stored in those plastic things in the first place.

A wave of the chopstick and the salad and its un-environmental container vanish. The girl glances around in confusion, searches the ground at her feet, then hops off the rail and peers into the water. If she tried the trash can next to the hat vendor, she'd score, although I doubt she'd want to dig soggy lettuce leaves out of the trash. She searches around for a few more seconds, even looking up, as if maybe she'll see a bird flying off with it. Finally she squints at her watch and frowns. Lunch break is probably over. She'll have to settle for a protein bar. The girl walks away and Jeni takes her place, one body closer to Ronald.

The next three are just as easy. A little girl's orange and silver pinwheel flies from her hand, onto the ground several feet away. She chases it and Jeni moves over. A security guard fidgets, his uniform suddenly itchy, thanks to the bits of grass I've transported under his collar, and he steps forward to scratch. Jeni slides into his spot. A fountain jet spurts up wildly, spraying a man and woman holding hands, causing them to leap back and brush water from their shirts—and, at last, Jeni is next to her prince. She's in place and "P" is taken care of. It really didn't need to be part of the code, but I knew she was nervous and I wanted to give her an easy, guaranteed victory right away. Thanks to our f.g.-client connection, I can feel her tiny surge of confidence, and there's a faint smile on her face—so I know this was the right thing to do.

Time for me to move in closer. I take the long way around the fountain and look for a spot a few bodies away from Jeni and Ronald. Close enough to listen in, far enough away not to be seen.

There's somebody at the rail where I want to be, a woman reading the free mall newsletter. Not for long, though. She suddenly spins around to look for whoever tapped her shoulder (no one), and I'm able to slip in. I retrieve a small pad and pencil from my shoulder bag and flip to a fresh page to sketch. After I've gotten a few lines on the page, I angle the pencil toward Ronald.

Jeni blinks down at the wallet in her hands, surprised, even though she knew this was the next step. " 'W,' " she says to herself in wonder. Ronald glances up for a second, not at Jeni, just in vague confusion. He knows something's wrong, but what? *We* know, Ronald. And soon *you'll* find out.

Jeni bends down and then straightens back up, holding out the wallet in both palms like a lotus flower. "Um . . ."

Come on, Jeni. "W." Wallet. You're staring right at it.

"Um . . ." Oh, no. "Walnut?"

Ronald, listening to his MP3 player, can't hear her, but a mouthed "walnut" looks enough like "wallet," I guess, and he does see the wallet in her hand.

He pulls out his earbud. "Hey! Wow, thanks. It must've fallen out." He takes the wallet from Jeni and stuffs it back in his pocket. "I don't know how that happened. I haven't moved since I got here."

"Um . . ."

My f.g. radar picks up Jeni's panic as it clashes with her yearning, fear trumping desire. I can sense her struggling, her fingers curling up again as she mentally recites the letters. This is the easy one, Jeni! I spin my pencil to make the bubbles in Ronald's Nutri-Fizzy fizz.

"Fizzy!" Jeni blurts out. Thank God.

"Huh? Oh, yeah. Cherry with the B-12 boost. My a.m. jolt. Hey! You work there, right? I recognize you."

"Uh . . ."

Ronald laughs. "Oh, yeah. Stupid question. You got the uniform on. Duh, man! I'm Ronald."

"Shoes . . ."

"Huh?"

"Um . . ."

I can't stand it any longer. I step away from the rail and

catch Jeni's eye. I draw an "L" in the air, but her blank look gets blanker, so I act it out, cheerleader style, one arm straight up, the other flung to the side. A couple of tween boys gape at me. I shoot them a glare and they avert their eyes.

"*Listening* . . . ," Jeni says finally, sighing it out like a punctured bike tire.

Ronald stares at her a beat, as if she's speaking in some strange code—which, actually, she is. "Okay, well. I gotta get back to work. Nice to meet you. You have a great day, okay?" *No, no, no.* They're so close.

I need to act fast. Luckily, the girl next to Jeni is texting, not paying attention, so she doesn't notice me flick my pencil in her direction. The wedge heel of Texting Girl's left sandal cracks, causing her to fall sideways, and she crashes into Jeni, who tumbles into Ronald. Domino love. But Ronald doesn't catch Jeni. The arms that were supposed to wrap around her fly up instead. He lets go of his phone, which sails free, soaring above the fountain pool. Ronald turns, following the phone with his eyes, throwing himself off-balance. His raised arms pinwheel . . .

If only Jeni had reached for him, grabbed an arm, a hand, the edge of his shirt—*anything*. Instead, Jeni jumps back and away from the fountain, her hands to her mouth, her eyes squinting in anticipation of the disaster that's coming . . .

And that a split second later is here.

SPLASH!

Everybody turns to look. Some people back up, some lean forward. The grass-infested security guard dashes into the fray and helps the bystanders haul Ronald out of the water.

So much for steering clear of slapstick. I grab Jeni's hand and drag her over the mini-bridge to the mini-lawn. Jeni's lobotomized shock gives way to despair. "I pushed him!"

"*Shhh.* Technically, *I* pushed him. Well, indirectly. I was trying to save the whole thing from falling apart. Trying and *failing.*"

"I'm sorry." Jeni sniffs and covers her mouth with her fists, as if to prevent a full-out wail.

I struggle between pity and irritation, but it's a close battle. "Don't apologize to me. It's not *my* wish. What happened back there? We rehearsed it a million times."

"I know! P.W.F.S.L.! P.W.F.S.L.! It's the only thing I could remember."

"What am I supposed to do? Write out a whole script for you to memorize?"

Jeni looks up, her fearful face taking on a hopeful glow. "Could you?"

"No. Because that wouldn't work. How do I know what Ronald is going to say? Advanced mind reading is not one of the f.g. skills."

"Oh." Jeni wipes her eyes with the back of her hand.

I find a tissue in my shoulder bag and give it to her. As I do, I catch a glimpse of twinkling light, coming from the direction of the movie theater.

And then I see *her*.

She peers out from behind one of the columns that hold up the movie theater marquee. She's eating a grape candy stick, her headband glinting even in the shadows. She smiles, coy, takes the candy stick from her mouth and salutes me with it.

"So it's hopeless?" Jeni asks.

I turn to her. "It's *not* hopeless. We're just getting started." I glance back at the movie theater, ready to give Ariella a defiant sneer.

But she's gone.

My sarcastic comment about writing a script gives me an idea. We'll go to Jump Kicks, and while Ronald waits on Jeni, I'll listen in and send her texts to tell her what to say. Having their romance begin in the store is better than the fountain, because instead of a glass slipper, it'll be an athletic shoe that the prince will be slipping onto the foot of his prospective princess. How modern-day-fairy-tale can you get? It's obviously what Ariella had planned with Fawn. Too bad it didn't work.

Jeni is having a lot more success this time. It's true that her responses to Ronald are a little delayed, the delivery of her lines is kind of wooden, and the number of "ums" and "uhs" is approaching astronomical, but at least the two of

144

them are having a conversation. It's only about shoes so far, but once Jeni relaxes, I'll send her more-personal questions to ask.

"Hi, I'm Sarah. Anything I can bring you to try on?" A woman in a red tracksuit has appeared at my side. She must've been in the back when we came in.

I swing a hand past a row of shoes. "You have these in a seven?"

"Which ones?"

"Um, all of them. In whatever colors you have. And maybe bring out all the six and a halves and seven and a halves too. To be safe."

Sarah stares at me for a second, skeptical, but then leaves to get the shoes. That should keep her out of the way until my work is done.

Opposite me, Jeni jogs in place in a pair of purple running shoes. Ronald laughs. Excellent! The ice is broken. Flirtation is imminent.

"Here's a couple to get you started." Sarah has returned, carrying a small armful of boxes. She lifts the lid off the top box.

Ugh. This means I actually have to do it. I have to take off my boots and pull on a pair of flimsy canvas things that don't even cover my ankles.

I unzip and lace up as slowly as I can, while doing my best to keep my ear tuned to Jeni and Ronald.

"Try walking around in them," Sarah insists. "See how they feel."

I know how they feel. Wrong. The skin on my calves has turned into a mass of goose bumps in the store's air-conditioning, and I feel off-kilter without my usual chunky heels.

I wobble around the store, never getting too far from Jeni. My cell goes off just as I hear Ronald ask, "So how long have you been working at Nutri-Fizzy?"

The prince has asked a personal question first! This could *not* be going better. My phone rings again: Flynn. Since Jeni can answer Ronald's question without my help, I take the call as I walk back to Sarah. "Hey," Flynn says, "so I haven't heard from you—"

"Hold on a sec." Jeni has yet to speak. I notice she's staring down—at her phone. You have *got* to be kidding me. She can't be waiting for me to text her the answer.

"Delaney?" Flynn's voice distracts me, and because my eyes are on Jeni, I'm not looking where I'm going. "I can't talk right—" I stumble into the boxes mid-sentence. As I fall, I catch a flash of Ronald's puzzled expression and a glimpse of Jeni's panic, and then I hear Jeni whisper, "I don't know."

This could not be going worse.

Sarah helps dig me out of the rubble. I grab my phone to send Jeni a text—but then I see Jeni yanking off the running shoe, shoving her own shoe back on.

"What happened?" Flynn's voice buzzes up at me. I forgot he was still on the line and I lift the phone to my ear. "Is everything okay?" he asks.

When is everything ever okay? When is anything ever not ridiculously, violently *not* okay?

"Everything's fine." The lies come automatically now. "I'll call you later."

I hang up and wave to Jeni. "Hold on!" I struggle to get the cross-trainers off, but she's already at the exit, mumbling, "I don't know, I don't know, I don't know," until she's drowned out by the door's cheerful "A customer has arrived!" chime.

Except this time it's the sad gong of the customer gone.

★   ★   ★

When I get back to Treasures, I text Flynn that I'd tipped over some store inventory that had been precariously stacked and that's why I couldn't talk earlier. I was proud of myself—it was a totally believable fabrication, and was even sort of true, because I didn't say which store. I'm making it a goal to find more ways to tell the truth in my lies so I won't always feel worse at the end of every conversation than I did at the start. I'm determined to try this out when Flynn calls back. But he doesn't call.

A couple of college-age girls come into the store, looking for sundresses to wear to a bridal shower, and while I help them, I struggle to think up a new strategy for getting Ronald and Jeni together. The ideas grow wilder and wilder, involving water balloons dropped from one of the store's upper balconies and the derailing of the trolley that occasionally carries tourists and lazy shoppers from the

Alcove to the Annex and back. Somehow I've gone from romantic comedy to disaster film.

"Ooh, that's nice," one of the girls says to the other, admiring the simple aqua shift her friend has tried on over her shorts and top. "It's like it was made for you." Right. Ronald and Jeni are made for each other. That's already been determined. I don't need to go crazy. I just need to let it happen.

Flynn and I didn't have a "meet cute." We had a "meet hostile." Well, I was hostile anyway. Then, when I was forced to join Yearbook, I got to know him better—and when he became my client, I spent even more time around him. . . .

Hmm. Jeni and Ronald *have* a place where their paths regularly cross: every morning at Nutri-Fizz. If I use a little magic to make sure Jeni is always the Fizz Master who takes Ronald's order, eventually the romance will happen, because, like I've told Jeni a million times, it's meant to be.

"Oh, yeah," I tell the girl in the aqua dress. "You can definitely stop looking. You found it. That is definitely the One."

★ ★ ★

Clang . . . Clang . . . Clang.

The clock on Taylor & Taylor's for Men strikes three. Jeni should be here any minute. She'd agreed to meet at the Ice Cream Cottage after her shift ended. I've grabbed a plastic spoon so I can grant a few small wishes while I wait.

What I can't wait for is to tell Jeni how easy and simple it's all going to be now. She'll be so relieved. No codes to

148

memorize, no scripted lines to read, no artificial scenarios to wade awkwardly through. She only has to do her job.

I might set up some coaching sessions with her off-hours, though, to help her with the art of conversation. And I probably should make her promise not to run off and hide whenever Ronald appears in the Nutri-Fizzy line, like she'd done with me. I may be stepping back, but this isn't going to work if Jeni doesn't step up, at least a little.

I feel a sudden chill and with it the sense that Ariella is watching me. I tell myself she doesn't matter—but that same self argues back: even if Ariella is wrong, she can still complicate things, and complications are exactly what I don't want any more of.

I glance around, but there's no sign of sparkle lurking behind vendor carts or peering out from pillars. I've just about convinced myself that the chill was only a blast of refrigerated air from the Ice Cream Cottage when I spot Fawn, maneuvering along the cobblestone walkway, in the direction of the faux side street where Jump Kicks is located. Her outfit has Ariella stamped all over it: goofy spring-green tulle miniskirt, chartreuse tube top and yellow kitten-heel slip-ons that are obviously causing her pain. Her frizzy hair is held up by a matching yellow clip and sprouts from the top of her head like a mushroom cloud.

She's like the Little Mermaid on land, wobbling on her new legs, yet eager and excited to join the party she's convinced she's been missing out on while trapped under the sea. Although she winces and lurches and squints, flailing her arms for balance, there's more confidence to her awkward stride than I've ever seen in Jeni's slow trudge.

I've got to stop her. She may be pathetic, but there's an adorableness to her pitifulness. Ronald might confuse feeling sorry for her with liking her, and that won't be good for anybody.

I'll wait until she's near the mini-lawn and then shove her, gently, onto the grass. All the parents and nannies will run to her aid as I disappear into the crowd. Nobody gets hurt. Everybody wins . . . in the long run.

I toss my spoon in the trash and slip around to the far side of the Pretzel Palace.

"Hi, Delaney!" Ariella appears in front of me, blocking my view of Fawn. She sneers as she stirs a strawberry shake. "How's it going with Janna?"

"Jeni. Fine. Great. Excellent, actually. Feel free to concede."

Ariella laughs. "You're so funny! I wish I had your sense of humor!" Her mock-friendly expression ices over. "I don't want anything *else* of yours, though."

"I really don't have time to talk to you. I'm meeting Jeni."

"Give up, Delaney. You know it's doomed. That fountain scene was a joke. And I know what happened at the shoe store too."

"I have no idea what you're talking about." I hope Jeni

isn't on her way yet. The last thing I need is for her to meet Ariella.

"Stand aside," Ariella declares, "and let the correct happy ending play out, or you're going to make your non-beneficiary miserable."

"I can't stand this!" Fawn steps between us, mushroom cloud askew, feet bare, clutching her yellow shoes in one hand. "It didn't work! Again!"

"Did you—"

"Yes! I did everything you said. I talked to him. I asked him about the music he likes. He answered—but he barely looked at me." Fawn pouts. "This is taking too much time away from my poetry."

"Priorities, Fawn. Don't make me repeat it again."

"Gee," I say, moving around to where Fawn can see me. "You seem . . . miserable."

"Shut up." Ariella pushes me away, then turns back to Fawn. "Let's talk about this somewhere more private."

"I hate these!" Fawn holds up the kitten-heel shoes, as if she hasn't heard Ariella. "They're like torture!"

"That's enough," Ariella hisses. She grabs Fawn by the wrist to silence her and then points a finger at me. "This would be over already if not for you. You're blocking my energy." She casts one last searing glare at me and then hauls Fawn off across the lawn, out of sight.

I smile. The war is almost won. There's merely this one final battle.

"Delaney?" I turn around to see Jeni approaching from behind me. She glances off in the direction Ariella and Fawn disappeared. "Wasn't that—"

"No," I say quickly. "Those were just some girls I know from school. Forget them. Wait until you hear my new—"

"I release you."

"What?"

Jeni stares at the ground. "I, um, hereby declare that I don't want my wish granted. I'm sorry."

"No, listen. I've figured it all out. It's going to be easy—"

"Our bond is now severed. Or whatever." She spins around and hurries back to the Fizzy Bar.

"Hold on." I catch up to her. "Let me tell you my new idea."

"It's too late. I said the magic words. You're free."

"I made that up."

Jeni pauses near the fountain. "But I can still tell you to stop . . . can't I?" This is more a statement than a question, the way she says it.

"Well, yeah. I guess. But you'll still have the wish."

"That's okay. It was better before. From afar. I don't belong with him." The fountain starts playing some horrible, ill-timed song about love gone wrong.

"You *do*."

Jeni shakes her head and resumes walking. The water jets spurt and sway to the repetitive old-timey verses of the song. This music is *not* helping.

"I'll still feel the wish too," I remind her as I tag along beside her.

"I'm sorry."

"I'll be linked to you forever. I won't be able to help anybody else."

We reach the entrance to the Nutri-Fizzy Bar. Jeni looks up and meets my eyes. "That might, you know . . . be a good thing." Her expression is sad and pitying. She's pitying *me*!

I'm so stunned that I don't even stop her as she disappears inside. It's like Flynn and Cadie all over again, but this time I've failed with the right wish, which means I've actually become a worse f.g. than I was before. How is that even possible?

chapter eleven

"Wow, are those really for sale?" I step down into the sunken living room to get a better view.

Nancy consults a booklet she was handed when we arrived. "Two hundred dollars apiece. Not bad, but I'm not sure of the resale potential."

I spin around in a 360 and count them. Thirty. Thirty two-foot-tall Statues of Liberty, standing proudly along a wide shelf that must've been built for them. I take a picture and send it to Flynn. Even though he hasn't called me in days. I'm trying not to worry about it. Ha.

When Nancy invited me to come along to the estate sale, I agreed because I needed a break from the mental loop that keeps playing in my head. Do I give up on Jeni? I can't, because I'm meant to grant her wish. I don't see how I can do that, though, since she doesn't *want* the wish. So I guess that means I have to give up. But I can't . . . etc.

The house is owned by some folk singer who's decided to move to Ireland and raise sheep. It's not some big movie-star mansion. It's in a nice but normal neighborhood, and from the outside it looks like all the other houses. But inside, it's definitely . . . interesting. Nancy's already loaded her pickup with furniture and we've only been through three rooms. "We better head upstairs," Nancy says. "The sale opens to the public in half an hour, and I don't want you to miss your chance." Nancy's on some list that gets her in early. It meant waking up at seven, but it's been worth it so far, both as a distraction and for the entertainment value. In addition to the Statues of Liberty, I've seen a couch shaped like a giant mouth, a creepy collection of dolls with dried apples for heads, and a library room with an entire wall of shelves devoted to *The Little Prince*. Over a hundred copies at least. Paperback and hardcover, in like forty different languages. "It's the owner's favorite book," an estate sale worker informed us, as if I couldn't have guessed that on my own.

Lourdes would love this place too. On the way up the spiral staircase to the second floor, I snap a couple of photos to send her: a tiny topiary shamrock on a built-in shelf and a mural of snakes on the wall that seem to slither past as you walk by. When we get upstairs, there are already a few other early shoppers in the master bedroom, rifling through the closets.

"Psst! Nancy!" A thin man at the end of the hall gestures to us.

"That's Ryan," Nancy whispers to me. "He helps run the sale. He always steers me to the best finds before everybody else."

Ryan leads us into a small guest room. The walls of this room are painted in wavy stripes of green and gold, like the surface of the ocean at dusk. The apartment I lived in with Mom had some cool stuff in it, but nothing too bizarre, and we couldn't paint the walls because it was a rental. Dad's house was lifeless when I moved in, but I've helped him raise it up to "tolerable," and I've improved my bedroom a lot, even with the kiddie décor that came with it. But this house is like the residential version of my overhauled vintage clothing room at Treasures—design by artistic impulse, without rules or limits. And it exists *here,* in the land of design by imitation and ostentation. Amazing. This is how *I* want to live someday—without the gruesome apple-head dolls, though.

"I've kept the others out until you got here," Ryan says, and then opens a door to reveal a walk-in closet that's almost as big as the guest room. Inside, it's all accessories: bins of purses and belts, stacks of see-through hatboxes, and an entire wall of shoes.

"I'll take those and those," Nancy says, pointing to a bin of purses and one tall stack of hats. "And give me both bins of belts." On the drive over, she'd explained to me that she buys first and examines later, especially when it comes to collections.

"Hey, I wanted to look through those," a woman says from the closet doorway.

Nancy hands the woman a business card from the store. "Come see me. I'll give you a good deal."

I'm bummed because the shoes are all sandals and pumps. Nancy had thought there'd be boots . . . but either they've been packed up to take to Ireland or they're in the master bedroom, where the other shoppers have probably already snagged the best ones. Nancy whispers something to Ryan, who smiles and steps over to a mirrored cabinet. He opens it . . .

Inside, there is nothing *but* boots. Cowboy and army and hiking and ankle and high-heeled; with buckles and zippers and snaps. Different colors, different materials, all well worn but perfect for remaking. Nancy flips through the booklet. "Hmm. Priced to sell." She winks at me. "We'll take them all."

★　★　★

I had to clear off a whole row of sandals at Treasures to make room for the boots. The deal is I have to put them on display, available for sale, until I've begun to work on re-making them. And I have to finish redesigning one pair before I can start on another. "You talked me into letting you have your boot-making business at the store, Delaney," Nancy explained on the drive back. "But I haven't seen you working on it much. I thought you needed something to light a fire under you."

She thinks I have artist's block—designer's block, rather—and I guess I do, sort of, but I can't explain to her *why* I haven't had time to make any. It's killing me that I could lose some of these boots before I get a chance at re-making them. And now I do have time. This should make me happy, and I was excited as we were leaving the sale, but being back at the mall is such a geographical reminder of everything that's gone wrong that my enthusiasm has crumbled. I'm hoping it will return once I unpack all the other accessories Nancy bought. There's one more box, filled with costume jewelry. It takes forever to untangle the twisted-up necklaces and unhook the bracelets that have gotten caught on each other's clasps. I hang each piece on a candelabra I've brought in from the main room. I'm almost finished and I'm admiring my work, when I spot it. At the bottom of the box, peeking out from underneath a strand of wooden beads, is an angel pin, glittering up at me as if it were smirking.

Things weren't bad enough, now I'm being mocked by jewelry.

I can picture the real Ariella, snickering with glee at my defeat—once she finds out about it. I snatch up the pin and try to break the wings off, to get some voodoo revenge. Maybe it was *her* energy blocking *me,* and if I can get her out of the way, Jeni will come back.

Unfortunately, the wings are soldered on to stay, and now I feel even worse than I did before. Not only because the pin's tiny wings have pressed painful indentations into my thumbs, but because it's like a symbolic victory for Ariella. She may not have stolen Ronald for Fawn yet, but she's succeeded in eliminating the opposition.

I bring the pin out to the counter. Nancy had bought two milk crates crammed with old paperback novels at the estate sale, and she has several of the books laid out in front of her. She skims through one and her eyes grow wide with interest.

"Hey, Nancy. Don't you think this would look better without wings?" If I can convince Nancy not to want the wings, this will qualify as a small wish—and off the wings will come with the wave of a chopstick. One mini-victory for me, which is better than nothing.

Nancy peers at the pin over the top of her reading glasses. "It's an angel, Delaney. It wouldn't have much point without the wings."

"Yeah, but, you know, certain people are turned off by the whole supernatural thing—or they don't want to make some overt religious statement. I think it'd be less offensive if I removed any part that seems, like, *celestial*."

Nancy stares at me curiously, and then her expression brightens with a thought. "Wasn't your friend looking for angels?"

"She is *not* my friend."

"Who's not your friend?" I spin around to find Flynn grinning at me. "You better not be talking about me." He lifts up the camera he's got strung around his neck and takes a photo of my shocked face. "I wanted to surprise you."

I'm so, so, so, so happy to see him, it's like a sudden fever. I want to grab him, hug him, clutch him. I was worried he was mad at me, but here he is, which means he missed me, I hope. So much has happened since I talked to him last—not that I can tell him about any of it. But you know what? It doesn't matter! Since I'm obviously never going to grant another big wish, I'll just mentally block out that part of my life. It'll be easy to keep it all in, as long as I stay focused on Flynn, Flynn, Flynn.

"Is this the famous Flynn?" Nancy asks.

Flynn's grin spreads to cover his whole face. "You've talked about me?"

My face turns my least favorite color: pink. "I may have mentioned some guy who never returns my texts."

"Yeah. I'm sorry," Flynn says, his face falling. "But I'm here to apologize . . . and take you out."

"We don't close until five."

Flynn looks at his watch. "Ten minutes . . ." He sighs and glances upward, thinking deeply. "Yes. It's worth the wait." He takes my hand. "And while I'm waiting, you can show me the boots you made from the designs you came up with at the library." He tugs me in the direction of the vintage clothing room, but I hold back.

160

"The ones I've finished are at home. I don't want to show you any that aren't done."

"Why not?"

Because I haven't even started any of them. "Because it's bad luck."

Flynn looks at me curiously.

"Delaney's been having some problems with procrastination," Nancy says helpfully—but she's not helping. "Too many breaks, in my opinion." She winks at me and all my goodwill toward her for taking me to the estate sale withers and dies.

Flynn grabs me by the waist and pulls me closer.

"Flynn . . ." I tilt my head toward Nancy.

"Oh, don't mind me," Nancy says. "There's a lot worse going on in here, believe me." She taps the top of her book, then puts her glasses on to read.

Instead of kissing me, Flynn keeps talking. "Maybe you could show me where the 'inventory' crashed down on you. I could help you stack it more safely."

Nancy looks up from the book and casts a questioning glance my way. Thankfully, Flynn has his back to her.

"It's all picked up," I tell him. "Strapped in. No danger of it falling again." Flynn keeps staring at me, as if he'd hoped I'd say something else. But what? I want to move *on* from this.

What I really want is for him to kiss me already, and for a second it seems like he's going to, but then—

"Oh my God, is that . . ." Flynn lets go of me and picks

up a dusty, prehistoric camera off a nearby bookshelf. Wow, that romantic moment lasted less than a quarter of a millisecond. Girlfriend versus camera: no contest.

"This is the Jackson X-7, Red series. I've never seen one of these in real life! Awesome." He inspects it from every angle, squinting through the viewfinder, gently advancing the shutter, his eyes glazing over with camera love, rendering me invisible. "Hey," he whispers. "You can use your employee discount for me, right?" Correction: not invisible, but of interest only for mercenary purposes.

"Ten percent of three thousand dollars isn't going to help you much."

"Three thousand dollars!" Flynn continues to study the camera. "I mean, I know it's rare and all, but the shutter advance is rusted and there's scratches on the—"

"Delaney's pulling your leg, Flynn," Nancy says. "If you're really interested in it—"

"Are you kidding? It's a *Jackson*. They only made these from 1957 to 1959—"

"Don't get him started," I warn Nancy.

She smiles. "It's yours," she tells Flynn.

"Really?" Flynn beams. "Do you have any more cameras?" He directs this to me.

"There's a bunch of crap in the armoires against the wall," I tell Flynn. "Help yourself. I'll go get my bag."

"And then I have a surprise for you."

"I thought *you* were the surprise."

"There's more." He grins and slips off to camera hunt.

I smile to myself. Doing small wishes will be enough f.g. action for me, because I can fill the client gap with boots and Flynn. From now on, I say yes to every date request he makes. I'll never have to think about Jeni or Ariella again. Well, I did think of them just now, but only for a second, and I'm banishing them from my thoughts for the rest of my life.

I toss the angel pin into a wicker basket filled with rings. Maybe one of them will slip around the angel's neck and choke it.

"Any five things. My treat." Flynn swings his hand out over the nearby stalls, palm up, the king offering his kingdom. A kingdom of junk.

Flynn has dragged me to the Bizarre, which is what I call the Bazaar (although I'm pretty sure I'm not the first person to come up with the nickname). The Bazaar is a part of the Annex that used to be a fruit and vegetable market, but now, instead of mangoes and avocados, the stands display baskets filled with cheap toys and bags of candy and sets of ceramic coasters with palm trees painted on them.

"This is my surprise? An unrecyclable bag filled with pointless plastic toys and defaced dead sea animals?" I pick up a sand dollar that's been covered with spirals of green and blue glitter glue.

"Nope. It's just the warm-up."

I take a sip of my lemonade and try not to sneeze. Flynn's bought us each a drink from a cart where a man cranks an old machine that squeezes the lemons fresh for each cup. Because nothing's played straight here, not even lemonade, there has to be a "twist," which means that there's every flavor of lemonade you can think of, from strawberry to kiwi-apricot. Flynn got a watermelon lemonade. I chose ginger, which is hot and is making my eyes water, but it's still way better than a Nutri-Fizzy. At least it tastes like something that came from nature and not a laboratory.

"I thought we were going *out*."

"We are out." Flynn waves his arms. "We're literally *outside*."

"I meant somewhere outside of the mall."

"Why do that when we're surrounded by riches?" He grabs my hand. "Here, I'll choose your presents for you." He leads me through the winding path made by the slender gaps between the stalls and stands and carts. As we zigzag through the crowd, my mood lightens, as if the failures and insecurities that have been piling up on me are peeling away, layer by layer. Part of it is the vibe in the Bazaar. The buzz is livelier here than in the main part of the mall, and the people are more animated. The slatted roof and closely packed stalls help to hold the atoms in and keep them circulating. The early evening summer light casts muted stripes onto the customers and the concrete floor, and the dropped temperature has injected an extra burst of exhilaration that matches the stinging zing of my lemonade.

One after the other, Flynn snatches up items, pays for them and then drops them into my hands: a keychain with tiny blue cowboy boots hanging from it; a bag of malted milk balls; a tin license plate with the name DELIA stamped on it (since there is no sticker, mug, bracelet or anything in the country that has *my* name. A million versions of "Kaitlynn/Katelynn/Caitlin" but no "Delaney" anywhere); a package of sugar straws; and a pink whistle.

"Not bad," I tell Flynn when his shopping spree is over. He snaps a picture of me holding my gifts.

"And . . ." He holds out a paper bag. "One hundred percent recyclable."

I take the bag. "I wish the whistle wasn't pink, though." I blow it to test it out. It lets out a shriek that gets everyone within a twenty-foot range staring and glaring. Nice.

Flynn winces. "It's meant to be ironic. And the sugar straws can double as wands."

"Thanks, Professor. I figured that one out." I point a green one toward a little girl whose wrist is too thick for the elastic bracelet she's picked up, and suddenly the bracelet fits perfectly. The little girl smiles. I smile. Flynn smiles and I give him a kiss without even thinking about it. Okay, that was good. That was an ideal b.f./g.f. moment. Casual and spontaneous and sweet. My mind in the moment, free of any worries, past, present or future.

For dinner Flynn suggests we go to this snack bar in the Bazaar called the Hot Top, which sells hot dogs with like three thousand different toppings. You can't just order a chili dog, for instance, because there's black bean chili, turkey chili, three-alarm chili, spicy mango chutney chili and something called "silly chili," which is "for the kids." And that's only the chili dogs—it'd take me three years to list all the other options. So much for getting out of the mall tonight.

I order a veggie dog with lime salsa, and Flynn gets the traditional (ketchup, mustard, relish—but I told him to hold the onions if he wanted to stay within three feet of me).

"This better not be the surprise," I say. "Eating hot dogs while a school of human sharks swarms behind us?" I flick my thumb over my shoulder, where salivating diners yell out their orders and shift their eyes from one end of the curved counter to the other, looking for a stool about to free up so they can dart in for the kill.

"No, it's much better. Are you ready?"

"I've been ready." If it's not a place or an activity, it's got to be a present. In the three months we've been going out, Flynn's only gotten me goofy gifts, like the whistle and the sugar straws. That's been fine with me, since necklaces with heart pendants and twinkly charm bracelets are not remotely my style. But if Flynn wants to get serious and sincere for a second and pledge his eternal devotion in gold or silver, I'll be totally supportive. I'd even be willing to actually wear whatever it is. "Okay, where is it?" I glance down at his camera bag and wonder which of its three thousand pockets the jewelry box is hiding in.

166

"It's not a thing. It's news."

"News?" News is not a gift. News is bad. Oil spills, terrorist bombings, TV show cancellations. I don't want news. I want a heart pendant.

"The paper's sending me and Skids to Costa Verde to cover the Pacific Southwest Extreme Water Sports Festival!"

See? News = bad. Always. "That's like five hours away. You're going to drive down there and back every day?"

"We're going to crash at Skids's Aunt Jennifer's and Uncle Dan's place."

Flynn doesn't seem to notice the dark mental cloud forming over my head. This isn't fitting in with my new plan. If he's not here, how can I fill up my time with him?

Flynn sits up straighter on his stool, buoyed by his excitement. "The festival goes on for a week and a half, but we'll probably stay after to see if there are any other newsworthy things going on in the area."

Ugh, that word again. "'Newsworthy,' meaning horrible stuff that'll make people even more depressed about the state of the world."

"The water festival's not horrible. It's, like, awesomely cool."

"Eye of the beholder." He's not putting me in the equation at all. My cloud is expanding, growing grimmer and gloomier.

"We get to post daily reports on the paper's website. They're going to create a whole separate page for us! How awesome is that?" Flynn's eyes are literally shining, his smile enormous. It's as if he thinks this is something to celebrate. Enthusiasm radiates from him like bursts of sunshine.

Meanwhile, my cloud is rumbling with impending lightning flashes. "When are you leaving?"

"Day after tomorrow. This is an awesome opportunity for me, Delaney. I'll be able to take some really awesome photos, with the sun and the water and everything. Action shots that are art. It's going to be *awesome*."

"You've officially exceeded your lifetime limit for the number of times you're permitted to use the word 'awesome.'"

Flynn's eyes dim a little as he narrows his gaze in on me. I can tell his mood is still high and he's mystified as to why I'm not sharing it. Can he be that clueless? Can he really not tell that the thunderstorm he's created over me is now drenching me, deflating my mood, dissolving me back into the pool of depression I thought I'd left behind?

Our hot dogs arrive. We eat in silence, the din from the crowd closing in.

"What if I want to call *you* awesome?" Flynn asks quietly, between bites.

"Don't even try it." The hot dog is peppery and sour, matching my mood.

"You're happy for me, though, right?"

"I'm thrilled."

"You have to be happy for me, Ms. Collins. It's in the

boyfriend/girlfriend rulebook. You're supposed to cheer me on."

I try to dig up some enthusiasm, but the only thing I succeed in unearthing is sarcasm. "Rah."

"Whoa. Delaney Collins Mood Level Alert: Orange." He leans on his elbow and tilts his face toward me. "You're really going to miss me that much?" I can smell the relish on his breath. I should've told him to leave that off too.

"I mean, you're busy too, Delaney. Right? With your job . . . and everything?" He's got the same questioning look in his eyes that he had at Treasures. Like there's something he's waiting for me to confess. What? I haven't done anything. I've withheld information, but there's no law against that. I don't think.

"I *am* busy," I say. "But I made time for you, even though you showed up without calling or anything, so you could take me out somewhere that's not even *out*, and then tell me that—surprise!—you're blowing me off."

"I'm not blowing you off."

Isn't he? I think back to when he threw me over for a washed-up lighthouse, and before that to when he took the job in the first place. And what about the ignored texts? Hasn't he been showing me that I'm not as important to him as I thought?

I've been so caught up in my client chaos that I missed it, but I see it now. He's been figuratively drifting away from me since school ended, and now he's literally drift-ing away, or rather, *driving* away, in Skids's car, off to their water-world extravaganza. Figuratively or literally, it's the same thing. He won't be here.

"We'll go on a real date when I get back," Flynn promises. "We'll go *out*."

"Mmm." I can't look at him. I swallow the last bite of my veggie dog, and only the sourness of the lime lingers, along with that vinegary aftertaste that makes you want to brush your teeth *right now*.

"There's an art walk right after I return," Flynn continues, "at a bunch of galleries down near the beach. I'll text you the date. We can go together, get ice cream after. I already asked for time off from work."

"What if aliens land?" I suck up the last drops of my ginger lemonade, and now all I taste is bitterness.

"We'll still go. There'll be plenty of time to snap shots of the little green guys after they take over the White House and start eating people." He leans in closer, trying to catch my eye, but there is no way I'm going to let it be caught. "Okay?" he asks.

This is the problem with needing people. They vanish as soon as you need them too much.

"Okay," I say, because it's the only thing I can say, and begin the process of de-needing Flynn. It's going to take some time, so best to get right on it. "Whatever."

Flynn sets down the last bite of his hot dog, wipes his hands on a napkin and swivels on his stool to face me. Then he spins my stool around, rests his palms on the vinyl on either side of my legs and brings his face to mine, his relish breath wafting at me. "It's not like I'm going away forever," he says. "I *am* coming back."

His words hit me in my chest and burst into a clenching heat that spreads up my neck to my face, and suddenly my eyes are burning with near tears. No, no, no. This goes against the de-need directive. I take a breath and attempt to tap back into my inner apathy. But before I can deny that I'll miss him, that his absence means anything to me at all, he's kissing me. The heat in my body intensifies and then cools down. The tears reverse and I don't even mind the mustard-relish taste of the kiss.

He does care.

Everything, for one moment, is perfect again.

"Hey, come on," a voice calls out from the crowd behind us. "If you're done, let somebody else sit down."

And then the moment's gone in an instant, cruelly yanked away from me, like always.

★ ★ ★

The sun's dropped out of sight, and all around the Bazaar, fluorescent bulbs snap on one by one, casting their glaring greenish glow.

Flynn and I hold hands as we walk and it all feels right, but in a detached way, like I'm watching us from the outside and recognizing, yeah, they're a couple. But inside it feels as if he's ahead of me, mentally moving away, taking steps toward leaving, on his way to gone. I can't get that moment during the kiss back, that feeling of safety and settledness. I squeeze his hand like maybe I can pump the feeling in. Flynn turns to me and smiles, misreading the squeeze. He doesn't know. He doesn't feel it. He's already gone. Skids is coming to pick Flynn up so they can plan for their trip. Flynn offered to have Skids give me a ride home, but I know I wouldn't be able to stand it: sitting in the car, listening to their excited plans about something that excludes me, that leaves me behind. So I texted Gina at the bookstore and she said she could give me a ride after she finishes work. Flynn and I kiss good-bye, but it's brief this time, a reflex. There are no more reassurances, only a "Text or call anytime," and then I'm alone again.

By some horrible twist of fate, I've stopped in front of a bin of plastic charms, and right on the top is a silver-painted angel. Smirking up at me.

The angel's only fifteen cents, though. Hmm.

After I pay for it, I grip the angel's wings between my thumbs and index fingers—*snap*. The wings come off so easily I almost feel like I have superpowers.

Almost.

Snap, snap, snap. I bought a whole bag of the tiny plastic angels before I left the Bazaar and now I'm breaking their precious little wings off one by one, or rather two by two, while Gina drives. *Snap, snap, snap.*

I can't help thinking "He loves me, he loves me not" as I break off each pair of wings.

I replace the chant with "I hate her, I hate her not,"

except that doesn't work because it should be *all* "I hate her." There's no "not."

"Is there anything wrong, Delaney?" I feel Gina's eyes on me. "Anything you'd like to talk about?"

Yes. How does love work? How do you know if a boy really cares about you when he says he does but doesn't act like he does, or rather he *does* act like he cares but not in the way you want him to? Why do things never go right for more than five minutes? Are you ever ahead? How can I have lots of self-esteem and none at the same time? Why is everything perfect in my imagination when I plan it out, but crap in reality? Why is snapping the wings off plastic voodoo Ariellas not making me feel any better?

"No."

Gina purses her lips for a second, not convinced. She doesn't say anything else, though. She doesn't ask me again. She doesn't press me to answer. This is a relief, because I don't want to talk.

I don't.

Really.

Snap.

chapter twelve

I sit at the kitchen counter and take a bite of Froot Loops as I scroll through my messages. Nothing. Except for the unanswered texts I've sent that remain ignored.

I thought I'd hear back from Lourdes by now, but I guess she's decided I'm not cool enough to hang out with. Not that I care. It's not like we were friends or anything. Posh and I are friends, but I've given up hope of ever getting a response from her. So that's no big deal.

And how is it a surprise that I've only had radio silence from Flynn? It's not.

I know he's busy, but what about the trip down to Costa Wherever? Skids was the one driving, so Flynn had plenty of time to call me. The only message I've gotten from him since he left is one "Hey" text, with a photo attached of a giant dead eel tangled up in seaweed, all rubbery and rotting—like I want to see *that*—and a link to a haiku Skids wrote about the eel in the *Sea Foam Weekly*'s online fiction section. I go online to Flynn and Skids's Extremely Stupid Water Sports page on the paper's website. As I do every time I visit the site, I scroll through the pictures, looking for some coded message, a sign that Flynn's trying to tell me something with the angle of the shot or the lighting or the subject. Maybe "I miss you, Delaney" written in the sand in the background of one of the photographs, behind the handstand surfer accepting his gold medal, for example, the words barely visible, but clear enough for me to see. But there's nothing. No message, secret or obvious, to prove he's not blowing me off.

So I guess that proves it.

In summary: deserted by friends, by boyfriend, by client. And you know what? Totally fine.

I pull up Facebook and check Posh's wall. Lots and lots of photos of her and Christopher, hugging and laughing and sharing pizza. I could click "like" on a few, to remind her I'm alive, but I *don't* "like," because it's not fair. I should be having a summer of romance too, and I'm not.

Although, as I said, I'm fine with that.

"Did you have breakfast?" Dad enters the kitchen, dressed in weekend-outing-wear: jeans, striped shirt and sneakers.

I lift up my bowl toward him and clank my spoon against it. "Right here, blind man. Unless that was a rhetorical question."

"Tone down the attitude until I've had my coffee, please." He pours a cup from the pot that he's programmed to start brewing the second his alarm goes off. "It wouldn't hurt you to put a little real fruit in there, you know."

"Yes, it would. It would cause me intense, agonizing physical pain."

Dad ignores me and retrieves a loaf of his multiseed, multigrain bread from the fridge. He lays six slices neatly on a cutting board.

"How much toast are you having?" I ask.

"I'm making sandwiches for the zoo."

"They have food there, you know."

"It's all processed. The sodium alone is ridiculous." He holds up the bag. "You want one to take to work?"

"No, thanks. I'm always afraid that sprouted-grain stuff will germinate in my stomach."

Dad twists the tie around the bag. "Funny. I've never heard of that happening."

"Two words: massive cover-up."

Dad smiles and returns the bread to the fridge. "I'm sorry you can't come with us. We'll do something on your day off next time."

The trip to the zoo is part of the continuous assault on Theo, following the theory that the more time Theo is forced to spend around Dad, the quicker it will break down Theo's resistance to Dad being in Gina's life. Sort of like a prisoner-of-war interrogation with a domestic twist.

I fish out my last few Froot Loops while Dad spreads mustard on the bread in delicate, precise sweeps. It actually *is* my day off, but when Dad first asked me to go, I said no because I thought I'd need the time for Jeni. Now I don't, so I *could* go, but spending the day watching Theo pout and scowl isn't going to cheer me up, so I decided to go into Treasures anyway. Fate may be screwing with me on every other level, but it's definitely created time for me to work on my boot designs.

I wish I could talk to Dad about Jeni. He's stopped asking me if I have a client, and we never talk about his either. Being an f.g. was the one thing that bonded us when I first moved here, and now it feels like it's pushing us apart. We joke around, but we don't talk about anything serious. If Mom thought there was something going on with me, she'd bug me until I caved, but Dad leaves me alone. It's as if whenever I say "Leave me alone," he takes it literally. Not that I care . . .

Except I *do* care. I care about it all. My force field is up, but care keeps creeping in, seeping through cracks I can't detect—because if I knew where they were, I'd patch them up.

Life used to be so simple, before all these other people came along.

"By the way, Posh's mom called me last night about sending some of the boxes that are in storage."

I hear nothing from Posh for weeks, but Dad gets calls from her mom? Calls about things that are personal to me and have nothing to do with Dad? That's so messed up. "No."

"Delaney—"

"It's *my* stuff. I want it to stay there." Because it's Mom's stuff too. It's a reminder that all that's left of her is stuff.

Dad puts the lid back on the mustard. "It can't stay there forever." I don't answer. "I'm not going to keep paying the storage fees."

"You owe me, for past child support."

"I paid child support, Delaney."

"The financial part, maybe. But there was emotional neglect. Pain and suffering."

Dad tightens the lid on the mustard and studies me, as if deciding whether to defend himself or apologize. Instead of doing either, he puts the mustard away. He keeps his attention on the inside of the fridge and gathers up the rest of his sandwich ingredients. "What if we have a couple of boxes shipped out to start?"

I'm about to press the automatic "no" again, but then I think, Maybe that's what I need. Just one or two things that belonged to Mom, that will summon up her strength for me, and will patch the cracks. Plus, there's still a lot of my boots back there, and I could use the inspiration.

"Okay. A couple."

"Okay." Although Dad's now focused on his sandwich-making again—layering cheese, ham, tomatoes and lettuce neatly onto each mustard-painted slice—I can tell he's relieved by my answer. "If you want a ride to the mall, honey, you should get ready. I met a new client yesterday, and I have to stop by his house to grant his wish."

The one thing I *do* know about Dad's clients is that there's been a lot of them this summer. This is like his fourth or fifth. I get that he's a professional and has been doing it even longer than Ariella, but he's the one who told *me* that magic is only a superficial fix, and who's writing a book on how you have to "accept the you that is you" or whatever. He's definitely not telling any of this to his clients. Instead, he grants their wishes the second he figures them out.

It's *shazam,* new clothes, and then *kapow,* girlfriend landed. *Abracadabra,* house decluttered, and then *kaboom,* ex-wife comes back. Did either of these rushed unions work? Who knows? Who cares? Dr. Hank definitely doesn't. He's too busy with his *own* personal life to care about his clients'.

"Gee, I hope the wish doesn't take more than two seconds. Wouldn't want your client's longing for happiness to keep you from the baboons."

Dad wraps the sandwiches up in parchment, carefully folding each end like it was advanced origami. "You know, Delaney, you're lucky you don't have a client yet. This way you can enjoy your summer and just have fun."

Ugh! He is so clueless about my life!

His cell rings, thankfully ending the conversation.

"No, Bob. I'm on my way now," he says, in the irritated "I have better things to do" voice he uses now for his clients, when he's not using it on me. "No, that's not going to work. Because I have plans today."

He's as bad as Ariella. They both abuse their powers because they want to get the wish over with. I may have crashed and burned, but at least I made an effort. Lots of efforts. It was Jeni who was the problem. It's not my fault she rejected her own happily-ever-after. . . .

Or is it?

Haven't I been doing the same thing as Dad and Ariella? Sure, I worked hard, but I was focusing only on the end result: Jeni + Ronald. But my job isn't to get Cinderella the prince, it's to convince Cinderella that she *deserves* the prince. And that takes more than just telling her over and over.

Once again Dad is the model for what *not* to do. So I guess he is helping me after all.

While Dad continues to bully his client, I carry my bowl to the sink. There's only milk left in it, dyed a disturbing shade of "Ariella pink." I tip the bowl and pour it out. Now that I know what I'm doing, Ariella's chances of winning this war are just like this milk: swirling down the drain.

★　★　★

I set the plate of berry-banana mini-muffins in front of Jeni and sit down across from her. "I'd like to thank you again for coming," I tell her.

After breakfast I texted Jeni and told her that we had to meet to formalize the severing of our bond—and that I'd lied about the bond-severance thing being a lie.

Jeni shifts her eyes back and forth between me and the muffins.

"Go ahead. Have one."

She picks one up and takes a tentative bite. She chews tensely, as if she's waiting for the poison to kick in. Is that what she thinks I'm planning? To sever the bond by killing her?

I grab one of the muffins and take a big bite to prove they're harmless. "See?" I say after I've swallowed. "Just fruit and nuts."

She has the morning off, so I suggested we meet at this bakery. I come here with Dad sometimes. The first time was when I proved to him that I shared his powers and that he was wrong about me not inheriting them. I always feel empowered here as a result, and it seemed a good place to embark on the Jeni Empowerment Plan as well.

"So, like I explained, we have to go through some steps to make it official, or else we'll be psychically chained together for eternity." Jeni chokes as some muffin crumbs go down the wrong way. I lean over and pat her back while she coughs to clear her throat. "And we don't want that to happen," I say, using my doom-laden voice. "Do we?"

"Um . . . no?"

"Correct. According to the f.g. bylaws, which were originally written in the twelfth century" (and which I have completely made up), "in a land now known as Denmark, in order for us to break our connection, I must help you in some other way, and leave you happier about yourself and your life than when we met. Only then can I move on to the next client, and you to your new destiny."

Jeni takes another tiny careful bite of muffin and chews. "You swear you're not going to trick me into running into Ronald?"

"I swear."

"Or vice versa?"

"This has nothing to do with him." For now, anyway.

"You won't try to talk me into it later?"

"I will never again mention his name—unless you do it first."

"I *won't*."

"Okay, then. We're on the same page—of a different fairy tale. In this one, the peasant girl finds her inner princess—and who cares about the prince?"

Jeni nods. "Okay."

"Okay. So. What are some things about you or your life that you wish were different?"

"Um . . . nothing?"

Oh Lord, it's like we've gone backward, to the first day.

Although . . . on that first day, she had a wish . . .

I spin my fork in the air. Jeni blinks. She knows something has changed.

"Check out your ponytail," I tell her.

She pulls the ends of her hair over her shoulder and gasps, stunned to see her brown hair streaked with strands of honey blond. "Highlights," she sighs happily. And then I know exactly what I need to do.

"Thank you." Jeni stands up, ready to go.

I hop up next to her and grab her arm. "Oh, we're not finished. Not nearly."

★　★　★

Jeni frowns as she holds the pale blue tie-dyed sundress in front of her.

"I don't think it . . . My legs are . . . I'm too short . . . There aren't any sleeves, so my arms . . ."

"Just try it on," I tell her. "It's a dress, not a tattoo. It can come off."

I swallow my frustration, because this is the new Delaney Collins, f.g., the patient, caring, mindful one. Jeni seemed almost eager when I offered to help her find some prettier clothes at Treasures, but every skirt, dress or tunic I hand to her is greeted with the same fear and panic that she showed with Ronald.

"Why do I have to try anything on, when you can just . . . wave the wand?"

"I told you, magic is temporary. I'm trying to give you some long-term life skills here."

"You did *this*." She strokes a strand of her highlighted hair.

"That was to make a point. You could do it yourself

with a box from the drugstore. We're here so I can show you how to do it all yourself, without me. I'll be gone, remember, on to the next client."

Jeni holds up the dress again. "I just think this is too . . ."

I take the dress from her hand. "Okay. Let's start over. Why don't *you* pick out some outfits you think you might like and try them on?" I point to the curtained corner where she can change. Even if what she chooses is *bleah* and/or *blech,* at least it'll get her out of the metaphorical potato sack she's wearing. Metaphorical *and* literal: oversized khakis; ugly, faded boy's T-shirt—and those awful clunky shoes. Once she's "off with the old," it'll be easier to get her "on with the new." Even if the "new" is vintage. "I'll be right back," I tell her. It's obvious I'm going to need more than clothes and accessories to lure Jeni out of her comfortable nest of dullness. I need *mood.*

In the main part of the store, Nancy is showing a young couple an armoire with rusty hinges. She doesn't seem to notice as I haul dusty floor lamps and tarnished mirrors to the vintage room and then return for more. On a bookshelf near the front door, I spot an old portable radio. Perfect— except when I snap open the back, it's empty. Nancy's now swiping the couple's credit card, and I see that the armoire has a big SOLD tag taped to it. I wait for the couple to finish paying and leave, and then I take the radio up to the counter.

"Do you have any batteries?" I ask Nancy. "I need two Cs."

Nancy files away the credit card receipt. I see enough of it to know she's made her big sale of the week. "I'm not paying you to play dress-up with your friends, Delaney."

"Jeni's a customer."

"Mm-hmm."

"And I'm making her a pair of boots." As soon as I say this, I realize I mean it.

Nancy smiles. "Boots" was the magic word. She reaches under the counter, retrieves a flashlight and unscrews the top. "Not too loud, all right? And nothing too *noisy*."

"I don't know what that means."

"I'll let you know." She drops the flashlight batteries into my hand.

Back in the vintage room, Jeni's standing in front of one of the mirrors, looking worried and lost. I'm not surprised she's so upset, because she's wearing a shapeless shift dress that is (1) ankle-length, (2) high-necked and (3) the color of baby puke.

"I'm ugly." Jeni's mouth curves down into a little-kid pout.

I load the batteries into the radio and turn it on. "No. It's the dress that's—" I stop myself, because she *did* pick it out and I don't want to insult her taste, even if she has none; that would probably put a dent in the Jeni Empowerment Plan. I spin the dial on the radio, but it's all New

Age jazz stations and soft rock. I settle on a techno-pop station because at least the songs have a beat. "That dress is the wrong color for you, that's all," I say finally. "Pale green works better against really dark brown skin or fair, pinky skin. You need warmer colors." I sort through some scarves and find the one I'm looking for. It's a jungle design of gold and orange. I drape it around Jeni's shoulders. "There. Much better." Jeni touches the ends lightly with her fingers, as if testing to see if it's real. "Let's get a better view." I use chairs to prop up two mirrors at opposing angles to a third, to form a three-way. I grab a pair of cowboy boots off the shelf. They're a faded rust color, with spirals stitched into them. "Try these." Jeni slips them on. I was prepared to use magic to make them fit, but I don't have to. They're exactly the right size. "See? Don't you think you look pretty?" Jeni blushes and her gaze drops. "Where's that inner princess we were talking about at breakfast?" Jeni doesn't answer. She just shakes her head. "Yeah, okay," I say. "That's what we have to work on. Not your wardrobe—your *attitude*." I put my hands on Jeni's shoulders and press them back, prompting her to look up and into the mirror. "You. Are. Pretty."

"Nooooo." She looks away.

"Okay, why not? What's wrong with you?"

"Everything. My hair . . . even with highlights, it's . . ."

"Do *not* say ugly."

"But . . ."

"It's *hair*, Jeni. It's a bunch of dead cells. If you do

186

something with it, it'll look good. Highlights are a start, but they're not the finish." With one hand, I sweep her hair up behind her head in a twist and use the other hand to pull a few strands free. It softens her whole look, making her dark eyes bigger and brighter, giving her a sophistication that surprises even me.

Jeni is awed. "How did you do that?"

"Did it look easy?"

"Yes."

"It *was*." I let her hair fall. "You don't need magic. You just need to take charge."

"I'd ditch the dress, though. It looks like she's been dipped in baby puke." Lourdes stands in the entranceway, dressed in another warrior-wear outfit: a dark, sleeveless denim shirtdress with frayed edges, three thick black leather belts with animal faces engraved on them, and muddy, scuffed-up red moccasins. "So what are we doing here? Makeover?"

"Delaney's my—"

"Friend," I say, cutting Jeni off and shooting her a "Do *not* say anything about me being an f.g., because this is proprietary information" look. It's a lot to convey in a glance, though, and Jeni stares back at me, utterly confused, but at least she doesn't say anything.

"It's not a makeover," I say. " 'Makeover' implies that there's something wrong with the person. It's an enhancement."

Lourdes considers this. "I like it. Everybody's got their

own style, right? Look at me." She waves a hand over her outfit, then flings her arm my way. "Look at *you*." What's that supposed to mean? "Still, you have to admit, the dress has to go," she says. "That sack wouldn't look good on a supermodel."

Jeni pouts. I'd been momentarily happy to see Lourdes, but that moment is gone. "Why don't we pick out some things together," I tell Jeni. "And Lourdes can belt shop or whatever she's here for."

"No way," Lourdes says. "I want in on the makeover. I mean 'enhancement.' " She picks up one of the lamps. "What's with these? Why don't you plug them in? Toss some scarves over them, create a mood." She does exactly this as she's talking and soon the room has taken on an amber glow.

"Oooo," Jeni murmurs under her breath.

"I was just about to do that," I tell Jeni. "That's why I brought them back—"

"And what's with the music?" Lourdes crouches down, spins the radio dial and tunes in a hip-hop station. She cranks up the volume, making the floor vibrate and the belts on the walls shake. "Now that's—"

"Noisy!" Nancy calls from the other room.

I march over to the radio and turn it down. Not off, though, because it's exactly the kind of music I'd been looking for earlier. "Look, Lourdes, I'm trying to—"

"All right, let's get started." Lourdes claps and swings

her hips in rhythm with the song. Jeni is staring at her with a mixture of fascination and future-roadkill-in-headlights. At least she's too stunned to flee for the exit. Lourdes dances over to a rack of dresses and sweeps several of them up in an embrace, rising onto her toes to lift the hangers free from the pole. She sashays back to Jeni and dumps them into her arms. "Start with those."

"All of them?" Jeni glances over at me, unsure.

I hate that Lourdes is right. I've been doing it again—rushing the process, trying to skip to the end instead of following all the steps. "Yes," I tell Jeni. "All of them. You can't tell what anything looks like on a hanger. You have to see what it looks like on you."

"Pretend it's a game," Lourdes says. "No pressure." She grabs a handful of scarves and tosses these on top of the dresses. " 'Dress-up day.' "

Jeni casts one last doubtful look between us and then reluctantly carries her pile over to the curtain.

"We make a good team," Lourdes says to me.

"You kind of forced your way onto the team."

"And you are *so* grateful I did."

"Eternally." I select some random tops for Jeni to try on next. Lourdes looks through the few new belts that have come in since her earlier shopping spree.

"Loved those photos from that estate sale," Lourdes says. "Sorry I haven't called. Boy trouble. How's the math tutoring going?"

"Better. How's it going with the guy?"

Lourdes examines a wide white patent leather belt. "I've given up. A million girls are after him. There's no point."

"You don't seem like the giving-up type."

"Shows how much you know, Boots." She says this in an "end of subject" way that I'm familiar with, because I use it all the time. But I never realized it makes the person listening want to know *more*.

"What's the holdup?" Lourdes calls out to Jeni. "We're ready for the fashion show out here."

"They all look bad. None of them look—"

"You've been trying things on without *showing* us?" Lourdes glances over at me.

"Jeni, you need to come out," I say. "Show us whatever you have on now."

"It's awful."

"Good! It'll be a reject, then. The more wrong outfits you try on, the closer you'll get to the one that's right." Silence from behind the curtain. "Jeni?"

"You won't laugh?"

"I could use a laugh," Lourdes says. "If you can make that happen, *please* come out. I'll owe you." More silence.

"In return," I say, "we'll make *you* laugh." I grab a stack of hats and pile them on my head. Lourdes smiles and ties a wrap skirt around her neck like a cape. I pull on a horrid polyester jacket in mustard yellow. Lourdes circles one leg with a feather boa and ties it in a bow below the knee.

"We're coming in." Lourdes and I each take one end

of the curtain and raise it up, revealing Jeni, dressed in a knee-length hot-pink crinoline skirt and stretched-out macramé sweater top, looking like some disco reject. "Oh my God, that *is* awful," Lourdes says. "What do you think, Boots?"

"Wretched," I say. "Positively wretched."

Jeni's flustered, but only for a second. Then she notices what *we're* wearing and she smiles. The smile turns into a giggle—and then we're all laughing.

We send her back in to change. She's still reluctant at first, and we have to drag her out again and again, but once she gets used to taking things off and dumping them in the reject pile, she relaxes. Her steps are a little less tentative each new time she comes out from behind the curtain. Soon, she walks right up to the mirror without us having to force her. Eventually, she *wants* to look in it. The different pieces start to come together. Old becomes new. I roll up the sleeves of a tunic Jeni's tried on, Lourdes ties a beaded belt around Jeni's waist, and Jeni smiles at the result. A smile that's not shy or reluctant or embarrassed, but happy . . . closing in on confident. I begin to see the *real* Jeni, the one who's been hidden all this time behind boring colors and downcast eyes and hesitation. My strategy is working. I finally feel as if I'm accomplishing something and that the f.g. thing isn't about victory for me. Well, not only for me.

I can actually help transform people—transform them in a way that doesn't require one wave of the wand.

"Shiny New Boots" by Art in Motion comes on the radio. Lourdes and I dance around Jeni, and Jeni sways, just a little, like she's trying it out, waiting to see if she'll die of embarrassment. When she doesn't die, the swaying grows slightly more detectable.

The song builds to the final verse. Lourdes hums along. I snap my fingers. Jeni does a spin. As the song rises to its last line, Jeni throws her arms open and belts out the last lyric. Lourdes and I stop dancing and stare.

Jeni's voice is gorgeous.

Jeni suddenly notices we're staring at her and she slaps her hand over her mouth, her eyes wide, her face flushed.

"Noisy!" Nancy calls again from the front. Then a second later: "But lovely!"

Our eyes meet in a three-way glance. We all burst into laughter at the same time and Jeni's shyness is shattered, like the glass case holding Sleeping Beauty.

chapter thirteen

"Never?" Lourdes asks for the third time, stirring the ice in her drained blood-orange lemonade. "You've never sung in front of *anybody*? Ever?" Jeni shakes her head. "Why not?"

"I don't know." Jeni takes a tiny bite of her soft pretzel. "I don't want people to stare at me?"

"It's not exactly an insult if they're staring at you because you're talented."

Jeni blushes and smiles down at the gum-spotted concrete floor of the Bazaar.

My lunch break is nearly over and I still haven't figured out a way to bring up Ronald. Since I'd promised, pledged, sworn not to, this makes it challenging.

I take a sip of my ginger lemonade. I'm not sure ginger was the right choice for the lemonade, because it reminds me of being here with Flynn. I put the cup down and try to concentrate on the problem in front of me.

"You don't get how lucky you are." Lourdes points her last bite of pumpernickel pretzel at Jeni. "When I sing, people throw sacks over my head. I could be used as a military weapon. A torture device."

Jeni laughs and I see it again, that inner sparkle that came out at Treasures. She's changed into her Fizzy uniform, but she's wearing a pair of big gold hoop earrings. Her hair is up, tied back with the orange jungle scarf. The lazy strips of sun coming through the roof slats cast a soft spotlight on the side of her face. She's stopped hiding from herself and stopped hiding herself from everybody else. She's not all the way there, but I can tell the door's been opened, and in time it'll swing all the way around on its hinges and never close again.

If only I'd *started* here, like I should have, it'd be an easy transition to fixing her up with Ronald. Now I have no idea how to get back on track. I've learned something for my next client, but I don't know if there'll be one, since I might be stuck with Jeni forever, both of us inching closer to full-on f.g.-generated fulfillment, but never quite getting there.

"You should try one of those open mike nights," Lourdes says to Jeni. "They're doing a talent show thing here at the mall. There's a poster for it in front of Brennan's. A friend of mine's going to be in it. Anybody can sign up."

"Oh, no," Jeni says. "That would be too scary."

"We'd go see you. Cheer you on. Right, Boots?"

"Yeah. Totally."

Lourdes stirs her melting ice and stares across the table at me. "What's with you, Boots? Join the conversation."

"I'm listening. Listening is a key element in conversation."

"Are you saying I'm talking too much?"

"If you were *listening,* you'd know that I *didn't* say that." Arguing with Lourdes wakes me up a little. It's like she's whamming handballs at me and I could duck—or slam them back. Slamming is more fun.

"Are you sad because it's over?" Jeni asks.

Lourdes glances between us. "What's over?"

"Nothing," I say, with a look to Jeni. I straighten up from my slumped position. "It's just post-pretzel carbo-crash."

"Jeni?" A pair of Nutri-Fizzy-uniform-clad kids approach the table. One male, one female. I recognize them from my Frequent Fizzy visits.

"Hi!" Jeni says enthusiastically, forgetting for a second to be shy. Then she remembers, blushes and stares down at her strawberry lemonade.

"Hey," the boy Fizz Master says. "We're going over to Mocha. They've got half-price coffee shakes until two."

Jeni nods and says nothing. I kick her under the table and tilt my head toward her coworkers. "Oh! Um, this is Delaney," Jeni says. "And Lourdes. Kevin and Cheyenne work with me at the Nutri-Fizzy Bar."

"Figured that part out," Lourdes says. This time I kick *her* under the table. She kicks me back.

"Hey," I say.

"Hey!" Lourdes says, directing it and a big smile at Kevin and Cheyenne.

Cheyenne nudges Kevin. "Tell Jeni about tomorrow night."

"Oh, yeah! A bunch of us are going out for karaoke, if you want to come."

"Yes!" I yell, and ignore Jeni's look of alarm. "That would be, like, *perfect*." Oh my God, I can't believe the universe is actually helping me for once.

"Uh, sure," Kevin says. "Anybody can come."

"Sorry," Lourdes says. "The nationwide bar against me singing in public remains in effect through the next millennium."

"Um, okay." Kevin exchanges a wary glance with Cheyenne. I shoot Lourdes a look. She smirks back. I don't think she realizes her effect on people.

"So it'll be me and Jeni," I tell Kevin. "We just need when and where."

Jeni has yet to speak. This is working for me at the moment, because she can't protest. I give Kevin my cell number so he can text me the information.

"We better get going," Cheyenne says. "We're on break."

"Why don't you go *with* them," I say to Jeni with a pointed stare. "I have to get back to work anyway. And Lourdes has to go—wherever it is she's going."

"Yeah. I'm late," Lourdes says. "For wherever. And you know how *that* is."

I stand and gesture at Lourdes to do the same. Jeni follows as we carry our trays over to a nearby trash can. I can feel her nervousness. It's like a buzzing in the air. "No backing out on the karaoke," I whisper to Jeni, out of earshot of Lourdes.

"But I'm—"

"This is part of the process we have to go through, okay? Now go get a coffee shake and have fun, like we did at the store. Try not to worry about tomorrow. Try not to think at all. It's going to go fine, I promise, and then you'll be off the hook. We'll be done."

★ ★ ★

Jeni has borrowed her parents' car to drive us to the karaoke place. She's made an effort with her clothes. She's in jeans, a T-shirt and sneakers, but the jeans are a pretty cobalt blue and not baggy, and the T-shirt has been embroidered with pearly beads along the collar. She's wearing the scarf from Treasures around her shoulders, and she has on the dangling earrings I bought for her at the craft show.

We enter the parking lot, across from what used to be a huge bowling alley, the length of an entire strip mall. It's been divided up and there's still bowling, in the middle part, but now one end is a video arcade and the other is where they have the karaoke.

As soon as she turns off the ignition, I hand Jeni the bag I brought with me. She asked about it when I got into the car. "I'll show you when we get there," I told her.

She opens it now. "Oh!" She lifts out the cowboy boots I'd made her try on, the sides now etched with stars, painted silver to match the spirals, and puts them on.

When we get out of the car, I inform her that it's not only stars I added to the boots. "I know I said I wasn't going to use magic to help you with this step of our bond severance process, but this is a special circumstance." Even though there's no one around us, I lower my voice to em-phasize the gravity and significance of what I say next. "I've put a powerful confidence-building spell on the boots. It'll kick in when you need it, like a timed-release vitamin."

Jeni absorbs this information, her eyes growing wide and then lowering to stare in awe at her magical boots. I hold back a smile.

She totally bought it.

Cheyenne shrieks out a rendition of "Hey, Soul Sister." She's definitely got the enthusiasm—hips sway, hands slap overhead—but no sense of pitch. I glance around to see how the rest of the crowd is reacting. There are about forty people in the place, scattered among the nine or ten tables in the room. The décor is a weird mix of glitzy and gritty.

Tinted lights are hung above the small stage, and they flash and swirl whenever the music is playing, and one whole wall is covered floor to ceiling with old LP covers.

It's dark, but the revolving lights make it possible to see that there's nobody preparing to boo Cheyenne, no one clutching their ears in pain. They're either chatting with each other or swaying along with the song.

It's a friendly bunch. Jeni will be more than fine. She doesn't seem to know this, though, because her left leg has been jiggling nervously since the moment we sat down. The heel of her cowboy boot makes soft *tap-tap-tap*s on the black-and-white-tiled floor.

Cheyenne finishes and Kevin cheers, joined by Hunter, another Fizz Master who has come along, and Hunter's boyfriend, Austin. I clap and Jeni follows my lead, but her claps are little hummingbird-fast slaps to match her tapping foot.

A girl and boy run up to the stage to follow Cheyenne. The order is decided by numbered tickets you're given when you pay. "We have the next one," Kevin tells the table. "Who wants to go?"

"Hey, Jeni," I say loudly. "You ready?"

Jeni shakes her head.

"Cool!" I say, as if she'd agreed. "We're ready to cheer you on." The others at the table offer their encouragement. The duo onstage bow to the applause of their friends.

I lean over toward Jeni. "Remember the boots," I whisper.

Jeni glances down, notices her foot tapping, and stops it. She looks back up at me and I give her a supportive smile. She stands—and then clutches onto my arm and gives it a tug.

"*I'm* not going," I say. Jeni nods. "No, I don't sing. Not my thing." Another staccato bob of the head from Jeni. "The boots," I hiss. Her fingers dig in. Maybe I did do a spell, but a bad one—one that's making her act possessed. She tugs again. Clearly, I have no choice. I stand up and let her drag me to the stage.

On the stage is a long rectangular box with a touch screen on it that flashes a list of songs. I randomly pick something and hand Jeni a microphone, hoping she'll let me just provide silent moral support. But no—she thrusts the other mike into my hand and then immediately punches the button on the screen that says "Duet." Lyrics pop up on a split screen. And mine are first. Of all the humiliations f.g.s have undergone for their clients, this has got to be the worst.

What can I do? I sing. I wish I could close my eyes and pretend I'm home alone, listening to my iPod, but if I close my eyes, I can't see the lyrics, and I don't know this song. It's something called "You've Got to Have Friends," which is too ironic, because if anybody here was my friend, they never would've let me get up on this stage in the first place. Luckily, the lights pointed toward us are too blinding for me to be able to see the horror of the crowd.

I never should've mentally mocked Cheyenne.

Finally, it's Jeni's turn, and at first I think she's not singing, only mouthing the words, but when I lean closer, I can hear her, barely.

She can do this, I know it, but *she* doesn't yet. Time to put the boots to work for real. I catch Jeni's eyes and tilt my microphone down, angling it her way. The silver stars on the boots spark and the leather glows. To the audience, it will seem like it's the lights creating the effect, but Jeni is close enough to see the magic.

It works. Jeni straightens up and her voice gets a little louder. She closes her eyes and I guess she does know the song, because she keeps singing, taking my lines too, and no way am I going to protest.

I step back to let her have center stage. She sings and sings, and it's like she sounded at Treasures, but better because now she has musical accompaniment and a real audience.

I smile to myself. All I did was a little routine Atom Manipulation to cause the sparks. I didn't add the confidence. Jeni did that herself.

After the song ends, Jeni bows shyly, blushing at the applause coming from both friends and strangers.

I feel a happy sense of completion. Maybe I wasn't lying to her about how the f.g.-client relationship works. Maybe getting her to this moment really is enough.

It takes my eyes a second to adjust to the bright lights out in the snack bar. I lean against the wall near a rack of gourmet potato chips and text Lourdes to tell her how it went. Jeni appears while I'm still typing. "Did you hear?" she asks, eyes gleaming.

"Yes, you sang great. It was hard to miss. I was onstage with you, remember?"

"I mean the applause."

"Yeah, I was there for that too."

Jeni hesitates. She picks up a bag of red pepper chips and thumbs the corner of it nervously. "Is it too late?"

"For what?"

"Is it . . . severed?"

I finish texting and look up at her. "Why? Don't you want it to be?"

"Well, I . . . I . . ."

I decide to make it easy for her, especially since otherwise it'll take all night for her to get it out. "There's always a grace period. In case the client changes her mind." I take the potato chips out of her hands. "It's going to work this time, Jeni, because we're going to let it happen naturally. No tricks."

"Do I have to say anything?"

"To Ronald? Eventually. You're not going to get very far if you never talk to him."

"No, I mean to, you know, reverse the severing of the bond."

"Oh, yeah . . . Definitely . . . It's, um, what I made you say way back at the start. That you're meant to be."

Another pause, and then, in the breathless whisper

she'd used for the words before, "Ronald and I are meant to be."

"Bond officially un-severed. We're back on."

The phone rings. It's Lourdes. "So you got her to sing?" she asks. "The 'enhancement' worked?"

I smile at Jeni. "Like magic."

chapter fourteen

Dad knocks on my door. "Let's get going!"

"Okay! I just have to put on my boots."

Things have been going so well with Jeni that I felt I could leave her alone for a day. I followed through on the plan I came up with after the fountain and Jump Kicks disasters. I time my breaks to coincide with Ronald's so I can slip over to Nutri-Fizzy and make sure he always orders from Jeni. Sometimes I use magic to send her notes—not telling her what to say, just reminding her to be herself and not stress.

But she doesn't really need the notes. Now that she's

gained some self-confidence, there's never even a hint that she's going to run away when he appears. She was shy at first, but each day she's a tiny bit more at ease. Each time Ronald reaches the counter, they chat a little longer. Yesterday I didn't have to do anything, because it was Ronald who let somebody in front of him so that it would be Jeni taking his order.

It was time to step back and see how she does on her own—which led me to agreeing to the Theo-Gina adventure. It's not like I had anything better to do.

★ ★ ★

Why couldn't I have found something better to do?

First there was a horrid 3-D animated movie about construction trucks that turn out to be aliens in disguise. Then it was on to lunch at the pizza chain next door. Since we've arrived, the conversation has consisted mainly of "How about one more bite, Theo?" and "I hate mushrooms," interspersed with glares from Theo tossed my way, as if I'd snatched his favorite toy, when I've taken nothing from him, not even Dad's or Gina's attention, which is all on him.

The proposed post-lunch activity is a visit to a batting cage, where I'll have nothing to do but watch Theo take out his anti-Hank issues on baseballs while Dad joins in and shows off his utter lack of athletic skill.

I'm considering faking a bout of food poisoning, when my phone rings: Lourdes.

"You free? I want to show you something."

"Yes!" I say. "Of course. Right away. I'll be at Treasures ASAP." I hang up and turn to Dad. "I have to get to the mall. It's an emergency."

Dad peers over at me suspiciously. "What kind of emergency?"

"Clothing related. There's a fashion designer who wants to use vintage in his fall line, and he needs me to help sort through the inventory for the best stuff. Nancy's totally clueless about that side of the business."

Dad still seems skeptical, even though my story is beyond believable. There are lots of designers who use vintage stuff. Maybe it's far-fetched that they'd be shopping at Treasures, but it would be less far-fetched than most of the things that have happened in my life.

Dad must be thinking along the same lines, because he gives in and drops me off on the way to the batting cage. Lourdes is waiting for me outside Treasures, a helmet under each arm. Except we're not going batting.

We head downtown on Lourdes's moped, and as we get closer, we leave the epic malls and fancy mansions behind. The buildings get taller and older, with sculpted cornices and Art Deco façades. There are Metro stops and city buses at every cross street, and trash and dirt. The sidewalks grow more crowded, and the pedestrians jostle each other aside, rushed and unsmiling.

I love it.

It's an eye-opening ride. At least until we turn down a street lined with warehouses and pull up in front of a big brick factory-looking building. Then Lourdes orders me to close my eyes and slaps her hands over them to make sure I can't see where we're going. She steers me down the sidewalk. "Thanks," I hear her say, and I feel someone brush past us. I can tell from the change of sounds that we've stepped inside. The first thing I notice is the smell: coffee. She's brought me to a coffee plant? I don't hear any machinery, though, only people talking and pop music playing softly in the background.

"Okay!" Lourdes pulls her hands away. I open my eyes.

"It's . . . It's . . . What is it?"

"Common Grounds. It's an artists' café." She says this as if there's one on every corner, but I've never seen anything like it, not even in New Jersey.

It does have the look of some of the places I'd gone to with Mom or Posh: exposed brick, exposed beams, long stainless-steel counter with the menu posted above on a blackboard.

But the tables aren't the usual café tables. There are two drafting tables, like architects use, a few large square tables with outlets in the center for laptop plugs, and a long wooden table down the middle of the room that looks like two huge doors laid end to end. There's a sewing machine on one end of the long table and carpentry clamps at the other.

At each of the four corners of the café are easels, and at the easels and tables are the artists: drawing, painting, sewing, sculpting, designing. The people all have dyed black or blue or magenta hair. They wear overalls or paint-spattered smocks or ripped jeans that I can tell they didn't buy that way, but that they ripped themselves. Some have multiple piercings, and some have multiple tattoos, and a lot of them wear boots. Boots!

"I thought you'd like it." Lourdes slaps me on the back. "Grab a table. I'll get us drinks. What do you want?" I ask for a chai latte and then make my way through the café, still in awe.

There are a few small normal-looking white tables scattered throughout the room, and I take a seat at a free one. I gaze around at all the artists, working separately but sharing a creative energy that seems to pulse through the café, from one easel and table to the next.

"Here you go." Lourdes hands me a tall black mug topped with frothy milk and takes a seat across from me. "Is this great or what? I saw a post about it online this morning. There're a couple of art schools in the neighborhood, so it's mostly the students who come here, plus some professional artists who live in the lofts nearby."

There's an old soup can in the middle of the table, filled with colored markers. Lourdes lifts out a green one and draws the outline of a boot on the table, upside down, so it's right side up for me. She wipes away an errant line and I realize that the tabletop is a big dry-erase board. "We have to come back when we have more time," she says. She hands me the pen. "But I had to show you."

I decorate the boot with random swirls and checks. Lourdes grabs a red pen and draws a series of stick figures doing acrobatics. We're quiet and listen to the sounds of creation: the hum of the sewing machine, the tap of fingers on laptop keys.

I'm filled with the same calm that comes with watching Jeni and Ronald flirt. I feel, for the first time in a while, that things are getting better instead of worse.

For instance, I haven't seen Ariella since that day Jeni tried to "sever our bond." I have seen Fawn occasionally, charging back from the shoe store, wearing sundresses that hang on her skinny frame, or halter tops and skintight capris, or short shorts that are so short that she has to stop every two seconds to tug them down. I feel sorry for Fawn, and I'm tempted to lure her into Treasures and find something for her to wear that would make her feel better about herself, not worse. I'll do it after Jeni and Ronald have walked off into the sunset and Ariella's finally admitted that her beneficiary hasn't benefited from her help at all.

If the universe really is spinning back in a pro-Delaney direction, then Flynn should be next. Maybe he's thinking about me right now, missing me, desperate to get back and tell me, over and over, extremely clearly, with lots of specific detail, how much I mean to him and how lucky he feels to have Delaney Collins, super f.g., as his g.f.

Anything is possible now. I mean, look—I've created

a whole new boot design without any effort! Without any thought, actually. Why shouldn't my relationship with Flynn be as thought- and effort-free?

My phone buzzes. Oh my God, it must be Flynn. I know it is. It has to be.

It's not. It's Jeni. The text is a half-gibberish mess of misspellings, missing words and nonexistent grammar. "What the . . . ?" I say. Lourdes stares at me curiously. "It's Jeni," I explain. "I think she's, um, been hit in the head or something. Let me just text her back." I type out a series of question marks and send. Her next message is just as nonsensical, except for one word that screams out from the screen. Not a word—a name. A name that causes both of Jeni's texts to become decipherable, her scrambled words unscrambling as I study them, the gaps filling in, until the meaning is completely clear: Ariella has gone *too* far.

The sky's turned pink when Lourdes drops me back at the mall. "I have this thing to go to," she says, "but I can be late."

"No, that's okay." I'd told Lourdes after Jeni's second text that she wasn't injured, just upset. "It's kind of personal. Better if it's only me."

"Call me if you need me," Lourdes says. She rides off and I hurry out of the parking lot, into the mall.

The daytime crowd's cleared out and the nighttime crowd has begun to arrive, like the changing of the guard. The shorts and strollers and packs of kids have traded up for women in party dresses, strappy high heels and bright lipstick, holding hands with men in sport coats or designer leather jackets or dress shirts with skinny ties. Older couples hurry to the movie theater to catch the first show because they have only so much time before they have to get back for the babysitter, and groups of friends bump shoulders on their way to happy hour, laughing loudly, *already* happy. I feel out of place, irritated by their contented contentment, the joy that wafts off them like perfume, while I stink of panic and dread. Jeni didn't answer my last text and I don't see her now as I get closer to the Nutri-Fizzy Bar, where they're closing up for the night. Has she been carried off in a straitjacket? Thrown herself in the fountain? Overdosed on thyme-flavored carbonated water?

But no, she's there. I see her through the window, helping Kevin lift a gas canister onto the Nutri-Fizzy machine.

"Jeni!" Jeni lets go of the canister when she sees me enter, causing Kevin to lose his balance and fall back against the counter. Another Fizz Master leaps into action and grabs the opposite side of the canister, while Jeni rushes past them, away from me. I grab a straw from the counter and aim it at the door to the back room. When Jeni pushes the lever handle down, it goes nowhere, locked from within. She grabs the lever with both hands, rattling it.

"Jeni, I need to talk to you."

Jeni gives up on the door, spins around and charges from behind the counter. Her head is down, not from shyness—from anger. I'm about to speak when she reaches up her arms and shoves me, hard, then storms past me. I hurry out the door after her.

Jeni's walking so fast, I have to run to catch up to her. "Whatever Ariella said to you, she was lying," I tell her. "She has an agenda."

Jeni stops, suddenly, and I shoot past her several strides before I've even realized it. Then I have to jog back. I really don't think being an f.g. is supposed to be this physically demanding. "She said she was a fairy godmother. She *showed* me." Jeni glares at me, a glare so filled with hurt and betrayal that even in the dimming light of the evening, it slices into me.

"Okay, well, *that's* true—"

"She said she's helping another girl get Ronald."

"Okay, well—"

"She said you're an 'inferior mutation of the profession.'"

"Inferior! I am so *not*—"

"And that you've never granted anybody's wish before."

"Okay, well, yes. *Technically*—"

Jeni pokes me in the shoulder. "*You're* the one who lied." It's a hard poke. I'm definitely going to have a bruise.

"I've *never* lied to you. I didn't tell you about Ariella, because she's *wrong*. The girl she's trying to help isn't the right one. *You* are." Jeni turns her face away from me just as the mall's streetlamps snap on. The light illuminates the conflicted expression on her face. I can tell she wants to believe me, or at least she *wants* to want to, but she can't quite get there. "It's her word against mine," I say. "And against what you *know* you feel."

"She said they were already together." Jeni's voice is a whisper, nearly lost among the echoes of the vanished happy-hour-goers. But even as soft as they are, the words cause my stomach to lurch.

"I'm sure she made it up, to throw you off."

"I texted him."

"Ronald?"

Jeni nods. "To invite him out with us tonight. He said he was *busy*."

"That doesn't prove anything."

"And I know who the girl is that the other fairy god-mother is granting the wish for. It's the girl we saw in the shoe store that first day. The one you *lied* about."

"That wasn't a lie. It was a minor fabrication for the purpose of—"

"Liar."

The clock tower chimes and Jeni gives me a smug look, like the ensuing gongs are symbolic proof that whatever magic spell I wove for her has ended. But I've come too far now to be undone by a clanging bell. It's just a clock. Midnight is hours away, so even symbolically, I still have time.

"I'm going to find Ariella," I tell Jeni. "And I'm going to talk to her and clear this up. Everything'll be fine. Wait here five minutes."

"I can't. I have to go back and help close up."

"Wait there, then," I say, and try to keep the exasperation out of my voice. "I'll be right back."

I dial Ariella's number and take a quick detour to glance into Jump Kicks. Ronald's chatting with two preteen boys, who are listening with rapt awe as he extols the benefits of spring-loaded heels. No Fawn, no Ariella, no impatient anticipation in Ronald's expression to suggest that he's a prince looking forward to his date with his princess.

I sigh in partial relief.

The Elegant Imprint, the card store where Fawn works, is still open, but there's no sign of Fawn. Or Ariella. "Excuse me," I ask the lady behind the counter. "I'm a friend of Fawn's. I was supposed to meet her and another friend here."

"Fawn left about an hour ago. I think she had to babysit."

A guy restocking stationery glances over. "Wasn't she going to that poetry thing?"

"I don't think that was tonight," the lady says. "Was it?"

"I think it might be."

"Hmm. I don't—"

"Was there another girl with her?" I ask, interrupting the endless debate.

They both shake their heads.

"She was by herself when she left," the lady says.

"I didn't see anybody else," the guy says. At least they agree on something, but it doesn't help me.

Back outside, I hit Redial on the phone and then search

up and down the mall's curved sidewalk, as if I'll be able to spot Ariella blinking like a human firefly, but the only bright beams come from the reflections of the streetlamps in the shop windows.

The fountain music crescendos and then ends, leaving only the trickling sound of the water jets as the next song cues up. There are just a few people out now, and they're in no hurry to get to bars or movies. They stroll slowly, talking softly, and in the whispering quiet, I hear the tinkling sound of wind chimes. I speed toward the sound, the clacking of my boot heels echoing along the cobblestone. Then I see her, and—oh my God—she *is* glowing like a firefly. But no, it's only light bouncing off the sequins on her angel jacket as she strides toward the half-moon driveway near the valet stand, where her mom's pointy-finned green car is idling. "Ariella!" I call out.

She pauses in front of the little table display of eye creams and body oils that sits outside of Potions. She waits and watches me as I approach, a smile on her face, her eyes gleaming, partly from the golden glow of the big globe light over Potions' front door and partly from an evil glee. "Hi, Delaney! What a nice surprise!"

I stop in front of her and catch my breath. "How could you do that?" I finally manage to say.

Ariella picks up a lotion bottle and pumps a couple of dollops into her palm. "Do what?" She rubs the lotion over the tops of her hands, like some diabolical TV cartoon villain getting ready to extract the brains out of kittens.

I fold my arms and say nothing. Ariella glances over her shoulder at her mother's car, where her mom is talking into her Bluetooth and gesturing with her hands, clearly in the middle of her own f.g. crisis. Assured that she has time to torment me, Ariella turns back and drops the smile.

"I did that poor girl a favor," Ariella says. "You were getting her hopes up when there's no chance for her."

"You're cheating."

"It's not a game, Delaney. You're playing with people's lives."

"I know that—" A white-smocked saleswoman steps out from the store. She smiles at us over her rectangular mock-doctor eyeglass frames.

"Can I interest you young ladies in a sample of our latest grapefruit blossom body scent?"

"No, thank you," I say coolly, and give her a "no sale" glare.

"I'd *love* to." Ariella sneers at me and then holds out her wrist for the woman to spritz.

"You have to come back with me right now and tell Jeni you were lying," I say, not caring that the saleslady overhears.

"Lying about what?" Ariella rubs her wrists together. She sniffs the scent and coos approvingly.

"Everything."

Ariella ignores me. "How much is it?" she asks the saleswoman.

"It's on sale today for fifteen dollars, and you get a free lip gloss with purchase."

Ariella thanks her and the woman smiles again, just at Ariella this time, before returning to the store. Ariella presses a wrist to the hollow of her neck. "I didn't lie about anything, Delaney. I *am* the superior fairy godmother. I have a lot more experience than you. Ronald belongs with Fawn. That's why they're on a date right now."

"I just saw Ronald at the shoe store."

"He's meeting Fawn there. In about . . ." She checks her phone. "Twenty minutes."

"Meeting her where?"

Ariella smirks at me.

"It can't be tonight," I insist. "You'd be there."

"I don't need to be there. Cinderella's fairy godmother didn't tag along with her to the ball."

A car horn beeps from the valet circle. "Ariella! Let's get going!" Ariella's mom leans out the car window. "Your father and Justine are waiting for us."

"I'm coming!" Ariella calls, and then turns back to me. "It's too late, Delaney. Give up. Accept the fact that you're never going to grant that girl's wish. Stop leading her on."

Ariella's mom spots me and waves. "Oh, hi, Delaney! We're going to Fiesta for Ariella's dad's birthday," her mom says. "Why don't you come with us?"

Ariella stiffens slightly when her mom mentions the birthday, and that's how I know Ariella would be with

Fawn if she could, which means she's *not* sure it's a done deal.

"No, thanks," I say. I wave back and in that split second, something occurs to me. It's as if, with the wave, I grabbed the thought out of the sky. I wait until Ariella has climbed into the car and then I give her the same patronizing smile she gave me. "I have other plans." I wave again and keep waving. Ariella's eyes stay on me as the car swings around to the street. It's hard to tell as her face moves into shadow, but I think I see a flicker of worry cross her face.

She may have the superior abilities and more experience, but she hasn't won yet.

As I exit the Elegant Imprint a few minutes later, I spot Jeni, emerging from the Fizzy Bar with a pack of her fellow Fizz Masters, now all in civilian clothes. I call out to her and she says something to Kevin and then walks over to me.

"What?" she demands. "What do you want to tell me? That she was telling the truth? They're on a date? It's over? You did lie? *What?*" One thing that Ariella has achieved with her betrayal is to get Jeni to finally speak up. There hasn't been one pause or hesitation in her speech since I arrived at the mall.

Jeni waits for my answer, while her Fizzy friends hover outside of the closed shop.

"I'm going to have to get back to you on that." I bring up my map app on my phone.

"I knew it! I knew I wasn't good enough for him. I told you that at the beginning."

"That's not true. And it's *not* over." I type in the address I got from the stationery guy at the store. "There's just been a small complication."

"Hey, Jeni," Kevin calls. "We'll meet you at the car."

"Okay. I'll be there in a second." Jeni turns back to me. "We're going to see *In Harmony* over at the Palace Theater. It's another one of those fake, lying romantic comedies, where everything works out. Fakely."

"Uh-huh." I study the map on the cell screen.

"I suggested one of the movies playing here—*Dark Forest*. You know, the one where this evil woodcutter is killing off all the fairy-tale creatures, in lots of bloody, gross ways. But I was outvoted."

"Mm-hmm." I expand the map, looking for a familiar cross street.

"I'm leaving now, Delaney. Thanks for wasting my time." She marches away toward the main parking structure. I scroll to the left on the cell screen, and among the highlighted landmarks, one stands out: the Palace Theater.

"Wait up!" I call out, and then run up beside her. Jeni looks up at me, a tiny flicker of hope in her eyes. It doesn't last long, because what I have to say is not what she wants to hear.

"I need a ride."

chapter fifteen

I thought poetry slams were in grungy coffeehouses, in seedy parts of town, down narrow alleyways, where you have to step over the sleeping homeless guy and duck around the quartet of jean-jacketed, greasy-haired smokers to get inside.

But this street is all glitter and glass, a wide boulevard lined with European clothing boutiques, and jewelry stores with empty velvet cases in the windows because the emeralds and rubies have been locked up in the vault for the night. The sun has set, yet I'm not cold. Either the breeze has died down or all the electricity being used on this boulevard is baking the air. The sky is that inky blue that comes a few minutes before it turns black—the part of the sky I can *see,* that is. The part that's not obscured by the glare of the brightly lit two-story storefronts that are all framed in wide bands of silver and gold, with the store names engraved in big block letters along the tops. I cannot possibly be in the right place. I check the name and address I got from the stationery guy again: Jasmine's. 138 North Piñon.

Yep. This is definitely it. Weird.

Jasmine's is one of the few places open. As soon as I step inside, it's obvious that it's not a coffeehouse. It's a tearoom. Straight ahead is a counter lined with tins of leafy dried buds. Labels hang on delicate silver chains with the names of the teas written in cursive: *Lemon Blossom Rose, Oolong Pearl Heaven, Black Currant Geranium*. Behind the counter a man with a TEA CONCIERGE pin on his pressed burgundy dress shirt stands at attention. Shelves with teapots and infusers and strainers and presses line the opposite wall, backlit by hidden lights.

This has *got* to be the wrong place. On the ride over, I persuaded Jeni to hold off on giving up, writing me off, believing that she would be heartbroken for life. I did this by telling her the truth. I admitted that Ariella *is* a super f.g., but I explained that this means there's something wrong if it's taken her this long to get Fawn and Ronald together. I confessed that Ariella and I had declared an f.g. war, which is why Ariella stuck with Fawn weeks after she should've known it was hopeless. And I even told

Jeni that, *yes,* Fawn and Ronald were apparently on a date tonight—but I also revealed that Ariella is not nearly as certain about the outcome of the date as she pretended with Jeni.

It took a while to convey it all, since I had to do it by text in order to keep it from the other four people in the car. I also had to type while crammed into one corner of the backseat, the door handle digging into my side so hard I still have the imprint.

"May I help you?" A thin woman with precision-cut black hair and wearing a cream shift dress, looking like one of the mannequins in the boutique next door, has materialized next to me.

"I'm trying to find this poetry thing, but I think I—"

"Oh, yes. The literary salon. Right this way." She swings an arm out to her left and leads me to a small doorway near the back of the store. *Literary salon?* I guess it's in the same section of the thesaurus as "poetry slam." My doubt returns when I peer inside the room and see lots of small tables and fancy-dressed people eating tiny cookies with their perfumey tea.

But then I notice there's a small stage at the far end of the room, where a girl in a belted silver dress and red strappy heels reads from a gingham-covered notebook.

"Mother, you don't listen.
Mother, you won't hear . . ."

She shakes her fist over her head, her poetry-filled rage clashing with her dance-party outfit.

*"Mother, I won't listen.
Mother, I won't care."*

The light is dimmer and warmer in this room than out where they sell the teas, and I can't tell if Fawn is here. Or Ronald. Maybe the guy at the Elegant Imprint gave me the address of the wrong poetry slam—although how many can there be? Maybe Fawn *is* babysitting. Maybe there's no date at all, and Ariella was making it up, and my f.g. radar or instinct or ESP or whatever is wrong.

"Mother, Mother, Mother . . . Let's talk."

Dance-Party Girl closes her notebook and bows to the ensuing claps.

"Hey! What are you doing here?"

I turn to see Lourdes standing behind me. "What are *you* doing here?" I ask.

"This is the thing I told you I had to go to." She seems to have dressed up a bit—for Lourdes. Her sack dress is less sacky and you can actually see some curves. She's wearing a collection of thin black and green leather wristbands instead of her usual thick scruffy cuffs, and matching thin black and green belts. Her hair is glossed back instead of spiky, and she's actually wearing earrings, long feathered things that brush against her neck.

"How's Jeni?" she asks.

"Oh, she's great. False alarm. She's going to the movies with some friends from the Fizzy place and they dropped me off here because I wanted to pick up some chai to make at home."

Up front, a guy in jeans and a backward baseball cap launches into a rhyming story about his dog, accompanied by some hip-hop moves.

"So, what's your story?" I ask Lourdes. "I didn't know you were into poetry."

"My friend Ronald's here. He's reading. I'm here to cheer."

"Ronald?"

"Kind of old-fashioned, I know. His middle name's Reginald. Can you believe it? He's named after his uncles. He keeps coming up with these new 'professional names' for his music career. The latest is 'Double-R,' which I told him sounds like a dude ranch." The tea drinkers applaud as Hip-Hop Guy hops off the stage. "There he is," Lourdes says, pointing toward the front. "Let's go."

Lourdes shoves me into the room. I'd intended to spy, from the back, but Lourdes drags me toward the stage. I spot Ronald at one of the tables near the front—but it's not Fawn with him. It's another girl. She's in a grayish sateen halter dress, hair held up in an elegant twist with about three hundred jeweled combs. Her bare shoulders, hunched over as she scribbles intently in a tiny lined note-book, have been dusted with bronzy glitter powder that shimmers in the glow from the table lamp.

I scan the room as Lourdes leads me through it. No Fawn. She must've left as soon as she saw Ronald with this other girl. It's a failure for Ariella, but it's not a victory for me, because now there's a new wish-granting obstacle I have to get rid of.

The girl with Ronald gets up to read. She glides to the stage in her metallic stilettos, and her dress catches the light, turning a peachy pink in one step, a silvery green in the next, like the pearly insides of mollusk shells.

Then she steps around to face the room, and my breath stops.

It *is* Fawn.

I'm stunned but not surprised. Somehow I suspected it all along, but after watching Fawn's fashion failures over the last few weeks, I didn't think Ariella would ever be capable of this successful of a transformation. Fawn didn't wobble once, and the dress is perfect for her willowy body. When Fawn squints down at her wee notebook, I think, *Aha! Ariella forgot to give her contacts*—but then Fawn lifts up a pair of stylish tortoiseshell eyeglasses and puts them on.

Ronald spots Lourdes and gestures for her to take the chair next to him. Lourdes pulls me down to the third chair, the one Fawn had been sitting in. Lourdes whispers something to Ronald and he gives me a friendly smile.

Fawn is close enough to see me, but her eyes are on her notebook and she begins.

"If Persephone is the goddess of spring,
Is Symphony the goddess of a summer night,
When the breeze is as soft as a feather
And the stars blink in harmony?"

This is not the usual "my life sucks" cry of angst. I get those. This, I don't get. Although, I have to admit, it seems deep.

"If Athena is the goddess of the forest,
Is Arena the goddess of the open fields of your life,
Spreading out before you,
Choices racing to the horizon?"

Whatever it means, I can tell Fawn feels it, and the intense, sincere way she reads it is mesmerizing.

"If Apollo is the god of the sun,
Is Hollow the god of heartbreak?
Is Follow the god of love left behind?"

Everybody's stopped talking and they're all staring. They're either blown away, or they're trying to figure out what it means too.

"On the sacred ledge of sacrilege, I make my offering
For a love restored, a heart healed,
And opportunity caught between two palms
Like fireflies on a summer night."

When she finishes, she closes her eyes. It seems to take her a few seconds to notice that the room has erupted with applause. She opens her eyes and blinks in surprise. It's like Jeni at the karaoke place. I feel as if Ariella has stolen my success and twisted it into her own—because unlike at the karaoke place, Ronald is here to see the magic happen. Fawn takes a little bow and steps off the stage. She does wobble this time, but she catches herself and slows her pace.

Ronald, standing, hoots and whistles, his hands whapping against each other in gunshot claps. This is not good.

Lourdes leaves to get another chair as Fawn nears. "That was off the hook, girl," Ronald says. "How did you come up with that? 'Sacred ledge of sacrilege.' You could write lyrics. We should collaborate."

Not good at all.

Fawn is blushing from the praise, and since she's taken her glasses off, it's not until she reaches the chair that she notices me.

"This is Delaney," Ronald says. "She's a friend of Lourdes, who's my friend. Lourdes will be back in a second."

"Uh . . ." Fawn grips the top of the empty chair but doesn't sit down. Behind her, the bow-tied emcee announces a tea break.

"Hey, Fawn," I say. "Great poem."

"Um . . ."

Ronald peers over at Fawn, worried. "You okay?"

"Uh, I . . ."

I wonder if some sort of vocal Object Transference has occurred and Jeni's inability to speak has transmuted to Fawn. Now, *that's* big magic. "Fawn and I have a mutual acquaintance," I say. I give her a big, nonthreatening smile. She cautiously pulls out the chair and sits.

Lourdes returns, carrying a tiny wire chair that she's gotten from the other room. She has a grim look on her face, like she might have had to slay someone to get it, but I don't see blood, so it must've been a verbal slaying. As soon as she sits, a waitress appears to take our order. Ronald and Fawn are already sharing (sharing!—*definitely* not good) a pot of green tea. Lourdes orders mint and a plate of mini-scones for the table. I'm too tense for another chai. I need a drink without caffeine, so I point to a random herbal tea on the menu, something with a lot of vowels in the name. It's either great or the weirdest thing in the tea shop, because the waitress raises her eyebrows in eager glee as she writes it down. Whatever. I have more urgent things to worry about. Like how to unplug this Fawn-Ronald connection that seems to have occurred.

"I'm gonna read the lyrics to the song I'm doing Saturday at that Alcove singing-competition thing," Ronald tells Lourdes. "It was Fawn's idea to test it out here, without the music." Ronald smiles at Fawn, who smiles back.

So *that's* how it happened. Fawn paid enough visits to the shoe store in her constantly changing wardrobe that she was able to get to know him better. Again, it feels like Ariella stole my strategy, although I don't think she did it intentionally. She was trying to get Ronald to fall for the dress. That didn't work—but the by-product was their bonding.

"Tell me it's not the song about your car," Lourdes says.

"It's symbolic, L. You're too literal. You miss all the layers."

"Mmm, yeah."

While they argue about the worthiness of Ronald's ode to auto, I turn to Fawn. "I really did like your poem, you know. How did you come up with it?" Fawn squints my way, like the question might have some hidden evil meaning. "Was it a dream or what?" She puts on her glasses, presumably to help her detect my true intentions. "I'm interested," I say sincerely, because although my priority is to keep her talking to me and not Ronald, I actually *am* curious how somebody can think up something so strange.

Fawn tilts her notebook up and considers the words she's written. "I never know how my poems evolve. I start with something, and it sort of . . . becomes something else." She reaches up to push her hair behind her ear, except there's no hair there, it's all swept up, the frizz hair-sprayed to a shellacked brilliance. Her fingers feel it to make sure it's there, and then her arm hovers a moment, as if it's not sure where to go now that this nervous tic has been taken away. Her hand flops back down. "That sounds dumb, doesn't it?"

"No," I say. "I know exactly what you mean. It's the same with me when I'm working on a pair of boots." I kick up a leg so she can see one of the "Suture" boots I'm wearing—zippers sewn up and down the sides in random patterns. "I get an idea for an image maybe, or a color, and then it builds, and the pencil moves and the design takes over."

"Yes!" Fawn declares, her myopic eyes shining. "It's like there's this invisible river, swimming with ideas, and if you're really into what you're writing, the current catches you, and you just . . . flow."

"That could be a poem, what you just said."

Fawn laughs. I notice doodles she's drawn up the sides of her notebook pages. "Are those illustrations?"

"Oh, no, I just do that when I'm thinking. Sometimes if I have an idea, and I can't figure out how to describe it, I draw it and it sort of lets my mind relax and then—"

I spin the notebook around to face me. "They're good, though." They are. "You should think of adding them to the poems. Illustrated verse. Do a chapbook, maybe. You could sell it at your store."

Fawn considers the doodles. "I haven't really done the publishing thing yet."

"Why not? What are you waiting for?"

Fawn pulls the notebook closer, protective.

"You just read your work aloud in front of strangers five minutes ago," I point out. "What's the difference?"

"They're poets."

"Not all of them. And they *all* clapped." She's as bad as Jeni. I wonder if this "hiding your talents" thing is a shared trait with all f.g. clients.

"You really think I'm good enough?"

"Definitely. I'd buy it. Everybody here would buy it. Print some copies and bring them to Treasures in the Annex, where I work. We'll sell them there too."

"Wow, thanks!"

"You need to follow your muse," I tell her, not adding that, ideally, she should follow it as far away from Ronald as possible. The waitress brings our scones and tea. She pours more hot water into Fawn and Ronald's teapot and this unfortunately replugs the Fawn-Ronald connection.

"Hey, Fawn," Ronald says. "Listen to this:

"There is a Voice, it's in my dreams.
I feel it calling out and crying, 'Can you hear me?'
A siren call. I start to fall.
Where is the Voice? I feel her singing right beside me.
Step into the light, out of the night.
We'll sing together and I'll have heaven right
  beside me."

"This is about his car?" I whisper to Lourdes.

She shakes her head. "This is a different one."

"I like it," Fawn says. "How about switch 'light' and 'night'? Make it something like 'Step from the night, into the light.' It's closer to the rhythm of the rest and it follows better narratively."

"Oh, yeah! Right!" Ronald makes a note.

I bite into a scone, grim. Now it'll start. Ronald glancing with grateful admiration at Fawn. Fawn beaming back, flattered by the adoration. Ronald may not have seen this as a date initially—why would he have invited Lourdes?—but it's become one.

Then, as I pour more tea, Ronald turns away from Fawn to show his rewritten lyrics to Lourdes. Fawn hunches back over her notebook, writing in more of her tiny looped scrawl. It's as if they've each forgotten the other was there. I take a sip of my multi-voweled tea, which tastes like I'm drinking sandalwood incense. It's disturbing—but not bad, actually. Or maybe I'm just cheered by the realization that I don't have to come up with a new way to block the bonding of these two human elements, Ronald and Fawn, because there is absolutely no chemistry between them at all.

He's seeking "the Voice." And who is the Voice? She's the Nutri-Fizzy clerk he sees every day. My phone buzzes. It's probably Dad, wondering where I am, even though I left him a message. But how perfect would it be if it was

Jeni? Right at the moment I can tell her I have written proof that *she* is the princess Ronald's been looking for.

I open the text. It's not Jeni, or Dad. It's better:

"Art walk tomorrow night? Aliens have promised to postpone invasion a week."

I text back: ":)!!!!!"

I swear to God I am so happy, I could even write a poem. I'd call it "Fairy-Tale Endings for Everybody."

chapter sixteen

Black velvet skirt, gauzy cap-sleeved top, gray diamond-patterned tights and "Twizzle" boots—the ones I scraped wavy vertical lines all around so the boots look like thick licorice sticks.

Something's missing.

I turn up the radio. I've tuned in some station that plays the same slow, old-fashioned jazz crooner tunes that the mall fountain does at night. Dangerously sappy, but I'm in a dangerously sappy mood, a romantic mood. Every hour of today has been better than yesterday, and I haven't even gotten to the best part yet.

Before I left the tea salon, I told Fawn about the *Sea*

Foam Weekly. I knew from Skids's gross dead-eel poem that they had a fiction page, and I offered to ask Flynn to ask Skids to put in a good word for her. I did this partly to prove to Fawn that I meant her no harm, and partly because I genuinely wanted to help her. I was feeling so happy, I wanted to share it, especially since Ariella was only giving her misery. Then I texted Ariella after Lourdes dropped me off at home. It was a preemptive strike, before Fawn could tell her I'd been at the tea salon. I said I was surrendering, that once I'd seen Fawn and Ronald together, I knew they were destined for each other, and that, as a true f.g., I had to step aside.

I didn't hear back until this morning, but Fawn must've confirmed that I didn't try to sabotage her, because in the voice mail she left, Ariella congratulated me for doing the right thing and offered to help me work on my powers so I can get "a real beneficiary" next time.

I was only semi-irritated by the call, because it was exactly what I wanted.

I met Jeni early, before her shift, at the mall office where the sign-ups were for the concert. The woman in the office brought the performance schedule up on her computer, and although registration had closed, with a little flick of a pen, I put Jeni's name on the list of singers. Jeni gave the woman the name of the song she wanted to sing, so they'd have the instrumentals loaded into their stereo system. I guess it's like a big karaoke machine.

Jeni and I are meeting again tomorrow morning, before

the concert, so I can help her get ready. She and Chey-enne are going shopping tonight for her dress, and I or-dered Jeni to steer clear of her usual shades-of-dull-brown choices and find something with color in it.

Maybe I should take my own advice for once.

The boxes haven't arrived from New Jersey yet, but I do have a pair of boots I brought with me when I moved here, which I've never worn. I drag them out from the back of my closet. They're the first pair of boots I ever made. They have pointed toes, which I usually hate, but when I try them on, they're not bad. I can definitely walk around a gallery in them. And they have color. There are cross-hatches of purple and silver along the sides, and around the top I'd cut small slits that I'd woven old hair ribbons through. Pale baby blue for the left boot, frosty mint-ice-cream green for the right. That's the main reason I stopped wearing them. The colors were a bit too friendly and un-intimidating.

When I look in the mirror, it's still not right. My boots take center stage, which would be okay any other day, but tonight I want Flynn's eyes to be up, on *me*.

I glance around the room, looking for ideas. My gaze lands on a pair of dolls. Each doll is dressed in a long satin cape—one baby blue, one mint-ice-cream green. Now I'm glad I haven't trashed any of the kiddie décor—it's all source material. I cut the capes into strips, tie them together, alternating the colors, making two long thin scarves. One I tie around my waist, the other around my hair. *Voilà.* I check it out in the mirror. This is definitely it, the perfect outfit for visiting an art gallery, because *je suis un objet d'art.*

I hear Dad, singing along with some eighties tune in his room as he gets ready for his own date. I'm not even annoyed. I'm happy for him. It's another fairy-tale ending. He and Gina are a good match. If I didn't like her, I wouldn't have fixed them up in the first place.

Dad leaves his room and his footsteps creak down the hall, and then it's just the faint clink of the piano and hiss of the snare drum from the song on the radio. Outside my window the lights in the yard blink off and on. I sit on my bed and, for once, instead of flashing back, trying to relive or correct a past that's gone, I see ahead, to tonight, to the ideal date, to the beginning of the rest of my flawless life.

Since it hasn't happened yet, there's not much detail to grasp—glimpses of Flynn smiling at me and holding my hand; me making some snide comment about a painting and Flynn laughing; us standing outside later in the yellow glow of a lamppost, having paused on the way to the car to wrap our arms around each other at exactly the same time, like it's part of a dance we practiced. The night is cool and misty, but the embrace warms us up. We pull apart for a second, so we can look in each other's eyes, and then we kiss . . . and it's flawless.

I'm holding my cell in my hand and I feel it vibrate before I hear the buzz. Flynn. Not canceling. Not blowing me off. He's here: "Your carriage awaits." I smile.

Tomorrow, Jeni can be the princess who finally snags her prince. Tonight, the f.g. gets to be Cinderella.

★ ★ ★

The fairy tale is not playing out properly.

There's a second, a moment, half a heartbeat, when I meet Flynn's eyes after I get into his car and I feel the tingling serenity from that night on the Ferris wheel, before we kissed.

But when we lean toward each other this time, it's as if an invisible air bag has exploded between us. Hesitation and nervousness and awkwardness fill the space, pressing us apart. We kiss, but it's off. My lips hit his cheek, my hair gets caught in the seat belt. He laughs, I laugh, although it isn't really funny.

I want him to shatter the awkwardness right there, tell me how much he's missed me. I'm waiting for the declaration of devotion I'd daydreamed about, but it doesn't come.

"So . . . ," Flynn says finally, but then he lets the rest of whatever he was going to say, if anything, just hang there.

So . . . *what?* Am I supposed to fill in the silence? I could demand to know why he didn't call during the whole time he was gone.

No. Too confrontational.

I could say it seems like he was pretty busy at his Extreme Water Sports thing, since he never had time to call me.

No. Too passive-aggressive.

Too bad this date isn't happening one day later, because then I could tell him, at last, about my f.g. success. But even though Jeni's wish is practically granted, it would be bad luck to say anything now.

I need to forget the f.g. stuff and think like a g.f. . . . I'll ask him about his trip, but without the "Why didn't you call" part. Just a nice, supportive "How did it go?"

"How—"

"We're here."

What? I spent the whole drive here lost in my inner monologue? Why didn't Flynn say anything?

He pulls into a metered parking space. This will be better anyway. We need to get out of the car, be together without seat belts and gearshifts and dead air separating us.

The date starts *now*.

As we walk through the galleries, Flynn explains who the artists are and what they're known for, but I feel like he's a guide giving me a tour. Most of the time, he doesn't look at me, but when he does, it's with a suspicious sideways glance, as if I might be a criminal he's seen on a wanted poster and he's not sure if he should call the police or make a citizen's arrest. We enter the next gallery, a group show, and make our way past the bizarre mix of sketches and sculptures and photos and paintings and tiny TVs playing staticky video loops, toward a framed photo that's one of the few pieces that doesn't have a crowd around it. Number 82: *untitled thought process*. It's a gray-and-brown blur against a bluish haze. It's either a flower or a building. Or maybe a dog. Hard to tell. There's a red dot stickered to the wall next to the number, which means somebody bought it. According to the price list we have, it cost $7,500.

"You could do that," I tell Flynn.

"That's not really my style. It's conceptual and I'm more naturalistic."

"Who cares—look how much money you could make."

"You can't just take an out-of-focus photograph and sell it for thousands of dollars," Flynn says. "It has to be part of a thematic plan."

"I know that. I'm joking." I *don't* know, but I *am* joking, or trying. It's like his sense of humor has gone MIA. The mood's gotten as tightly strung as the electronic violin music playing over the gallery speakers. Why is he being so un-Flynn-like? I'm afraid to ask, because what if the answer is something I don't want to know? What if he's feeling guilty because he met some Cadie-ish surfer girl on his trip and he wants to break up with me?

"I'm going to get another bottle of water," Flynn says casually, as if he's not about to destroy my whole life. "Want one?" I shake my head and Flynn moves off into the crowd. I notice for the first time that he's got a sport jacket on, a tweedy mix of dark green and mocha brown, and jeans that fit instead of the usual super-baggy ones.

He dressed up.

For me? Why, if he's breaking up with me? And for that matter, why take me out on a date? Is this some "Dating Guide for the Chivalrous" rule? Look your best and show your victim a good time before you dump her?

Untitled thought process is suddenly mobbed by fuzzy photo fans, so I escape through a doorway into a small room with only one artwork in it, lit eerily from above by a single amber light angled down from the ceiling.

It's a large wall-to-wall photograph of a doll, just its head, against a black background. It has a baby-doll face, with pink cheeks and round, eyelashed hazel eyes, but its long, shiny red hair is teased up high on top and falls around its face in big question-mark curls.

It's a photo, but it doesn't look real. There's something off about it, ghoulish. Its eyes stare right into mine, like it's reading my mind—reading the parts of it even I can't see.

"Oh, hey, here you are. They were out of water." Flynn steps up beside me. "Oh, yeah. This is cool. I've seen some of the other ones in this series. It's a mirror image. Look—see?" He holds up his hand in front of the photo to hide one side of it and then moves his hand to hide the other side. "The artist photographed one half of the face and then copied it, in the reverse, to the other side. It's perfectly symmetrical. That's what makes it so disturbing. Awesome, huh?"

I can't look at it anymore. It's stirring up something I don't need stirred. I turn to Flynn, who's still studying the photo, and I see that under the jacket, he's wearing a bright white dress shirt over a forest-green T-shirt, both brand-new. The whole outfit is definitely straight from the Date-Wear for Male Teens section of the department store.

Snippets of things I want to say dart around my brain,

slipping by too fast for me to grab anything complete, fully formed. "How many more galleries?" is what I say finally, but it isn't the right thing. It's not what I meant to say at all, and the way it comes out is all wrong too. It should be an innocent question, something asked out of curiosity, not a complaint, which is how it sounds. Maybe it's just the echo in the room that makes it sound that way.

Flynn takes in a breath, sighs out, and slumps his shoulders in a way that is so Flynn, it squeezes my heart.

"Let's skip the rest," he says. He sounds defeated, as if he's been struggling all night to put off some horrible decision and he's finally accepted that he can't wait any longer.

But I hope it's only the echo.

★ ★ ★

Each time we've exited a gallery, the ocean, which is visible down the narrow side streets, has darkened one shade. Turquoise to teal. Teal to deep blue. Now the water is a rich violet, with curves of silver from the moonlight reflecting off its waves. It's such a romantic setting! This was supposed to be a night to match the Ferris wheel. It's like fate and the universe are at war—one side pro-Delaney, one side anti-Delaney—and I don't get a say at all.

Flynn takes my hand, which confuses me even more, until I feel his grip tighten and see his shoulders sag farther, and then I *know*. He's about to do it. He's getting up his nerve. He's going to dump me.

I pull free from his grasp. "Say it already!" My voice

carries off down the street, waking a sleeping seagull, which squawks and flies off.

Flynn stares at me a second and then sighs. "It's true, then."

Wait, that's my line. "What's true?"

"I didn't want to believe it, but you were so weird on the drive from your house tonight, and I knew *something* was going on. All summer you've been pulling away."

"*I've* been pulling away?" What's he talking about? "That's not—"

"Every time we're together, you seem more distant."

"I don't—"

"I go away for, like, weeks, and you don't text or call or email or anything."

Have I stepped into Opposite Day? This is all backward. It's me who's supposed to be saying these things to *him*. He's stolen my lines. "You never texted or called *me*."

"I did so. I sent you that photo."

"Of a dead eel."

"Yeah, and you never responded."

"How am I supposed to respond to a dead eel?"

"I don't know. With a joke maybe? It's like your sense of humor has gone MIA."

Another line stolen! "*I'm* not the one—"

"Never mind, I know that's not why you've been so distant. It's because . . ." Flynn looks away. "It's because of you and Ronald."

"Ronald?" How does he know about Ronald? Has he been spying on me?

"Yeah. Your client."

"He's not my client. He's . . . the prince."

Flynn turns back to me, suddenly angry. "Right. So, you admit it."

"You're not listening. *Jeni* is my client. Ronald is the guy she likes."

"Jeni?" Flynn says this in a snide, skeptical tone, like I just now made the name up.

"Yes, Jeni Gold. She works at Nutri-Fizzy. At the mall. She was really shy, and she had a crush on this guy who works at a shoe store, and so I helped her, with earrings, and other stuff, and now she sings." Flynn stares at me, skepticism transforming into pure disbelief. "Wait, that didn't come out well." If it were one day later, I would have already told him all this, in a coherent and mesmerizing way, illuminated by memorable detail, with planned pauses for his gasps of awe and wonder. This is not how it was supposed to go.

"I don't want to hear any more of your lies." Flynn spins around and marches toward the car, his shoulders now unslumped.

Why am I constantly having to run after people and defend myself? Calling me a liar has become the theme of the summer.

"I'm not lying!" I run to catch up to him.

"I thought you couldn't talk about your clients, because it was all confidential." Flynn takes his keys from the pocket of his new date-wear jacket.

"I made that up."

He unlocks the car. "In other words, you lied."

"Not exactly."

"Hmm. Well, 'making something up' is pretty much the definition of lying. *Exactly*."

Flynn climbs into the car. I yank on the passenger door, and he takes his time unlocking it. So much for chivalry.

Flynn won't look at me as I get in. He turns on the ignition before I've even closed the door.

"Flynn, listen—"

"Tell me," he says as he pulls out, "that day at the library, when you said you had to run off to work on your boot designs because you were so inspired—was that true?"

"No, but—"

"Was the time you hung up on me really because inventory from your storeroom fell on you?"

"No—"

"When you wouldn't let me look at the boots you'd made at Treasures, was that because there actually *weren't* any?"

"No—I mean yes." This is just like my argument with Jeni. Nobody lets me finish. It makes it impossible to think clearly.

Outside the passenger window, the last glimpse of moonlit ocean disappears as Flynn turns onto another street, taking us away from what should have been a magical summer night.

My mind clears. But before I continue with my defense, I have a question of my own.

"How did you find out about Ronald?"

"Does it matter?"

"Yes, it matters. If you were spying on me, the only time I was ever anywhere near Ronald was at the poetry slam, and—"

Flynn lets loose another sigh, but this one is less sad and defeated than frustrated that he's being forced to continue the conversation, but too bad. "I wasn't spying on you. I got this call, right before I picked you up tonight . . ."

And icy dread stabs through my whole body. I've felt this dread before, always right before I find out—

". . . from somebody named Ariella."

I knew it! Why did I even bother to call her and concede? I should have known she'd find out about the concert, somehow. She must have tiny f.g.-cams installed all around the mall.

"You can't listen to her," I tell Flynn. "She's an f.g. too, but she's—it's a long story, but basically she has this client—although she's got the wish wrong, because— Wait, how did she get your phone number?"

"She called the paper and they forwarded her number and I called her and she called me back. Who cares?"

What was I thinking, giving Fawn information Ariella

could use against me? I was trying to help Fawn publish her stupid poetry, but why? She's not my client. Her happiness is of no use to me. "Tell me what Ariella said, exactly."

"She said that there are some fairy godmothers who have this . . . flaw. It comes from their DNA being screwed up—they're the second daughter, or they inherited the ability from their father instead of their mother—"

"That's not—"

"*And* that this flaw causes them to fall for the person they're granting the wish for."

"I'm going to kill her."

"So it *is* true."

"No, it's *not.*"

"It happened with me."

"That was . . . I had it wrong then, that's why. And anyway, I told you, Ronald isn't my client. Jeni is my client."

"Right. 'Jeni.' "

"Stop saying that like she's a figment of my imagination. Wait—I'll show you." I turn on my phone. "I should've taken pictures of her at karaoke."

"You went out to karaoke?"

"Yeah, long story. Hold on, let me see if she's on Facebook." I type in her name. "Oh my God. There are like two thousand Jennifer Golds."

"How convenient."

"I'm not lying! I'll call her. You can talk to her." I bring up Jeni's number. Flynn stops at a stoplight and I hold the phone in front of Flynn's face. "See? 'Jeni Gold.' Right there."

He pushes my arm away. "That doesn't prove anything."

I hit Call and put the phone on speaker. Jeni's voice mail comes on. Unfortunately, it's one of those generic computerized voice messages that only give the number, no name. "Call me," I say into the phone. "It's urgent." As I hang up, I come up with another idea, a better one, the one I should have thought of first. "Come to the mall tomorrow," I tell Flynn. "You'll meet her and you'll see what's going on. I'll show you that—"

"I'm not coming to the mall, Delaney."

"Why not?"

"Because I'm working."

"What does that matter, when our relationship—"

"We're here." Flynn points out the window at my house.

Again? It's like the route between home and the galleries exists in some time warp. "You have to come tomorrow, Flynn. You'll see you're wrong about everything. Ariella and Ronald and Jeni and Fawn—"

"Fawn? Who's Fawn?"

"She's Ariella's client. It's a long story."

"Yeah, right. You keep saying that. You have this whole long story about your summer adventures, going to karaoke and poetry slams, interacting with all these people you've never told me about. . . ."

"I was going to tell you, after tomorrow. All of it. Lourdes too, and the artists' café. You would love that place. Let me see if I can find it online." I pick up my phone again.

"I think we should take a break for a while."

What? No. I put the phone down and turn to him, but he's staring out the windshield, his hands on the wheel.

"I *told* you, Ronald—"

"Forget about him," Flynn says, his voice now sad, no longer angry. "It's not about him anymore. It's about you, telling me nothing about what's going on in your life."

"That's because you're working all the time. You're the one not sharing. You're the one who stood me up to photograph a dead lighthouse."

"That was over a month ago! You've been standing me up all summer. Metaphorically." Flynn leans back in his seat, impressed with himself at his clever phrasing— although it sounds more like something I'd say, which means he's stolen yet another line from me, even if I never said it or thought it.

"There were reasons," I tell him.

"Oh, yeah? What were they?"

Flynn's eyes are in shadow, but I can feel the intensity of his gaze, almost as if he's the one who has the supernatural powers.

He definitely has the power to cloud my mind, because now I can't remember the reasons. I know they were good ones—reasons that felt smart and right at the time. Something about not wanting him to look down on me? That can't be it, because how could his opinion of me be any lower than it is now?

"Can we go back and start over?" I ask.

"Not unless you have some way of erasing our memories too." He must think I'm considering it, and maybe I am, a little, because he quickly says, "I'm *not* wishing it." He sighs. "Why don't we talk in like a month," he says.

"A *month*?"

"Yeah. School will be starting again, and we'll have to see each other then anyway. This way we'll have lots of time to think about things."

Things? What things? Another stab of dread hits me, this one less a slam than a creeping, gnawing fear.

I know what he really means. He wants to begin the process of de-needing *me*. And by the time school starts, the process will be complete.

"Okay?" Flynn asks.

Not okay. Not. Okay.

But for some reason, I'm not able to speak. Thoughts come to me, but they're replays of everything I've already said. I have no new argument. No defense. And because of the whole unfair time-travel impossibility problem, no idea of how to go back and prevent the decision that I know he's already made.

"Good night, Delaney."

I unlock the seat belt, but it's become an extremely complicated maneuver for some reason. It takes like three hours for me to even find the button to push. I see my hand reach for the door handle and I hear myself say, "Good night." But what I see is through a fog, what I hear is through a haze. When I step inside the house, the muffled rumble of Flynn's car pulling away is joined by a high-pitched sound. An unnatural sound. A sound that pierces my aural haze and restores my hearing to normal, but which makes the horror of this night even more horrible.

It's a . . . giggle. Make that multiple giggles. *Giggling.* It's coming from the living room and it's followed by murmurs and the rustle of shifting bodies.

"Delaney?" Dad calls. "You can come in, honey."

How thoughtful. They've forced themselves to pause their—ugh, gross, I don't want to think about it, but how can I help it?—make-out session, so that I can enter and be witness to their romantic bliss.

It's as bad as I pictured. Worse. Dad and Gina sit on the couch, hip to hip. Gina tugs on her skirt and smoothes the surface. I noticed Dad's hair is all messed up on one side. Their faces are glowing and it's not from the lamp on the end table. It's that fireworks-inside glow that I will never experience again.

"How was your date?"

How can he even ask me that? How can he throw his happiness in my face and then mock my misery with his cheerful clichéd question?

"Delaney?"

"You two are *disgusting.*" I rocket down the hall at

twice the speed of light, propelled by a fuel of rage and despair—which, if I could harness it, would eliminate the need for pollution-causing energy sources and solve global warming. The sound of my door slamming catches up to me only after I am already on the bed, facedown, screaming into the lace bedspread. My mattress vibrates as it struggles to absorb the eardrum-shattering and earth-shattering decibels.

The doorknob rattles. "*Delaney*. You come out here and apologize."

I try to summon up another scream, but apparently I've depleted my scream stores. I stay facedown, gulping at the tiny bursts of air that I can breathe in through the layers of bedding.

I hear Gina and Dad murmuring and then Gina speaks. "Delaney? Is everything okay?"

I contemplate self-suffocation, but my lungs rebel and I flip over onto my back, gasping for breath.

Another knock, this one just a light tap. "I'm going to take Gina home. I won't be long."

More murmuring as their footsteps recede, and a few moments later, the front door clicks closed. Outside, the car engine starts, and then that sound too fades away.

I open my eyes and gaze at Mom's earrings dangling overhead from the lace canopy eyelets. I don't have any lights on in the room, so I can barely see them. Occasionally a bead catches the wink of the lights in the yard and twinkles.

I roll to one side. On the windowsill sit the gifts that Flynn bought me at the Bazaar, the nonedible ones: the pink whistle, the DELIA license plate, the keychain with the boots. Below, on top of the bookshelf, is Rufus, the blue stuffed dog from the carnival I went to with Flynn. He rescued it after I threw it away. The gifts remind me of the kinds of things I find at the bottom of the boxes that Nancy brings into the store. Random worthless items that you can't believe anybody would buy or keep.

Now I understand. It's not the object, it's what it means. It's not the gift, it's the giver. Once the giver and meaning are gone, then, like a spell broken, it all turns back into junk.

I lower my gaze to the dolls. I meet their eyes, but these dolls aren't like the one in the photo at the gallery. They're lifeless. They have no message for me.

My cell rings. Oh God, oh God. Please, please, please. Flynn, Flynn, Flynn.

Jeni. Because when, ever, has a call been from the person I expected or wanted it to be from?

"You're too late," I tell her.

"Oh, I'm sorry. Did I wake you up?"

"What? No. I'm talking about my voice-mail message."

"Did you call me? I missed it. I was at karaoke with Kevin and everybody."

"Good idea. Practicing. How did it go?" I'm not really interested, but it's surprisingly easy to fake it. Maybe the scream drained all emotion from me, permanently. I'm now an automaton. This is way better than self-suffocation. There's no physical discomfort.

"Fine," Jeni says. "But, you know, I'm not sure any-more about tomorrow—"

"*Stop.*" Okay, so I guess there *is* some emotion left. "Listen to me, Jeni. This is last-minute jitters. That's all."

"Maybe, but—"

"No maybe. Your destiny's in motion—you committed to it, remember? You don't have a choice anymore."

"I don't?"

"No. Now say it."

"Um, I'm going to sing tomorrow?"

"Not that. *You know.*"

"Uh . . . right. Ronald and I are meant to be."

"Good. If you feel nervous again, just repeat those words. I'll see you in the morning."

The war isn't over. Ariella might have ruined my life, but there's still time to ruin hers.

chapter seventeen

I pace back and forth between the paper towel dispenser and the door. Jeni should be here by now. She knew we were meeting in the Bazaar's ladies' room, but she's already two minutes late. No—make that three.

I'd faked sleep when Dad got back from taking Gina home, even though I was so awake, it was like I'd had five double chais. I stayed up until dawn, making sketches. The ideas were finally coming.

Boots with spikes. Boots with metal toes filed to a point. Boots with broken chain links hanging from them, the links' edges jagged and sharp.

I don't think the kids at school are going to like many

of these, but supervillains will love them. And who cares anyway? If people don't like them, they don't have to buy them.

In the morning, I wrote Dad a note, apologizing, and explaining that I'd been in a bad mood because I caught my boot on the corner of Flynn's car door and ripped the leather. Then I snuck out before Dad was up and skated the whole way to the mall on my roller boots. The sky was overcast and misty, as if the dampness of the sea air from last night had followed me home. All summer I'm wishing the sun would take a break for five minutes, please, and then today, the one day I need the light and warmth, it hides behind a huge cloud that's unrolled across the entire sky, coloring everything a shivery gray.

The trip took almost an hour, but I wasn't even tired. To be safe, I ordered a triple chai at the coffee place in the Bazaar, to go with the two croissants I bought. While I caffeined and carbed up, I did some Internet searching for other small lethal objects I could attach to my new line of villain boots, until it was time to meet Jeni.

"Delaney?" Jeni peeks her head into the ladies' room.

"You're four minutes late!"

Jeni trudges in, slumped and frowning. No surprise why. Her rust-colored halter dress is too loose in the waist, her eye shadow is a hideous orange and clashes with her hot-pink lipstick, and she doesn't have any mascara on at all. "This is all wrong," she moans.

"Don't worry, I'll fix it." I pull out my chopstick, but

at that moment, a group of women in shorts, fanny packs and matching green "Sunshine Tours" T-shirts burst in, complaining about the cloudy weather and the lack of celebrity sightings. They separate and disappear into the stalls. I slip the chopstick into my belt to work on Jeni's hair, which I can do without magic. She's put it up, but the butterfly clip has slipped to the side, like it's about to make a break for it, spread its wings and fly away.

"I've been saying . . . *you know* . . . all morning," Jeni whispers. "But it's not working."

The green T-shirts emerge from the stalls and fan out to the sinks. Their chatter fades as they toss their towels and exit, leaving Jeni and me alone again.

"You're here and that means it *is* working," I tell her. "It's totally understandable to be nervous, but I can tell that inside you're ready."

"I am?"

"Totally and completely," I say. But I'm not as sure as I sound. Jeni's hair is better, but the butterfly clip is still lopsided. It'll be easier to fix everything at once. I tap the chopstick against my teeth, mentally adding up the repairs I need to do. This is going to require some big magic. Bigger than just taking in the waist on the dress and softening Jeni's makeup.

Ariella is still out there somewhere, plotting, scheming. Gearing up her magic for top performance, which means my magic needs to be even better.

What I have to do is bring about a total physical

metamorphosis. Yes, it will be superficial and temporary, but sometimes that's called for. Generations of f.g.s have transformed pathetic peasant girls into dazzling royalty, so why have I resisted? It's what I was born to do.

My arm sweeps through the air as if I'm throwing a dagger, but the chopstick never leaves my hand. The bones from my shoulder to my wrist electrify, a thousand volts of energy zapping up through them. The chopstick flashes like a lightsaber.

Forget trying to be a super f.g.—I'm an f.g. Jedi.

Jeni sees herself in the mirror and lets out a startled cry. Her hands flail around her as if she wants to touch herself to make sure it's all real but is afraid of what will happen if she does. "This is . . . This isn't . . . It's . . . I look . . ."

"Like a princess."

"Uh . . ."

The shiny bronze dress wraps around her body like a second skin, curving up from her ankles to her hips to her chest, showing off cleavage that's probably never seen the light of day until now. Her hair is swept into a twist that defies gravity, glittery hairclips cascading upward. Her eye makeup is sultry and grown-up; her lips are a glossy cherry red. Her bronze nails match the dress and the dangling ruby earrings match her crimson stilettos. She's better than a princess. She's a movie star.

"This seems too . . . too . . ."

"It's what you've been asking me to do. Use my magic on you."

"I wasn't thinking it'd be so . . . so *so*."

"Cinderella never would've gotten the prince if she'd shown up to the ball in rags."

"I wasn't wearing rags. That dress was from Jean and Jane. Cheyenne helped me pick it out. It cost almost forty dollars."

"It was off the rack. It wasn't a dress that would make a prince ask you to dance."

Jeni's kohl-lined eyes grow even wider with worry. "I didn't know there was dancing too."

"That's just a metaphor. The point is you're perfect. *Finally*. Let's go."

I take her arm and drag her out of the ladies' room before she can start in on another hesitation-filled protest. As we wind our way through the Bazaar stalls, heads turn. Snack eaters and knickknack shoppers stare. Jeni is totally out of place among the shorts and tees, a diamond in a pile of plastic beads. I can sense Jeni cringing in embarrassment behind me, but this will be a great story to tell a reporter someday when she and Ronald are famous singers and have luxury dressing rooms wherever they go.

When we get to the Alcove, the sky is still gray, yet even in the hazy light, Jeni's dress is blinding. There are goose bumps on her arms from the cold or nerves, or both. There are more stares, but I pick up speed, tugging Jeni along. I have to put all my energy into clutching onto her, because I'm feeling shaky suddenly, weak. It must be the aftereffects of doing so much big magic at once. My body's not used to it.

A crowd's already formed. There are people sitting on folding beach chairs and blankets and sprawled out on the grass. Along the periphery it's standing room only. At the far end of the lawn, a platform's been erected over the stage, raising it about five feet higher. Huge black speakers are parked at the back of the stage. Their wires snake along the ground and are clamped onto the bottoms of poles that stand at each corner like giant Tinkertoys. A huge white cloth stretches between the poles, forming a cover from the sun, if it ever shows up.

A few guys in the crowd spot Jeni and whistle. Her face reddens and her gaze drops to the ground.

"Come on," I say. "We're almost there."

We arrive at the side of the stage, where a velvet rope barrier sets off a waiting area for the singers. Two teens in khaki shorts and black T-shirts, wearing headsets and holding clipboards, sign people in. I prod Jeni toward the girl teen. "Jeni Gold?" Jeni says, as if she's hoping her name won't be on there. But the girl nods and makes a checkmark on her sheet. Jeni glances around at the simple summer dresses and skirts on her female competitors. A few of them look our way and whisper.

"Ignore them," I tell Jeni. "They're just jealous because you stand out."

"But I don't want to—"

"Yes, you do. That's how you win."

I spot Ronald at the edge of the group. He's listening to his iPod, his face fierce with concentration. I steer Jeni toward him and his eyes pop open wide when he sees her. He seems about to whistle, on boy-automatic, but then checks himself. He pulls out his earbud. "Hey, well, *okay*, then," he says in admiration. "You look nice." Jeni smiles and blushes. Exactly as I predicted, the dress has hooked him. Once he hears her sing, it will all be over.

Thank God. I can almost relax. Almost.

At one end of the stage, a guy I recognize from a cable entertainment news show reads through a couple of stapled sheets of paper that look like a script. His hair is slick with gel and he's wearing a gray suit that you can tell costs more than ten pairs of new designer boots. One of the clipboard people hands him a stack of index cards. Hmm . . . I retrieve my chopstick from my boot as Slick steps up to the microphone. "Hey! Who wants to hear some music?" he yells. The crowd cheers and hoots. I back up a little, moving behind a hand-holding couple and making sure no one's looking my way. "All right! You're in the right place, then! I'm Diego Chen and I'm here to introduce you to the singing stars of tomorrow, at the Third Annual Alcove's Amateur Singer Celebration and Competition. We've got over twenty talented young men and women here to perform for you today. So let's start the music! Our first singer is . . ."

I aim the chopstick between the arms of the couple in front of me. Diego raises the first index card and reads it. "Jeni Gold! Give it up for Jeni!"

Jeni's eyes go wide in surprise at being first, but I had to do it before she lost her nerve and dropped out. Then it occurs to me that she could still drop out, make a dash for it, even though it'd be pretty hard to run in those shoes. I "excuse me, excuse me" my way through the crowd toward the stage, so I can cut off any escape attempts. I'm still pressing my way through the crush when I see Ronald lean over and say something to Jeni. He takes her arm and guides her to the steps. I sigh in relief.

Diego reaches down from the stage to take Jeni's hand. She's moving pretty slow and I don't think it's only nerves. I may have made the dress a little too tight. I'm not going to mess with it now, though, because she's not fleeing. She's onstage and she's going to sing and it's all going to be more than fine.

"Oh my God, is that Jeni?" Lourdes slips up next to me. "What happened to her?" Lourdes asks, tilting her head toward the stage.

"What are you talking about?"

"Are you looped on Nutri-Fizzies? She looks like a contestant on that show *Fashion Crimes*."

"She does not. Everybody's staring at her. Look."

"That's what I'm saying." Lourdes studies my face. "Please tell me you're not responsible for this."

"She needed . . . something."

262

"What happened to 'I don't do makeovers, I do enhancements'?"

"The enhancement wasn't enough."

"Enough for what?"

"She needed to be prettier, okay?"

Up onstage, Jeni tilts the microphone down, leans in and says, with more clarity and confidence than I'd ever have expected, even with the dress, "I'm Jeni Gold. I'm sixteen. I go to Flores High School in Mission Lago and I'll be singing 'I Will Always Love You.'"

Lourdes is still glaring at me. "Wow, Boots. I'm pretty good at sussing people out, but I sussed you all wrong."

I keep my eyes on Jeni. "You don't understand. If I didn't do it, I'd lose."

"What're you talking about? *You're* not competing. Jeni is. So what are you winning, exactly?"

"Watch. You'll see." But when I glance over toward Lourdes, she's gone. Whatever. If she's going to be that way, she'll just be *in* the way.

Jeni starts to sing. Her voice soars out of the speakers like a living thing, wrapping around the whole audience and putting them into an awe-fueled trance. She's even better than she was at the karaoke place. But there's something different. Something missing. It's like there's no joy in it, but that can't be right. I'm just too far away to see.

And no one else seems to notice. Shoppers stop to listen and Nutri-Fizzy customers give up their precious places in line to join the outskirts of the crowd, which is swelling, expanding with each note that Jeni sings. A few of Jeni's uniform-clad coworkers emerge from the Fizzy Bar to watch their fellow Fizz-Master-turned-diva.

The only reaction I'm interested in, though, is Ronald's. I rise up onto my toes and find him. His eyes are on Jeni, and I can tell that she's the only thing he sees. He's mesmerized. It's exactly as I planned. He believes she's the Voice.

I won. I did it! *Me.*

"Delaney Collins." Ariella marches through the crowd, dragging Fawn by the wrist. "What is going on here?"

Ha! She's too late.

"Oh, you mean the concert?" I ask innocently. "It's a singing competition. They have it every year, I guess. I'm here because I so enjoy listening to—"

"I know why you're here. Because your delusions about your abilities have led you to manipulations of villainous proportions."

I thrust my chopstick in her face. "You should talk. Nice try with that call to my boyfriend. He saw right through your lies," I lie.

"I thought we were just getting a soda," Fawn says, glancing around worriedly.

Ariella ignores her and points a lemon stick at me. "And I saw right through *you* pretending to concede, and your attempts to throw off Fawn with your fake enthusiasm about her writing."

"It wasn't fake," I assure Fawn. "I totally meant it. You're very talented."

"Thank you."

Ariella pushes Fawn to the side. "Do *not* speak to her."

Onstage, Jeni reaches the finale, her voice thunderous, and I have to yell to be heard. "It's over, Ariella."

"I'm not even supposed to be on break right now," Fawn whines, her protest failing to penetrate the f.g. hostility that's heated up between Ariella and me.

"It's never over until I get what I want." Ariella spins around and yanks Fawn after her. Fawn slams into me like the end of a cracked whip and I fall backward into the people behind me, whose protests are drowned out by the applause that erupts as Jeni finishes her song.

By the time I haul myself up to standing, I've lost sight of Ariella and Fawn. I push my way out of the crowd and race around the mall's cobblestone walkway toward the back of the stage. While two girls sing an a cappella song about the glories of friendship and sisterhood, I study the crowd and spot the top of a blond head bobbing through the densely packed SRO area along the outskirts of the lawn, a mop of frizzy hair following close behind. Without thinking or planning, the act triggered by impulse and desperation, I point my chopstick their way. Even though I don't know exactly what I'm trying to do and I have no specific intention, the two heads jerk up for a second and then drop out of sight. The people around them rustle and shift, and I know Ariella and Fawn have both gone down—tripped or stumbled or . . . something.

It's unnerving how easy that was. My heart rate has sped up, as if I've been zapped with those paddle things you see on medical shows, when the doctors try to electro-shock people back to life. The chopstick is unnaturally warm in my hand, like an overheated appliance.

I shake off the dizziness and elbow my way to Ronald and Jeni, who are chatting near the back of the stage.

"No, girl. I'm telling you. You've got it locked up. We might as well all go home."

"Oh, I don't—"

"Jeni wants to sing backup for you!" I call out, over the head of the clipboard girl blocking me. Ronald and Jeni glance my way, both confused.

"I do?" Jeni asks.

"Yes. You told me. Remember?" Clipboard Girl steps aside to let me closer, and now only the velvet rope separates us.

"It's an original song, though," Ronald says. "Jeni doesn't know the words." Onstage, the sisterhood duo finishes to cheers.

"Here." I snatch one of the CONTESTANTS ONLY photocopied signs posted on the velvet rope poles. "Write them down." I subtly flick my chopstick toward the Clipboard Girl, and her pen appears in Ronald's hand.

"How did that—"

"A lucky breeze. Don't overthink it. You're up next."

"Don't we have to sign up as a duo?" Ronald asks.

"Don't worry about that. It's handled." I turn my back to Ronald. The chopstick's gotten hot again. I blow on it to cool it off and then direct it at Diego.

"Write," I hiss over my shoulder at Ronald. "You've got five seconds."

"But he hasn't called—"

"Our next act is another singing duo," Diego announces. "Let's hear some love for Double-R and—hey!—Jeni Gold! Making a repeat performance."

Hoots from the rear of the crowd rise above the applause, and I see Kevin and Cheyenne spinning their arms in the air in support. Jeni waves to them as Ronald escorts her up onto the stage. I clap along and try to blink away the headache that's suddenly clamped down on either side of my head.

Ronald introduces himself. "Y'all may know some of my YouTube videos from when I was R-Squared. Today I'm performing a new tune—I mean *we're* performing it"—he smiles at Jeni—"for the first time. So be kind, people."

There are claps of encouragement. But then a wave of hush ripples through the crowd, with murmurs in its wake. At first I notice only the auburn hair, swept up into a loose bun, dappled with sparkling jeweled pins. Even from here I can see that the pins are winged—fairy pins. People move aside, giving Fawn room, and soon there's a wide corridor around her, as if she's a princess making her way through the peasants. Ariella, her f.g.-in-waiting, is right behind her. She twirls two candy sticks, one lemon, one grape, like majorette batons, casting her magic everywhere. The crew members, caught in the spell, step aside to let Fawn pass, and she glides up the steps to the stage. I point the chopstick at her, but nothing happens. Maybe it really *is* overheated.

Ronald stares at her, dazzled. Fawn's eyes are glazed over as if she's in a trance. She whispers something in Ronald's ear. "I guess I have *two* backup singers now," he says into the microphone. Jeni seems to wilt behind him.

No! I shake off the pain of my headache and summon up every ounce of energy I have, like a marathoner on the last leg of a race. I wave the chopstick at Jeni. I instantly feel the tingle and then the snap of an electroshock and I know it's working again. Jeni's dress shimmers, shifting through every shade of the yellow-orange-red end of the spectrum. The crowd "oohs," as if this is part of the act, and Ronald's attention transfers back to Jeni.

But this isn't enough. For all I know, Ariella has given Fawn a voice—a Voice. I can't believe that kind of magic is even possible, but with everything that's happened today, I'm not sure there's anything that's not possible.

I've got to get Fawn off the stage. I twist the wrist of my chopsticked hand and one of the speaker cables swirls up into the air and lassoes around Fawn. The chopstick is burning hot now, but I clamp my fingers down around it and hold on, the searing pain in my hand canceling out some of my headache. The "oohs" become "aahs" at this new special effect, but then there's a burst of purple light—the flash from a grape candy stick—and the cable snaps. One end smashes into a speaker, sending off sparks. The other flies up to the overhead tarp, igniting a flame that soon spreads.

Oh my God. I've been acting on instinct, but neither my subconscious nor my conscious knows what to do now, other than watch, in a daze.

The audience, having realized that this is *not* part of the show, shrieks and scatters, gathering up their blankets and snacks as they go.

A crew member shakes a Coke can and sprays the sugared flame retardant up at the fire, putting it out, but the tarp has burned loose from its frame and it falls in singed sheets. Ronald grabs Fawn and Jeni and pulls them out of the way, out of sight.

People run past me, but all I see is Ariella, being pushed back from the stage by crew members as she waves her candy sticks wildly. She spins around, looking for Fawn, and her eyes lock on mine.

Ariella raises the grape stick at me in an accusation. I point my chopstick at her as a reflex, in self-defense. My arm is still a live wire and the energy moves through it without effort. Currents zap through the air. My whole body becomes electrified and the burning pain in my hand is so intense that it doesn't feel hot anymore, it feels numbingly cold. Two mini-bolts of lightning meet overhead. They flash and burst into a single firework explosion. I watch, jittery and breathless, as spider legs of sparkles arch up toward the sky and then curve down, their twinkles dimming and diminishing before dissolving into smoke and vapor, leaving only the acrid firecracker smell of sulfur in the air.

Far away, on the other side of the fountain, Kevin and Cheyenne lead Jeni away. She's back in her off-the-rack dress, and there's someone else with her, someone in a peasant dress whose hair has never been frizzier.

"What's *up* with you two?" Ronald steps between us, glaring first at Ariella, then at me. "You wrecked my act, man. Why?"

"I didn't—" I start to protest.

"I *know* you did," he says. "You and that freaky chopstick."

The chopstick—where is it? My hand is empty, the palm now mysteriously pain-free. Then I notice, on the ground, a shriveled line of black lying on a strip of burned grass. I lean down to touch the black and it turns to ash.

I look over at Ariella, who is scowling down at her own hands, which are covered in a black sticky mass flecked with flakes of purple and yellow. She tries to wipe it off, but her palms get stuck together. She tugs and pulls and finally wrenches them apart. "Tell her," she orders Ronald, and points one carbon-coated hand at me. "Tell her Fawn's the one you love."

"Fawn?" Ronald asks, confused. "Are you—"

"Tell *her*," I interrupt. "Tell her that Jeni is the Voice. Jeni is the *One*."

Ronald doesn't answer for a minute. "*That's* what this was all about?" He gazes back and forth between us, his expression a mix of irritation and disbelief. I want to protest more. I want to insist. But my conviction melts away like Ariella's candy sticks.

"I like Fawn okay," Ronald says. "She's an amazing writer. Kind of intense, though. Jeni's sweet, and her voice—yeah, wow. But there's no more than 'like' there for either of them. I already got a girl. I mean, I don't *have* her—maybe I never will—but she'll always be the one. The One. Get it?" He shakes his head, snorts out a half laugh. "This sure is a mess. But you know what? I am *definitely* writing a song about it."

Ronald tromps off across the trampled grass, leaving Ariella and me staring at each other. Ariella glances down at her melted-candy-covered hands again, but she doesn't seem angry or frustrated anymore, just tired.

"Our powers are gone, you know," she says.

"How do you—"

"Can't you tell? Try. Go on."

I pick up a plastic knife from the grass, dropped by a fleeing picnicker. I aim it toward the stage, where two crew members are yanking at a corner of the singed tarp that's gotten tangled up in the collapsed poles.

Nothing happens. Not to the tarp. Not to me. Whatever

it was that allowed me to turn my thoughts into energy—into magic—isn't there anymore.

"You messed with the universe and *this* is what you have brought to pass." Ariella swings her sticky hands out, indicating the ashy disaster around us. Up near the stage, members of the mall's maintenance staff arrive to help the concert crew members decide what to clean up first.

"You did this too," I say. "We're co-brought-to-passers."

"No. Your magic screwed up the ions, and the atmosphere got all cloudy or gunked up or *something,* and everything went haywire. You're probably descended from some *anti*–fairy godmother. The black-hole opposite. Like angels and demons. Like when somebody takes a flash photo and you close your eyes and all the bright colors are dark and all the dark are—"

"Powers, no powers, whatever. We both had the wish wrong, which means neither of us is a real f.g."

"I will *never* believe that."

A security guard has joined the cleanup crew. Onstage, a guy gathering up speaker cables points our way.

Ariella and I see this at the same time. Our eyes meet for a second, and then we each run off in a different direction. We don't look back, or at least I don't. I don't know what Ariella does. It doesn't matter what she does. Nothing about her matters anymore.

chapter eighteen

It's barely past noon when I skate up to the front door, but the gray sky has gone so dark it's practically black now. Maybe we did screw up the ions in the atmosphere.

I dig around in my shoulder bag for the key. I don't care what time it is, I need to be in bed, under the covers, way under, buried deep where none of this day, this week, this summer, this year, my whole *life*, can find me. I'm going to haul everything out of the trunk at the foot of the bed: both extra blankets, the comforter, and the stupid quilt Dad bought me with the nursery-rhyme characters. The more layers I have over me, the better the chance of hiding from yet another cascade of instant replays.

Not really replays, though—freeze-frames. Memories that come in blinks. A collection of still images. They're not the obvious ones, the big moments, the things you'd think I'd remember the most—the midair explosion of colliding f.g. magic, the collapse of the tarp, the stampeding crowd. Instead, it's the details I didn't notice at the time but that have now emerged from the background like 3-D pop-ups. Fawn's shock after I'd roped her with a cable; Jeni's wide-eyed terror when the tarp caught fire; Lourdes's disappointed frown; Ronald's baffled stare.

And Ariella's final glance to me as she ran off, a mix of fury and confusion.

All faces. Portraits of horror. If there was a way to develop them on film, I could have an art show that would way out-creep those mirror dolls.

I'm at the door to my bedroom when Dad rushes out of his office. "Delaney. Wait—" He cuts off his warning, because it's too late. I've seen them.

Stacked up in front of my bookshelves, their tops taped, their sides labeled in Posh's mom's handwriting, are the boxes.

The boxes.

Why didn't I follow my first instinct and forbid Dad to let Posh's mom send them? Why didn't I call Posh and tell her I changed my mind? In what universe would seeing these make me feel better? Not in this Delaney-hating universe, that's for sure.

"Those are only the ones with your things in them. The

rest are in the garage." Dad puts a hand on my shoulder, so lightly I can barely feel it. Or maybe I've lost the ability to feel anything. Along with the other abilities I've lost.

"It's gone." My voice is raspy. I'm shaky again, but this isn't the magic-related, screwed-up-ions shakiness from earlier. This shakiness is from natural, not supernatural, causes.

"What's gone?"

I stare at the boxes. *"Everything."* My voice cracks on the last syllable. Dad's arms are around me before I even realize I'm crying. So much for not feeling anything. Soon it's like my whole body is sobbing, and it has nothing to do with Ariella or Jeni or losing the magic, or it does, but it's more than that. I'm worried I'll never be able to stop, that I'll be crying for the rest of my life until I die of it. "I don't know why I'm crying," I choke out.

"Oh, honey." Dad pats my back. "It's about time."

The sky was unable to hold it in any longer either and gave it up five seconds after I did, and now it's pouring outside, the rain coming down in heaving sobs.

I'm curled up in one corner of the couch in the den, the Mother Goose quilt from my bedroom wrapped around me, drinking hot cocoa like it's the middle of winter. I'm drained. Literally. Crying so hard emptied out every drop of energy I had. And with the tears came every secret, doubt, fear and experience I'd been holding in all summer. Like the sobs, it all gushed out. I couldn't control it.

"Do you think my powers are gone for good?" I take a bite of my cinnamon doughnut, still warm from the toaster oven.

"I don't know, Delaney." Dad is sitting next to me. He takes a sip of his coffee. "I've never heard of this happening. Two fairy godmothers sensing the same wish for two different clients? That shouldn't be possible. And you shouldn't be able to use your magic in ways that don't serve the wish either, much less use it on each other."

"Ariella said I was the anti-f.g., but I think we both were. We didn't grant any wishes—we *crushed* them. Including wishes that didn't even come from our clients." There was Ronald, for example, plus all of the Alcove Idol wannabes who never even made it to the stage.

Dad's phone rings. "It's Gina," he says. "I'll call her back." He sends the call to voice mail. "I'm sorry you had to go through all this alone, honey, and I'm sorry I haven't been paying better attention this summer. You act so independent, I forget sometimes how young you are."

"You say that like I'm a baby. I can take care of myself."

"See? That's what I mean." Dad pats my quilt-covered knee. "That act. It's very convincing."

"It's not an act."

He smiles. "Gina and I are taking Theo out. Why don't you come with us?"

"No, thanks," I say. "You guys have fun. I'm too tired to do anything but sit here and watch TV and not move at all."

"I'm not leaving you alone." Dad glances away from me for a second toward the hallway—toward my room. I know what he's thinking.

"Because of the boxes? You think they're going to come alive and eat me?"

"I'm only concerned—"

"I'm not going to open them tonight. I told you, I'm too tired."

I have no idea what I've said that makes Dad jump up from the couch as if he's suddenly solved some problem that's been plaguing the human race since caveman days. "Guess what? You're coming with us."

"Did you hear anything I just said, Dad?"

"I heard you. And that's why you're coming."

"You missed a word. You heard 'I want to come' when what I said is 'I *don't* want to come.' 'Don't.' That's the word you missed." Dad ignores me, picks up his phone and dials. "I'm not going out in the rain," I say as he raises the phone to his ear. "I'm weak from everything that's happened. My immunity is low. I'll catch pneumonia."

Dad gazes over my head to the window behind me. "It stopped." He returns his focus to the phone. "Hi . . . Uh-huh. Sure." I shift around and push myself up onto my knees so I can see outside. It's not only stopped raining, the sky is clear and bright and blue. There's not even one wisp of a cloud. "About twenty minutes, okay?" It's as if a gigantic painted stage backdrop, one that extends to every corner of the horizon, has been plunked down over the stormy skies from ten minutes ago. "Delaney's coming with us," Dad says to Gina, and a millisecond later, a beam of sunlight hits an evaporating puddle and bounces up, directly into my eyes.

I swear, the sun here definitely has it in for me.

★ ★ ★

Outside of the window, the ocean speeds past. The sky is pink, with one skinny strip of clouds where the earth curves away—all that's left of the storm from earlier. It's hard to look at the ocean and not remember the darkening sky over the art galleries. It was only last night, but it feels like months ago, years ago. Time really is weird.

"Theo, buddy, can you knock it off?"

"Sorry."

Theo sits next to me in the backseat of Dad's car, playing his naval war game, kicking Dad's seat and sulking. Dinner was some fast-food chicken place, where Theo stuffed down his sandwich before we'd even gotten to the table. Then he spent the rest of the time playing one of the restaurant's video games. I'm surprisingly not annoyed by Theo tonight. He's not kicking the back of *my* seat, after all. Plus, it may be that I'm still too exhausted to summon up irritation about anything. But I can also see my younger self in him. Although my experience was different, I can relate to his frustration over feeling let down by life.

"Hey, Theo," I say. "You want to play twenty questions?"

"No."

I guess just because I have empathy for him, it doesn't mean we'll be bonding anytime soon.

"Wow, Theo. Look at that building." Gina points through the windshield toward our destination, an ancient hotel that looms on the horizon, a castle in the sand. "Neat, isn't it?"

Theo grunts. Dad pulls into the gravel parking lot. "Here at last!" he announces cheerfully. I think most of his elation comes from his relief that Theo's sneaker will no longer be ramming into his tailbone every other second.

As we walk up the stone path to the hotel, Dad provides a Wikipedia warm-up to the exciting event ahead: a display of ships in bottles in the hotel's huge lobby. "This collection dates back to the early nineteenth century," Dad informs us. "The bottles all belong to one family, and most of them were built by family members, many of whom were even younger than you, Theo, when they created them."

"How about that, Theo?" Gina leans down to Theo, who is still torpedoing virtual ships. "Interesting, huh?"

"Whatever."

We reach a forked path that veers off in one direction toward the hotel and in the other toward a seaside string of dessert shops. "Dad? I'm going to go get an ice cream." As empathetic as I may be feeling, I have to draw the line at being trapped inside with Theo, ships in bottles *and* Dad reading aloud from every posted placard in the exhibit.

"Are you sure, honey?" Dad says. "You'll miss the ships."

"Positive. I'll be over where the tables are. I'll save you guys seats." I hurry down the other path before Dad can come up with a reason to stop me. After I get my ice cream, I sit down at one of the tables closest to the sea, right where the concrete stops at the sand. I put my feet up on a free chair. Dad and I have come out here a few times this summer, but it's always been during the day, when the place is clogged with flip-floppers dragging surfboards and dripping with seaweed. It's better now, when the swimmers and sunbathers are packing up to go home.

They were out of mint chocolate chip, so I ordered a mocha chip, which isn't awful, but it's not a cheery flavor. It's dark and bitter, something you choose after you've gotten too mature and sophisticated for mint chocolate chip and ice cream is more about style and sophistication than fun or frivolity. It's appropriate for today, symbolic of my belated wising up, like me choosing to wear plain black boots. Not even a zipper, because, of course, I don't need to carry a chopstick anymore.

The sea is calm, sending only a few lazy waves to shore every once in a while. They roll up onto the sand slowly, way too tired to make an effort. The sky is even pinker now, Ariella pink. I'd rather be reminded of Flynn.

"Pretty view."

I look up as Gina takes a seat across from me. She smiles and licks the top of a double-scoop waffle cone. "Butter pecan and chocolate chunk," Gina says, nodding at her cone. "Neither of which are on my diet." She puts her feet up on the other empty chair and leans back, so that we're parallel, both staring out at the water. "Red sky at night, sailor's delight."

"I guess," I say. I glance back toward the avenue of iced desserts. "Where are Theo and Dad?"

"They're still looking at the exhibit. I thought I'd give them some guy time together."

"You sure that's a good idea? It may lead to a battle on the high seas. A bloody one."

Gina laughs. "Believe it or not, Theo likes your dad."

"Oh! So *that's* why he was trying to give Dad permanent spinal damage on the drive here."

"Theo's just a little . . . guarded. He doesn't like showing his feelings because he's afraid of being hurt. Perhaps you've had some experience with that yourself."

"Hmm."

"Luckily, as we get older, we learn that it's good to let your guard down sometimes. Especially with the people you care about and who care about you."

"You sound like Dr. Hank. You could write your own book."

Gina smiles and takes another bite of ice cream. "It's no secret I'm a fan of your dad's, both personally and professionally. And I admit I'm a bit addicted to the self-help genre. But, you know, sometimes you *need* help. It's hard to figure it all out on your own."

"Millions of readers would agree." I pop the last bite of my cone in my mouth. Gina finishes off her butter pecan and starts in on the chocolate chunk. "Your dad told me what happened. I'm sorry about your fight with Flynn."

"Wow, I keep it in all summer, and he can't even hold off on spilling all my private information for one day."

"Oh, it goes back further than that. Ever since we started dating, you're all he talks about, Delaney. 'Should I ask her how things are going with Flynn or should I wait until she brings it up?' 'Should I try to spend more time with her or should I respect her independence?' 'I don't want her to think I'm invading her privacy.' 'I don't want her to resent me.' 'I don't want her to think I'm uncool.'"

"I'm sorry, but that last one is a hopeless pipe dream."

Gina smiles. "I told him that." She takes a bite of her waffle cone and chews. "I also told him that he should be sharing all these concerns about your relationship with *you*. Like maybe you should do with Flynn."

"Too late now."

"Is it?"

"Um . . . yes. Didn't Dad tell you the part where Flynn says it's over?"

"He didn't. Your dad said Flynn told you he wanted to take some time and think about things. Did Flynn actually say 'It's over'?"

"No, but—"

"Delaney, listen to me." Gina swings her feet off the chair and turns around to face me. "You and your dad are proof that it's never too late to repair something, especially something that's only fractured, not broken."

"Wow, you *should* write a book, because you have the platitudes down amazingly well."

"Thank you. And will you at least think about what I've said? And don't say 'Whatever,' because I get enough of that from Theo. Parents have tolerance for only so many 'whatevers' before they crack, and I still have to get through Theo's teen years."

I say, "Okay," even though I'm not sure I mean it. I know it's too late, no matter what Gina thinks.

"And I also want you to call me or text me or come by the bookstore any time you want to talk about anything. I've had my heart broken quite a few times, so I can speak from experience. And I'm much better at keeping a secret than your dad is."

My eyes meet hers, for only a second, but I can see the sincerity and caring in them. They're the eyes of a mom, even if it's not *my* mom. Ugh, I'm sensing tears again. How is that possible, when I'm totally dehydrated from my earlier crying jag? Gina is still looking my way with her concerned-mom gaze. "Will you do that, Delaney?"

This is something I think I can say okay to and mean it, but what I actually say is:

"Whatever."

Gina laughs, and I laugh, and it's way better than almost crying.

★ ★ ★

Shouldn't I be exhausted? Unable to keep my eyes open? Instead, I can't keep them closed. The lids pop back up so my gaze falls, again, on the boxes, eerily lit by a beam of moonlight coming through my bedroom window.

I roll over to my other side and face the door, but now my eyes won't close at all.

Fine. I'll unpack them.

In the light of my Snow White lamp, I tear the tape off the top box and open it. Inside is a stack of my skirts, neatly folded in half. I don't remember packing these, but maybe I didn't. Posh and her mom helped me and they did most of it. I was in a daze, moving on automatic. My eyes begin to glaze over at the memory, and I can't let that happen or I won't get the boxes unpacked—and I *have* to. It feels urgent now.

Underneath the skirts are tops and rolled-up leggings. I open my closet and my dresser drawers and put everything away. One box down. I keep going, tearing through the tape, breaking down the empty boxes as I go. This is good. I'm almost done. I feel much better.

I set aside one box for the things that don't fit. I don't mean they don't fit me. I mean they don't belong in this world: a down vest, heavy wool ribbed tights, winter gloves. I'm not sure if I should give them away, take them to Treasures or keep them in case I go back for a visit in winter. I'll decide later.

I open the final box. It's all boots. Five pairs. My Moonlight boots with the streaks of silver. The ones with the snaps up each side. Two pairs of ankle boots. The green suede boots with the cork heels. I line them up neatly in my closet next to the ones I brought with me.

Done. I can sleep now.

So why am I even more awake than when I started?

It's the boots, probably. I'll sketch for a while and that'll help me chill out.

I grab my sketchbook off the bookshelf and climb back into bed. I open to a blank page and . . . do nothing.

Because this isn't it. This isn't the thing I need to do now. What I need to do now is finish what I started. I'm not done yet.

★ ★ ★

The sky is all stars. Distant strings of twinkling lights blinking out of the blackness. My Moonlight boots crunch through the grass and then clack across the concrete slabs of the driveway. I've never been inside the garage, because Dad parks the car out front and because there was never any reason to go in. Until now.

The motion-sensor light above the garage door clicks on, casting creepy shadows on the pavement. The windows in the garage door are like eyes, black and glinting, and when I reach for the door handle, they seem to flash in menacing anticipation. My heart speeds up and my shoulders tense, as if I've walked into the middle of a horror movie. I expect a violin-heavy soundtrack to screech in any second.

This is stupid. It's just a garage. I grab the handle with both hands and haul it up. As the door rises, shadows unfold inside, like hard-cornered geometric shapes painted along the floor in shades of gray. I quickly flick the light switch on.

There's no hockey-masked killer crouching in the corner about to pounce. No rotting zombie corpse with its teeth bared, about to hurl itself at me. No ghosts drifting along the ceiling. No slime dripping from the walls.

What *is* there seems a lot scarier, though.

I postpone going in and gaze around at anything but the boxes. Yet practically everything in the garage is boxes. There are folded-up moving boxes stacked up in the back, plastic tubs labeled "Taxes" and "Christmas Decorations" and "Computer Cables," and cartons of Dad's books, each with a photocopy of the book cover taped on the side. The Dr. Hank clones stare at me with their can-do expressions, nagging at me to get going, to do what I came in here to do. "I'm going to, don't worry," I tell the tiny two-dimensional faces.

I pick up a folding beach chair that's leaning against the wall, under the light switch. I unfold it, revealing its cheerful orange-and-yellow-striped lattice seat, totally out of place in this shadowy garage. The frame clacks down on the concrete and the sound focuses me. I turn the chair so my back is facing the Dr. Hanks and sit down. Like the boxes in my room, the ones out here are taped and neatly labeled in Posh's mom's handwriting: *Books. Clothes. Personal Items.* I reach out my hands to the top box—*Misc.,* which seems safe—but I don't open it. Instead, I let my palms rest on top of the cardboard, as if I can absorb whatever there is of Mom inside them. I know there's nothing. It's been almost a year since she died and it's only inanimate objects and it wasn't like Mom even packed them. All I feel is that hold-your-breath anxiety that comes before you're about to get a flu shot or rip off the Band-Aid: pain is coming and you want it over with, at the same time as you don't want it to come at all.

I force myself to rip the Band-Aid off. I tear back the tape, pull apart the flaps, press them down to the side of the box and look in. I wait for the sting, but it doesn't come.

There's no pain. I lift the items out and set them on the floor. Books we both read, things we bought together, a glass jar of coins we both added to. I still don't feel anything. Maybe my emotional explosion with Dad earlier today was like an inoculation and gave me temporary immunity. I continue to unpack. A bunch of pens rubberbanded together, some lined notepads, a roll of stamps. More books. A couple of ceramic vases, a set of coasters, a glass paperweight with dried flowers inside it. At the bottom of the box, swaddled in bubble wrap, is a small globe lamp, made of clear red glass, with a tiny teardrop bulb inside. We bought it at the last yard sale we went to, but we hadn't figured out a good place to plug it in. It sat on top of a cluttered shelf in the living room, waiting.

It's this, a stupid lamp, that does it—triggers a trip to the past and brings Mom back. But I'm on the outside looking in. I can see us on the couch, doing something boring like watching TV. I want to warm myself in the memory, but I can't help noticing how vulnerable we look, just the two of us, alone against the world. The little lamp sits nearby, and it seems like it's glowing, without electricity. Glowing like a warning light: Watch out! Danger ahead!

Now the pain comes. The anesthesia has definitely worn off. It's a deep, aching, throbbing pain, like a toothache times ten thousand. I turn my gaze away from the lamp, hoping this will clear the vision, and the pain with it, and look for something—anything—to take my attention.

My eyes land on a sliver of red poking out from behind a stack of Dr. Hank boxes at the far end of the garage, way at the back where the light dips again into shadow. I stand up and the beach chair scrapes against the concrete, loud and echoey. There's more scraping and clunking as I push aside plastic bins, clearing a path and sending tiny particles of dust into the air, where they sparkle in the light from the overhead bulb.

The red thing is a long metal rod. There are five of them, one straight, the other four curved and linked by cobwebs. There are indentations where they fit together and holes where screws would go. I shove another bin out of the way and notice a thick clear plastic bag, with a coil of rope inside, the color of straw, and a large piece of canvas, denim blue, faded from where the sun filtered in from the garage window.

It's a puzzle, but the pieces all come together in my head, like the answer to a test question on spatial thinking.

Is that a . . . It *is*. It's a swing set. But why does Dad have a swing set . . . ?

I figure it out before I finish asking myself the question, because "Duh, Delaney. Why do you think?" Because he had a daughter. She was on the other side of the country and he hardly ever saw her, but he wanted to see her. He wanted her to visit, and if she ever did, he'd have her bedroom all Disneyfied for her and he'd have a swing set out back. Just in case she came.

We *weren't* alone. The world was right outside the door, but Mom kept the door closed, and locked, and I did the same thing, believing she was right.

Sounds of the night I didn't notice before filter in: crickets, a cat meowing somewhere, the rustle of a faint breeze through the palms in the yard of the house behind us. I'm not alone now either. The world is all around me. People leave, but there are always more coming. The catch is that you have to open the door to let them in.

Oh God. Now *I'm* starting to sound like Dr. Hank. I guess I can't avoid it. I *am* his daughter.

I wade back through the boxes to the front of the

garage. I pick up the lamp but leave everything else, and then I flip off the light. The garage door creaks as I pull it shut, the shadows lengthening and covering the boxes and their contents like a blanket, where they'll be safe until Dad and I can return and unpack everything together.

chapter nineteen

I can't believe I'm sitting outside in the sun willingly. But here I am, leaning over the picnic table, sketching as the morning sun rises up from behind the bougainvillea-covered wall at the back of the yard.

The sketch I'm doing isn't boots. It's a plan for a space. It's what the garage will look like after I've turned it into a studio. My Treasures job is only for the summer and it's not like I've gotten much accomplished there anyway, boot-wise. So I'm going to concentrate on leaving Nancy the best vintage clothing room possible before the job ends, and bring all my boot-making tools and supplies home. If

I work hard, next year I won't need a summer job, because I'll have a business.

Dad and I haven't gone through the boxes in the garage yet, but we're going to start next weekend. At breakfast, we talked about the stuff still in storage in New Jersey: the furniture and the rest of Mom's things. Before I even finished my second Pop-Tart, Dad had booted up his laptop and bought tickets for us to go to New Jersey the week of Labor Day.

At first I'd felt that sense of slasher-movie foreboding that had come when I opened the garage door. But it didn't take me as long this time to remind myself that I wasn't going alone. Dad would be with me. And Posh would be there waiting.

"Oh my God, Delaney! Oh my God!" Posh squealed into the phone when I called her. "I can't wait! I've missed you so much!" It'll be weird to see her again after so much has changed in my life, and in hers. But after everything that's happened this summer, I can handle weird. Weird will be a relief.

A breeze rustles through the bougainvillea. In the distance, the floppy mop tops of several gawky palm trees sway on their spindly necks. That would be a great design for a pair of boots. A skinny palm tree carved along each calf, with the palm fronds reaching out toward the front and the back. I could also create a series of boots decorated with bougainvillea vines: one pair for each color of leaf blooms—fuchsia, lavender, orange, pale pink and lipstick red like the one in our yard. A whole California collection.

I flip the page in my sketchbook. There's no way I'm letting a single moment of inspiration get away anymore.

"Delaney!" Dad calls from the back door.

"I'm not hungry! I'll get lunch later."

"There's somebody at the door for you."

My first thought is Flynn. My second thought is that no way is it Flynn. He would've called first, and even a call is too much to hope for.

"Actually, it's two people."

Two people?

★ ★ ★

"Hello," Ariella says while glaring at me from the doorstep, her voice so frosty with hostility that I expect ice crystals to form in the space between us.

"Hello," I say back, trying extremely hard to make my voice even icier.

Behind Ariella is an older woman, who rolls her eyes at our hello-off. "Introduce us, please, Ariella." The woman has a French accent, which should spark a horrifying flashback to the evil Madame Kessler, my French teacher at Allegro High, but unlike Madame K, who bites down on every word like she wants to decapitate it, this woman speaks as if the words are flowing through thick maple syrup.

"Delaney, this is my grandmother," Ariella mumbles. "Grandma, this is Delaney Collins."

"I'm pleased to meet you, young lady." She doesn't have Madame K's troll face either. Ariella's grandmother has soft, bronzy skin, and her wrinkles are the kind that come from crinkly smiling eyes, not scowls. Her hair is pinned up in a French twist and she wears a long, cap-sleeved sundress with blooming lilies printed on it. "I have spoken with your father and he has given me permission to steal you away for a small time."

I glance back at Dad, who is standing behind me in the foyer. He's got one of his Dr.-Hank-knows-best looks on his face, so there's no way I'm getting out of this. I follow Ariella and her grandmother down to the street.

Ariella's grandmother's car is another old-fashioned one, but it's not stretched out and sharp-edged like her mom's. This car is all curves and bright stainless-steel accents on its polished chocolate-brown surface. At first it looks like there's only a front seat, and I cringe, because I really don't want to be squeezed up against Ariella Patterson, even for a "small time." But then Ariella leans in and pulls up on a handle I didn't initially notice, revealing the backseat.

"Both of you in the back," her grandmother orders.

As we buckle up, I notice there's something different about Ariella, but I'm not sure what. Pink headband, pink polka-dotted top, lacy pink skirt, iridescent pink flip-flops—it's all there . . . except . . . "Where's your peppermint stick?"

Ariella shrugs.

"Lime stick? Orange? Pineapple-coconut?"

"They don't taste the same without the magic."

Her grandmother starts the car and pulls out. "Where are we going?" I ask her.

"Where do you think?" Ariella's grandmother replies. "We are going to the mall."

★ ★ ★

Ariella's grandmother has one hand clamped down on my left shoulder and the other on Ariella's right as she guides us into Wonderland.

"You two are not finished," she had told us in the car. "A fairy godmother does not abandon a beneficiary."

A few shreds of yesterday's disaster are still around: tiny scorched squares of mini-lawn have been fenced off with string tied to orange flags, to protect the freshly seeded sod inside, and the Tinkertoy rods that held the tarp are stacked in a neat pile, ready to be carried away.

As Ariella's grandmother steers us around vendor carts, shoppers look on, curious as to why Ariella and I are wincing underneath the apparently affectionate semi-embrace of this pretty older lady. That's because they can't see the fingernails digging in. We near the fountain, which is playing a happy, everything-will-be-fine song. It's like the fountain's playlist has been programmed for the greatest possible ironic counterpoint to whatever is going on in my life. Eerie, really.

"Who is first?" Ariella's grandmother asks.

"Her." Ariella points at me. "We're closer to her

beneficiary." Ariella swings her arm from me to the endless Nutri-Fizzy line.

For once, I'm relieved the line is so long. I'll have time to psych myself up.

"Well, we are *not* waiting in that line." Ariella's grandmother prods us forward. So much for that hope. We've reached the entrance and Ariella's grandmother has just uttered a commanding *"Pardon"* to the people at the front of the line, when the Nutri-Fizzy door bursts open and Jeni comes running out, arms wide.

"Delaney!" She grabs me in a bear hug. Ariella's grandmother lets go of my shoulder and the blood flows back into where it had been cut off, but my lungs are now being crushed by Jeni. I get it—she's going to squeeze me to death, like a boa constrictor.

"I'm sorry," I choke out.

Jeni lets me go. "About what?" She looks genuinely confused by the question.

"Um, well, for ruining your song with Ronald and nearly setting you on fire."

"Oh, that." Jeni waves this away as if I'd accidentally bumped into her and not humiliated her in public while almost killing her.

"And for being wrong from the start about Ronald . . . he's not your Prince Charming."

I tense up for the scream, the cry of agony, the angry shove that will send me crashing backward into Ariella and her grandmother. None of these things happens.

296

"I already know that," she says, looking at me like I'm five steps behind in the conversation. It feels more like ten. She already knows . . . ?

"Hey, J.J." Kevin strolls up behind me, backpack slung over his Nutri-Fizzy uniform.

"Hey." Jeni smiles shyly. I watch as he walks right up to her and kisses her. No hesitation. Just leans in and kisses her right on the lips. And she's not surprised. "Can you cover for me for a minute?" she asks him when the kiss has ended.

"You bet. Take your time." He winks at her, grins at me and strolls off toward the entrance.

Ariella's grandmother whispers something to Ariella. Ariella shrugs and throws her hands up in the air. Her grandmother leads her away a few feet, leaving me alone with Jeni.

"When did *this* happen?" I ask Jeni.

"Yesterday." Her eyes mist up in an ecstatic memory of I don't want to know what. Although I kind of do.

"Yesterday?"

"Well, before, actually. The night before. Remember, I told you we went out to karaoke again? Kevin drove me home and there was something, well . . . I'd been thinking about him for a while. He's so nice and we talk all the time and it's so easy, and he makes me laugh. We were in the car, and I felt like maybe we were going to kiss, that he wanted to, and I did too. But then I thought about Ronald, and I was worried that if he liked me now, I'd hurt his feelings, and I was confused. That's what I was trying to tell you, before the concert."

"So you don't like Ronald?"

"Of course I like him! He's nice and a great singer and I like his songs. But I don't *like* him."

"But your wish—"

"It never seemed believable, the way it does with Kevin. Kevin's my real wish. Can't you feel it?"

I try, then shake my head. "My powers are gone. Which is for the best, I guess, since I'm a crappy f.g., obviously."

"But it's because of you that I got my real wish! Yesterday, after everything happened, Kevin was so nice, cheering me up, and so I told him. I told him I liked him. And then he said he liked me too! And then, well . . ." She giggles and her gaze drops, like it used to, but not in the same way. It's coy, self-aware, no longer the action of somebody who's trying to disappear. She raises her eyes again and meets mine. "I never would've talked to him in the first place if not for you, Delaney. I wouldn't have all the friends I have now. I'd still be afraid to try new things, new clothes, believe in myself. You're a great fairy godmother. The best one I could have asked for." She hugs me again. "I better go. Kevin's waiting. Will you be okay?"

"Uh, sure. Don't worry about me," I tell her. She smiles and runs back to work, to her boyfriend, to the happily-ever-after I never could have predicted.

"Well, that was . . . unusual." I turn to see Ariella's

grandmother right behind me, with Ariella glowering next to her. "You are very lucky it worked out this way, young lady. You understand that?"

I nod.

"Good. We continue."

And then it happens again. When we arrive at the Elegant Imprint, Fawn rushes out and hugs me. *Me!* Ariella's glower intensifies, turning her cheeks a scary, scorching shade of hot pink.

"They're going to put three of my poems on that newspaper website you told me about! And I used some of my illustrations to make greeting cards, and the manager said she would sell them at the store! Thank you, Delaney. Without you, I never would have had the courage to do any of this."

Ariella is now steaming. Any second, puffs of fury are going to shoot from her ears. Her grandmother pats her shoulder soothingly, but this doesn't help—possibly because it's the same shoulder she'd been squeezing to death earlier.

Then Fawn hugs Ariella too. Ariella's anger diminishes and her cheeks resume their usual pastel pink color. "Thank you," Fawn tells her. "This whole ordeal has taught me that my writing is way more important to me than boys. I hope Ronald doesn't feel too bad about me not liking him back. Will you tell him for me?"

Ariella pauses, not sure how to answer. "But he——"

"Sure," I say. "We'll break it to him gently."

Fawn smiles, gives us all a little happy wave and returns to the store. Ariella's grandmother folds her arms. "*Extremely* unusual."

★ ★ ★

It's like instant replays, with new players substituted in each time, because here comes Ronald, bursting out of Jump Kicks. No hug this time, though. Instead, he throws up his hands in a defensive mode. "Hey, we don't need any trouble here."

"We're only here to say we're sorry," I explain. Ariella's grandmother had insisted we apologize to Ronald too.

"Right," Ariella says. "I would've said it first if I'd had the chance." She glares at me. I sneer back. Ariella's grandmother makes a pinching gesture with her thumb and index finger and we both quickly spin forward to face Ronald.

He lowers his hands. "Truth is, you did me a favor," he says.

"We did?" Ariella perks up and sneaks a peek at her grandmother, who lets out a huff of disbelief.

"Yeah. You girls almost wipe out the whole mall just to get me together with the wrong girl—wrong girl times *two*—and I can't work up my nerve to tell the girl I really like how I feel? Forget that." He turns to me. "The 'follow your muse' stuff you said to Fawn at the poetry slam—it

300

got to me. I wrote a song and sent it to my girl. I'm just waiting for her answer. I never would've done that if not for you."

"If not for *both* of us," Ariella insists.

"Sure. Whatever. I gotta get to work. You all take care now."

Ariella's grandmother takes in a deep breath and lets out a long, exasperated sigh. "This day was not what I expected." She taps a finger against her lips, pensive.

"Do we get our powers back now?" Ariella asks.

Her grandmother doesn't answer. Instead, she says, "Perhaps we have all learned something today. Ariella?"

Ariella frowns. "Delaney won."

Her grandmother shakes her head. "No, that's not—"

"She granted everybody's wish!" Ariella flings her arms out in frustration. "Three! In a row! Without magic!"

"Not on purpose," I protest.

"Girls." Ariella's grandmother waves the discussion away as if it were not worth commenting on. "Delaney? What did we learn?"

"That nobody needs a fairy godmother. F.g.s just get in the way."

"No, no, no!" Ariella's grandmother shuts her eyes for a moment, then reaches out to place her hands on our shoulders. I cringe, but she sets her hands down lightly this time. She guides us back through the mall, toward the fountain. "You young people with your hurry and your 'more, more, bigger, better.' You dilute the purpose and meaning of our work. You need to have patience. Look at me. I take a year sometimes with one beneficiary."

"I thought that was because you were old," Ariella says.

"*No.* It is because doing a proper job takes time. A wish is a nuanced thing. It needs to be teased out. Carefully. The initial yearning you feel with your beneficiary is only the first, superficial layer. The true wish is deep down, in the soul." I should ask her to give this lecture to Dad. He needs it. "It is quite exhausting, yes. But this is why it may take me five or even six months between beneficiaries, to rebuild my strength and sensitivity."

Wow, and I was worried about three months going by between clients. If only I'd met Ariella's grandmother first, not Ariella. When we reach the fountain, Ariella's grandmother stops and steps around to face us. "You two don't realize how fortunate you are to have stumbled into each other's lives. You should be allies, not enemies. I'm going to let you have a few minutes to yourselves while I shop for a sarong." She walks off toward Fiji Escapes.

Ariella doesn't speak and neither do I. Does Ariella's grandmother expect us to become friends now? That seems beyond the power of even her magic. Ariella turns to face the fountain and puts her hands on the top of the stone wall. I lean my back against it and send a text to Lourdes: "I'm sorry. Call me. I have a lot to tell you." Because I don't know what else to do, I turn around and face the fountain too. It's between songs, so the jets are low. Their little bubbles of water create soft ripples along the surface. It's pretty and peaceful, and I realize I don't feel suffocated here in Wonderland anymore. I know now that it's just one small part of my new hometown, of my new life.

"You did win, you know," Ariella says.

"You helped."

Ariella lets out a sad laugh. "No, I didn't. I'm nothing without magic. But you don't need your powers back. It's like *you're* the wand."

I think about this. It's sort of what I'd been trying to do, but I'm not sure it counts if I still can't get the wish right. "I don't feel very magical," I tell her. "And don't forget, Ronald hasn't actually gotten his wish. The girl he likes could turn him down and he'll be worse off than he was before. It happens."

My cell *pings*. I glance at the screen: Lourdes, returning my text.

"It didn't happen *this* time," Ariella says before I can read the text. I look up from the phone and Ariella tilts her head toward the movie theater. In the shadow of the marquee, Ronald holds someone's hand in both of his. He pulls the girl to him, bringing her into view.

"Oh my God, it's Lourdes!" I say. Lourdes leans toward Ronald and their foreheads touch, their silhouettes forming the outline of a heart. I check her text: "I have a lot to tell *you*."

"You know her?" Ariella asks.

"Yeah. And I knew she and Ronald were friends—and she was always talking about this guy she liked, but I never . . . I should've figured it out."

Ariella throws up her hands. "You granted her wish too! That's four. Actually, Jeni's boyfriend makes it five."

"If you're going to count them up that way, then you have to double all of yours. That puts you way over a hundred."

Ariella brightens for a moment, but her happiness doesn't last. "I'll never have another one, though."

If I had a wand that worked and I could grant a big wish for anybody, I'd restore Ariella's powers. I realize now how much more the magic means to her than it ever has to me.

"How about we go over to Treasures," I suggest. "We can call your grandmother and tell her to meet us there."

"No, thanks."

"But I found an angel pin for you. It's a really well-made pin. No way will the wings ever snap off."

Ariella gives me a puzzled look. "Maybe later. You have other things to do."

"Me? No, I—"

"Boo," a voice whispers from behind me. Flynn!

I spin around, and it's really him, standing right in front of me. "I thought . . . How . . . I don't . . ." Oh my God, I've turned into the old Jeni.

"Ariella called me this morning. We had a *long* talk. She

wouldn't let me off the phone until I swore to come here and see you."

"She can be very persuasive." I look around, but she's vanished. The fountain jets have grown taller, gearing up for their next musical number, and I wonder for a second if she's somehow dissolved into drops of water, fairy-like.

"So, I'm here, Delaney, but—"

"Oh my God. There's my client! See?" Behind Flynn, Jeni and Kevin emerge from the Nutri-Fizzy Bar, arm in arm, on their morning break. "Jeni!" I call out. Jeni waves.

"So that's Ronald with her?" Flynn asks.

"No, that's Kevin. Ronald's over there." I gesture toward the movie theater, where Ronald and Lourdes now have their arms wrapped around each other and are deep in new-love conversation.

"I don't get it. Is that girl a different client?"

"No, that's Lourdes. There *was* another client, Fawn, but she was— Oh, there she is." I point across the fountain toward the mini-lawn, where Fawn walks with Ariella, who is intently reading something from Fawn's notebook. "I guess she wanted to apologize on her own," I say.

"Who?"

"Ariella."

The fountain song starts, this one all violins and trumpets and a chorus singing about throwing coins in the fountain to make wishes come true—which is probably a better way to do it. No human—or rather, f.g.—error.

Flynn shakes his head. "You know, this is really—"

"I know. But I can explain it all. And the only reason I didn't tell you what's been going on all summer is that I didn't want you to think I was a loser."

"Why would I—"

"Because I made such a big deal about being an f.g. and everything, like I was so special, when really, everything was going wrong. I just wanted to wait to tell you until everything was going right."

Flynn studies me, the water jets swaying behind him. "Why would you think I would care about that?"

"Because the whole g.f. thing is new to me."

"Don't you mean f.g.?"

"No."

Flynn thinks a second and then smiles, getting it. "The b.f. thing is new to me too, you know. And I guess I should confess that the reason I didn't invite you to come with us that night when we went to see the lighthouse was because I didn't want you to know that at the beginning of the summer, Skids and I were just gofers. I was carrying camera bags, not taking photos, and Skids was getting coffee. I didn't tell you, because I didn't want you to think *I* was a loser."

I can't believe this. "So you let me think your job was more important than me?" Flynn shrugs apologetically. "Loser!" I say, but it's hard not to laugh when I say it.

"Sorry." Flynn grins his adorable crooked grin.

"So . . . ," I say.

"So . . . ," Flynn says.

Now what? Do I make the first move? Does he? Will this stupid bubble of resistance between us never burst? Will we stand here like this for all eternity, like the bronze statues on the mini-lawn?

"Flynn, I—" Suddenly something yanks at the back of my boot and my ankle twists. I lose my balance and tumble into Flynn, who catches me in his arms.

"Are you okay?"

"What was *that*?" I glance down, but there's nothing there. No hand grabbing me, no reason for me to fall at all. . . . As I raise my eyes, the fountain jets lower and I spot Ariella and Fawn, watching me from the other side of the fountain. Ariella holds up a bamboo skewer from a nearby vendor cart selling cooking supplies. She shouts at me and although I can't hear her over the violins, I can read her lips: "It works!" And then she and Fawn vanish behind a wall of water as the fountain jets rise up for the finale of the song.

I smile. Her magic powers have returned. But how could she make me fall if I wasn't wishing it?

I straighten up, but Flynn keeps his arms around me. Okay, maybe I *did* wish it.

Our faces are inches apart and his eyes stare into mine. His gaze holds me as close and firm as his embrace. "I'm ready to tell you everything," I whisper.

"Later," Flynn says, and then he kisses me. For a second, I can't help wondering if my powers have returned too.

But then the internal fireworks begin, and I forget about my powers. I kiss Flynn and forget about pretty much everything except for this kiss, which I'm determined to commit to memory, even though I know it's only the first of many, many to come. So many I won't have time to flash back to them, or flash forward. I'll be living them in the present.

We come up for air as the song ends. Next to us, three little kids toss pennies into the fountain. The coins arc through the air and then drop into the tiled pond, sending up drops of water that sparkle like the wishes they carry.

And then we kiss again.

about the author

If Kathy McCullough had one wish, it would be for world peace—or a continuously self-replenishing bar of chocolate. A graduate of Cornell University, she lives in Los Angeles, where she works as a novelist and screenwriter. Reviews praised her first novel about Delaney Collins, *Don't Expect Magic,* including *Kirkus Reviews,* "Brilliantly timed moments of situational comedy . . . plenty to like in this debut" and *School Library Journal,* "Those looking for the magic that lies within will want to read it again." Visit Kathy online at kathymcculloughbooks.com or follow her on Twitter at @kathymccullough.